Nestlé Book Prize – Gold Award
Guardian Children's Fiction Prize

SHORTLISTED for the
Whitbread Children's Book of the Year
WHSmith People's Choice Awards

Praise for A WEB OF AIR:

*"A good introduction to one of the most
impressive series in children's literature"*
Daily Telegraph

*"[One] of the most talented and inventive of contemporary
writers. [Reeve has] a remarkable ability to combine a
strong, engaging and beautifully paced storyline with a
passion for argument and ideas: makes much of what
passes for young adult fiction seem very thin indeed"*
Robert Dunbar, Irish Times

*"A brilliantly imagined world, told with
Reeve's distinctive verve"*
Top Pick – Children's Bookseller

*"I love this series, with its unforgettable characters and
rich descriptions that make you see everyday objects
through completely different eyes. A Web of Air will
remind you why Philip Reeve has won so many awards
and proves that he has produced a series worthy
of sitting alongside Philip Pullman's Dark Materials
in the annals of teen fantasy"*
Waterstone's Books Quarterly

*"Atmospheric, well-tuned and gripping, this is a fine
tale for adventure-loving ten-year-olds"*
Philip Womack, Literary Review

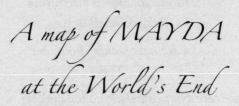

A map of MAYDA
at the World's End

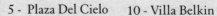

THE RAGGED ISLES

THURSDAY ISLAND

Shipyard

By Philip Reeve

Mortal Engines quartet:

Mortal Engines
Predator's Gold
Infernal Devices
A Darkling Plain

Fever Crumb series:

Fever Crumb
A Web of Air
Scrivener's Moon

Goblins series:

Goblins
Goblins vs Dwarves
Goblin Quest

Larklight series:

Larklight
Starcross
Mothstorm

Railhead series:

Railhead
Black Light Express

Other novels:

No Such Thing As Dragons
Here Lies Arthur

Books for younger readers, written with Sarah McIntyre:

Oliver and the Seawigs
Cakes in Space
Pugs of the Frozen North
Jinks & O'Hare Funfair Repair

Philip Reeve was born in Brighton in 1966. He worked in a bookshop for many years before becoming an illustrator and then an author. His debut novel, *Mortal Engines*, the first in the award-winning epic series, was an instant bestseller and won the Smarties Gold Award. The Mortal Engines Quartet and its three subsequent prequels cemented his place as one of Britain's best-loved authors. In 2008 he won the CILIP Carnegie Medal with *Here Lies Arthur*.

His recent works include the Railhead trilogy and a series of books for younger children, co-written and illustrated by Sarah McIntyre. A movie version of *Mortal Engines* is in production for release in 2018. He lives with his wide and son on Dartmoor.

www.philip-reeve.com

A WEB OF AIR

PHILIP REEVE

SCHOLASTIC

Scholastic Children's Books
An imprint of Scholastic Ltd
Euston House, 24 Eversholt Street, London, NW1 1DB, UK
Registered office: Westfield Road, Southam, Warwickshire, CV47 0RA
SCHOLASTIC and associated logos are trademarks and/or
registered trademarks of Scholastic Inc.

First published in the UK by Scholastic Ltd, 2010
This edition published 2017

ISBN 978 1407 18022 9

A CIP catalogue record for this book
is available from the British Library.

Printed by CPI Group (UK) Ltd, Croydon, CR0 4YY
Papers used by Scholastic Children's Books are made
from wood grown in sustainable forests.

1 3 5 7 9 10 8 6 4 2

www.scholastic.co.uk

To John Lambert,
and his Eigenbrain.

CONTENTS

1

THURSDAY'S CHILD

omething was upsetting the angels. Usually at that hour Arlo found dozens of them fluttering along the beach, scuffling their little bony hands through the mounds of drying seaweed to scare up crabs and sand fleas which they caught and crunched in their toothy beaks. Most mornings, when he came in sight, dozens of them would start calling to him, their scratchy voices rising above the boom of the breaking surf: "A-a-arlo! Snacks? Snacksies?"

But that morning the beach was silent and deserted. The tide had gone a long way out, and even the sea was quiet. Despite the heat the sky was grey, and had a strange look; as if the clouds had somehow curdled. Glancing up as he climbed his secret path on to the island's high, rocky spine, Arlo thought that this was what a fish might see if it looked up from inside the sea at the underbelly of the waves. His grandfather had grumbled that a storm was on the way.

He scrambled up on to the island's summit, hoping to find cooler air and some angels to talk to. No one had time for him at home that morning. His mother was busy with the new baby, which was grizzling at the heat. Father was down at the shipyards, overseeing the work on Senhor Leonidas's new copper-bottomed schooner. Grandfather was

1

at work in his study. Arlo didn't really mind. He preferred it up here, on his own. He'd always been a solitary, thoughtful boy.

Following goat tracks through the gorse and heather, he approached the old, abandoned watchtower, which stood on a crag high above the harbour. From there he could look down into his family's shipyards. The new schooner lay like a toy in the large pen with other ships, xebecs and barquentines and fine fast sloops, built or half built, in the lesser pens around it. Offshore, the sea was scabbed with islands, but most of them were just barren rocks and angel-rookeries, none as big or pleasant as Thursday Island. Away in the east, dark against the hazy shoreline of the mainland, squatted a conical crater. Smoke hung above it in the hot and strangely windless air, making it look as if it were getting ready to erupt. But it was no volcano. It had been formed in the long-ago by some powerful weapon of the Ancients, and the smoke came from the chimneys of the city that was built on its inner slopes. Mayda-at-the-World's-End was the finest city in the world, and Arlo's family were its finest shipwrights, even if they did choose to live outside it, safe and private here upon their island.

He left the tower and climbed a little higher, intent on the tiny white specks which were the sails of fishing boats scattered around Mayda's harbour mouth, and suddenly, as he reached the stones at the very top of the island, angels were soaring past him, their wide white wings whizzing and soughing as they tore though the air. A few of them recognized him and he heard them call his name: "A-aa-arlo! A-aa-arlo! W-a-a-a-a-ve!" So he waved, and they swung past him and out

2

across the sea and back again, following curious zigzag flight paths as if they were trying to elude a predator. He glanced up, expecting to see a hawk or sea eagle hanging in the sky's top, but there was nothing, only those curdled clouds.

He watched the angels for a while, trying to understand the way they tipped and twitched their wings to steer themselves. He pulled two leaves from a bush, found a forked twig of heather on the ground, and spent a little while constructing an angel of his own. He climbed on a rock and threw it like a dart, and just for a moment its leaf-wings spread to catch the air and he thought it would fly, but it only fell. He lost interest in it before it even hit the ground, and looked away westwards, sensing something.

Above all the black stacks and wherries where the angels roosted, fretful clouds of them were twisting, turning the sky into a soup of wings. And beyond them, far off across the ocean. . .

Something had gone wrong with the horizon.

Just then his favourite of the angels, the fledgling he called Weasel, landed beside him like a feather football. Arlo groped in his pocket for the crusts of stale bread he always brought with him, expecting Weasel to ask for snacks. But Weasel just made the same noise the others were all making. "Wa-a-ave!"

"What? What's that, Weasel?"

"Wa-ave come!" Weasel had more words in him than the others of his flock. He was learning not to let his bird-voice stretch them out of shape. Grandfather said he was a throwback, almost as clever as the angels of old. He hopped from foot to foot and fluffed out his feathers and waggled his fingers in alarm, trying to

3

make Arlo understand. "Wa-ave come here! Danger! Big-big!"

"A *wave*?" said Arlo, and looked again to the west, from where a sudden wind had started blowing.

The horizon heaved and darkened. It swelled into the sky. Arlo listened. He could hear the hammers at the shipyards, and the maids laughing in the house, and a distant sound that lay beneath it all, so vast and low that he wondered if it had always been there. Perhaps this was the noise the world made, turning round on its axis. But how had he never noticed it before?

"Wa-a-a-a-ave!" screamed all the angels, and the sky flexed and shuddered and Arlo understood, and then he was up and running. But how can you hope to outrun the horizon?

After ten paces he looked back and saw it clearly; a blade of grey water sweeping towards him over the face of the sea. It hit the outermost of the islands and there was a brief explosion of spindrift and they were gone and the wave came on, white and broken now, like a range of snow-covered mountains uprooted and running mad.

"Wa-a-a-ave!" he started to shout, just like the angels, as brainless as an angel in his terror. But who could hear him, above the world-filling voice of the sea?

He ran and tripped and fell and rolled and scrambled back through the heather, out on to the crag where the watchtower stood. A hundred feet below him the men in the shipyards were setting down their tools, standing, starting to run. From down there he doubted they could see the wave, but they must be able to hear it. . .

There was a smack like thunder as it struck the cliffs

at the island's western end. White spray shot high into the sky, and dropped on Arlo as a storm of rain. The weight of it punched him back against the stones of the watchtower wall. It plastered him there; and past him rolled the wave, or part of it, a fat, foam-marbled snake of sea squeezing itself through the straits that separated Thursday Island from its neighbours, lapping at the high crag where he stood.

And when it was gone, the thunder and the spray and the long, shingle-sucking, white, roaring, hissing rush of it, he peeled himself from the tower's side already knowing what he was going to see. Or, rather, not see. Because his home, his family, the shipyards and the ships which they had held were all gone, swiped aside by the sea's paw and dragged down into drowning deeps so bottomless that not a spar or a splinter or a scrap of cloth would ever surface, and he was alone on Thursday Island with the angels.

2

IN MAYDA-AT-THE-WORLD'S-END

n the long, lilac twilight of a midsummer's evening, Ruan Solent ran between the land-barges which were parked up on the fairground behind the busy harbour.

In London, where Ruan came from, these barges were called "Summertown", and he'd looked forward every year to their arrival. Now he was a part of their convoy, a traveller himself, and he knew that their proper name was Bargetown, and that they kept rolling through every season, not just summer, carrying their shops and entertainments all over Europa; even here, to Mayda-at-the-World's-End.

The fairground where they had parked was a weed-speckled empty lot between tall warehouses, swept clear of buildings by the great wave that had struck the World's End nearly ten years before, the same wave which broke over Thursday Island and destroyed the shipyards there. But Ruan was only ten, and he had arrived in Mayda just that afternoon. He had never heard of Thursday Island. He had heard people talk about the giant wave (the *Ondra del Mãe* they called it in these parts) but it was an unreal and storybookish thing to him; just another colourful disaster out of history.

Anyway, Ruan had more immediate disasters to worry about. His land-barge, the travelling theatre called *Persimmon's Electric Lyceum*, was supposed to raise its curtain at sundown, and already the sky was freckled with the first pale stars and in the steep streets of the city the lamps were being lit. So Ruan was rushing, weaving, burrowing his way through the crowd of sightseers and shoppers that swirled between the barges. Behind him he could hear his friends Max and Fergus bellowing through their brass trumpets to attract an audience. "Take your places at the *Lyceum*! Take your places for *Niall Strong-Arm* or *The Conquest of the Moon!*" Some of the people Ruan was pushing past looked interested, and started to make their way towards his barge, but Ruan just ran even faster away from it. He knew that without him and his fleet feet and bony elbows, the show could not begin.

"'Scuse me!" he hollered, as he jabbed and ducked his way past a fat, silky merchant. "Scoozi! Scoozey-mwa!" he shouted, bulldozing onwards. (He was a much-travelled boy, and knew a little of all the languages of Europa.) He was as thin as a pipe-cleaner sculpture and as brown as a hazelnut, with a dandelion-clock of sun-blond hair and a sudden white grin that helped people forgive him when he bumped into them. Maydan fisherfolk in their temple-going best looked down and made way for him. Pretty ladies smiled sweet smiles as they stepped aside to let him pass. "'Scuse me!" he kept on shouting. "Scoozey-mwa!"

All afternoon the barges had been crawling into Mayda, edging their way out along the zigzag causeway which tethered the crater to the mainland, squeezing through a cleft in its wall into the city. The *Lyceum* had been one of the first to arrive, and while her crew were busy setting out the stage and seating, other barges had parked up all around her; not just the familiar ones which had been travelling with Bargetown all season but a second convoy too, come down from Nowhere and the Caps Del Norte to set up shop here at the World's End.

Ruan recognized one of the newcomers; an old blue travelling market called the *Rolling Stone*. It was such a recent arrival that its engines were still cooling and sea-spray from the causeway crossing dripped like rain off its wheel arches and its underparts, but its merchants had already set out their wares, and a queue of eager shoppers was edging up its gangplank. Ruan scurried up past them to the turnstiles at the top, where one of the men on duty tried to stop him squirming underneath, but the other said, "Oh, let him through, Allan, it's only that Solent boy from Persimmon's theatre. . ."

He waved a thank you, running out on to the market-deck. It was crammed with stalls and little cluttered shops, already busy with shoppers under its fluttering awnings. A woman blocked Ruan's way, holding up a bolt of cloth against herself and asking her bored husband his opinion. "You ought to go and see the play, master," Ruan told him, swerving past. "It starts in a couple o' minutes." And right on his cue his words were answered by a distant farting of brass bugles from the far end of Bargetown, announcing that the *Lyceum* was preparing to raise its curtains.

Ruan knew that by now the audience would have gathered in front of the apron-shaped stage which extended from the theatre's stern. The first night in a new town always meant a big crowd. The seats would

8

be full, and people would be sitting on the ground too, or standing at the back, or watching from the windows of nearby buildings. Max and Fergus would be going round with their cash-satchels, selling last-minute tickets. The closed curtains would look calm and classy, and give no hint of the panic boiling behind them, where Ambrose Persimmon would be trying out his big stage voice, "Me, me, me, me, me-me-mee!" while Alisoun Froy helped him into his first-act costume. Fern, Ruan's small sister, would be sneezing in the fog of face powder that filled the ladies' dressing room as she hared this way and that among the racks of hanging gowns on frantic errands for frantic actresses. Mistress Persimmon would have lost her tiara as usual and Lillibet would be sobbing that she had put on weight and couldn't fasten the hooks and eyes on the back of her bodice . . . and all that effort, all that fuss and worry would be for nothing if Ruan didn't make it back within the next two minutes!

At the untidy sternward end of the market-deck was a stall called *Squinter's Old-Tech Improbabilities*. Its owner, Mort Squinter, was haggling about something with a large man in a broad-brimmed hat and travel-stained blue cloak. Ruan waited a bit, bouncing from foot to foot with impatience, then interrupted. "If you please, Master Squinter, we need some copper wire."

"Ain't you got none of your own?" asked Squinter, squinting down at him.

"We *did* have, Master Squinter, but AP used it to make his costume more magnificent and he forgot to tell us and now there's none left and a fuse has blown and we must do the show in darkness unless you can help us. Mistress Persimmon said you'd be sure to help. . ."

(Mistress Persimmon had said nothing of the sort, but everyone on the *Lyceum* knew that Mort Squinter was in love with their leading actress; kept her portrait under his pillow and kissed it each night before he went to sleep. Ruan guessed that his request might go down better if it seemed to come from her.)

"Well," said the love-struck Squinter, blushing as he rummaged through the stacks of tiny wooden drawers behind his counter. "It's not cheap, your actual copper, not nowadays when so much is shipping north to London. But of course if it's for Laura Persimmon. . ." He looked to his other customer, hoping the man wouldn't lose interest and wander off to try some other stall while he was busy with Ruan. "Beg pardon for the interruption, sir. This boy's from Persimmon's *Lyceum*, at the far end o' the line. We travelled with 'em all last season. They have a wench from London who arranges their 'lectric lamps and stage-effects and such, and there's never a performance goes by without this lad of hers comes scavenging for some piece of 'tech or other. It's not as if Laura Persimmon ain't radiant enough without old-fangled lights shining on her."

"She knows the secrets of electricity then, this Londoner?" the traveller asked. "What is her name?"

Squinter, still nosing in those drawers, scratched his head and said, "She's called Fever Biscuit. No, Fever Crumble. . ."

"Fever *Crumb*," said Ruan firmly, and the traveller turned and stared down at him with a look that was

10

difficult to fathom.

"Aha!" said Master Squinter triumphantly, holding up a scrap of cardboard around which a few inches of wire was wound. Ruan snatched it from him with a mumbled thank you and was gone, vanishing back into the crowd before Squinter could finish shouting, "What about payment?"

"Ask AP after the show!" Ruan yelled over his shoulder. Squinter shouted something else, but by then Ruan was halfway down the gangplank, visible only as a ripple of disturbance moving away through the crowds. "'Scuse me – scoozey – scoozey-mwa. . ."

The *Lyceum*'s stage-front reared up dark against a sky stitched all over with stars as bright as moth holes in an awning. The curtains billowed and filled in the soft breeze as if they were breathing. The crowd quieted, sensing that things were about to begin. They all knew the story of the play, for it was based on the old legend of the astro-knight Niall Strong-Arm, who flew to the moon in Apollo's fiery chariot and won the love of the moon-goddess. What they were wondering was, how would the Persimmon company fit a fiery chariot and the moon's white gardens on to that tiny speck of stage?

Well, not at all, thought Ruan. Not unless he was quick. He flung himself up the steps at the backstage entrance and fell through the hatch into the bustle and commotion within. The air was thick with the smells of greasepaint and armpits, the tiny, stuffy corridors a maze of shadows and confusion, lit by bobbing lanterns. Alisoun Froy was kneeling at the shrine, saying a pre-show prayer to the goddess Rada, who was supposed to watch over all theatre people. As Ruan dodged past her, Mad King Elvis of America loomed out of the darkness ahead of him with his rhinestone armour all a-glitter and his vast black wig grazing the passage walls on either side. "Oh, this is just *too* beastly, darling!" he complained. "It's a disaster! This would never have happened if we had stuck to using oil-lamps and reflectors! Why did AP ever agree to let the girl electrify us?"

Ruan squeezed past him without answering. Cosmo Lightely always found something to panic about before curtain-up. He passed Dymphna and Lillibet too, who were complaining in whispers that their careers would be ruined, and then Fern, who was to play one of the ladies-in-waiting in Scene Two and was busy practising her single line – "Yes, my lady. *Yes*, my lady. Yes, my lady!" – in different voices with her toy dog Noodle Poodle for an audience. He scrambled down a companion ladder and ran aft past the wood-stacks and through the engine-room where the big boilers slept in silence and the batteries hummed. Then along a tight passageway and into the cramped burrow beneath the stage where Fever Crumb was waiting for him.

And where Fever was, everything felt calm, even when it was a minute past curtain and not a footlight or a spotlight or a backstage glim lit anywhere in the *Lyceum* and you could hear the crowd outside starting to make that mumbling, sullen sound that comes off disappointed crowds and the heavy footsteps of Master Persimmon crossing and recrossing the stage above your head as he paced about waiting to begin his first soliloquy.

Fever came to meet him, lighting the way with the pocket torch she'd made for herself. She took the wire and smiled a thank you at him. She was fairly new to smiling, having been brought up among Engineers who did not approve of it, and she wasn't really very good at it; she kept her lips tightly closed and her mouth went down at one end and up at the other. Some people might not have recognized it as a smile at all, but Ruan knew what it meant. He stood there feeling proud and happy, holding the torch for her while she went to the open fuse-box, her clever fingers unwrapping the precise length of wire that she needed and twirling it round and round till it broke off the coil.

She had already stripped out the blown fuse. She wrapped the wire round this terminal, then round that, making a bridge for the 'lectric particles to swarm across, while Ruan watched her. She was sixteen; tall and bony with a strange face that was all angles and large, watchful eyes that didn't match; one green, one brown. Her hair, which she punished with a hard brush every morning and scraped back into the tightest of buns, was every shade of fair from white to honey, and her old grey linen shirt and canvas trousers were smeared with oil and grease and stained with sweat. In Ruan's opinion (which no one ever asked for, him being only ten) there was no one in the world as lovely as Fever Crumb.

She glanced at him with a little frown, as if she wondered why he was staring at her, then reached for the lever on the wall that turned the power on. Anyone else would have crossed their fingers for luck at that moment, or said a prayer to Rada, but not Fever Crumb. She knew that crossing her fingers couldn't affect the universe, and she was always telling Ruan and his sister that there were no such things as gods or goddesses. But Ruan couldn't help himself; he crossed as many fingers as he could, behind his back where Fever couldn't see, and he said a prayer as well, not just to Rada but to the gods of far-off London too; Poskitt and Mad Isa and the Duke. . .

The lever came down. The dim red working lights winked on. From outside came a noise like a big wave breaking, and Ruan realized that it was the sound of the audience applauding as the curtains suddenly flamed blood-red in the glare of Fever's lights.

Few people in Mayda had ever seen such lights as those before. The knowledge of electricity had survived from Ancient times before the Downsizing, but like all the old knowledge it was spread unevenly. Great cities such as London had buildings made of stone and salvage-plastic and lit at night by 'lectric lanterns, but on the wild Atlantic coasts of World's End in those days you were more likely to find grass-roofed huts and tallow candles. In some of the settlements which Bargetown had visited that season people thought that its land-barges were magic, and were wary of approaching too close for fear of the demons they thought they heard a-growling and a-griping in their engine-rooms.

The Maydans were not so primitive as that, but they had a distrust of technology and they mostly did without engines and devices. They had never seen anything like the clean, bright light that burst upon them as the *Lyceum* opened its curtains.

The light grew brighter still, illuminating a stage dressed as a castle, with purple-headed mountains (painted by Ruan and Fergus Bucket) stretching off into a smokey distance. A wind was blowing (that was Max Froy standing in the wings, huffing into a conch shell and fanning dead leaves across the set). Clouds sailed across the painted sky, thanks to an invention of Fever's own; a disc with cloud shapes cut in it spinning in front of one of her floodlights. Dappled by their shifting shadows, Niall Strong-Arm paced the battlements, a figure out of legend sprung to life, looking slightly older than most people had imagined him, but splendid nonetheless, with all those trails and squirlicues of melted-down copper wire gleaming on his armour and the gold visor on his helmet shining in the glow of the extraordinary lamps. Awed, the audience fell silent as he began his first speech.

Fever and Ruan, crouched in the crawl space beneath him, had other surprises in store. Tall jars full of salt water surrounded them, each with an electric terminal in its base and another dangling into it on a wire. Electricity flowed from one terminal to the other through the water, completing a circuit which kept the lamps alight. But night was meant to be falling in the play, so while Cosmo Lightely entered and started to tell Sir Niall of his plan to conquer the Moon, Ruan pulled a cord which raised the dangling terminals higher and higher up inside the jars. With more water to flow through, the current grew weaker, partly

15

spending itself as heat. The jars steamed. Up onstage the light grew dimmer and dimmer. Cosmo raised one rhinestone arm and told the astro-knight, *"So go you, good Sir Niall, to the Moon / And tell its guardian goddess even she / Must to Good King Elvis bend her knee."* Then Fever flipped a switch that turned on a masked spotlight and threw a perfect crescent moon on to the sky above the cardboard parapets.

Crouched between the simmering jars, she heard the audience's sigh and knew that she'd astonished them again. That pleased her. Unlike Ruan, she'd never fallen for the magic of the theatre, and still thought that plays were so much silly nonsense. But she hoped that maybe there would be someone out there in that crowd who would be more moved by the brilliance of her lights than by the silly love story unfolding under them, and would look into electricity for themselves and come to see how simple it was, really, to generate and harness. Then she would have played a small part in restoring science and reason to this backward portion of the world.

Or maybe that was just an excuse, a kindly lie she told herself to help her deal with the fact that Fever Crumb, trained in the ways of science and reason by London's Order of Engineers, had spent two years travelling across Europa on a mobile theatre and helping its crew of actors stage their foolish shows.

She switched on her torch to check her crumpled copy of the playscript, even though she knew the show by heart. There was a short scene front-of-curtain with Max Froy as the clown before Niall Strong-Arm climbed aboard the fiery chariot, when the red spotlight and the fire effect would be required. Time to fetch a cup of water from the pail in the corner. If the Maydans liked her moon then the fiery chariot should *really* please them. . .

Yes, it was an unlikely job for an Engineer, but she liked to think that she did it rather well.

3

STRANGE ANGELS

fter the show there was a party. There was always a party, after every show. When she first came aboard the *Lyceum*, a refugee from London with two newly orphaned children in her care, Fever had been shocked at the way the crew stayed up so late after each performance, drinking and laughing and telling again their well-worn stories of previous shows. But like so many irrational things, she had been forced to accept it. Something about the performances left the Persimmon company elated and filled with energy. If they had gone to bed they would not have slept. They needed to meet their audience, and be told how wonderful the play had been. They needed the praise and approval of strangers the way that ordinary people needed food.

Fern and Ruan loved those gatherings. They liked to listen in on grown-up conversations which they only half understood, and play excitable games with their friends from other barges or the local children, new friends whose languages they might not even speak, and whose names they would forget tomorrow or next week when the theatre packed itself away again and Bargetown moved on. But Fever always stayed at the edge of the talk, a little apart, careful not to meet anyone's eye in case they assumed that she was inviting them to praise her (which she found embarrassing) or just to talk to her (which was worse). She did not want to have to tell them that she came from London, and then go again through all the weary stories about the new Lord Mayor and his strange plans to set the city moving. She did not want to hear people tell her that she had the most remarkable eyes and bone structure, and to have to explain that her mother was a Scriven mutant.

The worst thing about the parties were the young men, who would watch her across the crowd and then come sidling up to ask her if she wanted to dance with them, or go out for a walk, or a meal. She was getting tired of explaining that she was an Engineer and had no interest in their foolish mating rituals.

That night she waited until the moon was well past its zenith before she called Ruan and Fern away and took them, complaining, to their bunks. All the way to the tiny cabin which they shared they kept telling her that they were not tired, no, not the least bit tired at all, and might they not stay up for just five minutes more? But they could barely fit the words into the spaces between their yawns, and their eyelids were already drooping while they brushed their teeth. Still protesting, they scrambled into their narrow bunks. Ruan curled up on his side, Fern snuggled down with Noodle Poodle, and within a few minutes they were both asleep, quite untroubled by the din of voices and a skreeling fiddle which Fever knew *she* could not hope to sleep through.

She went softly out of the children's cabin and slid the door shut. She felt no qualms about leaving them alone. They were theatre children, and the whole company was their family. If they woke and needed anything while she was gone they could go to Mistress Persimmon, or Lillibet, or Dymphna, or Alisoun Froy. Meanwhile, what Fever needed was fresh air, and silence.

She went into her own cabin to fetch her coat; the white Engineer's coat which Alisoun Froy, the *Lyceum*'s costumier, had made to replace the mud-stained, bloodstained, ripped and sodden red one Fever had been wearing two years before when she first came aboard. Then she climbed out of the barge and set off into the streets behind the harbour, climbing steadily up long stairs and steep, cobbled alleyways. It was never really very dark, not at this time of year, in these latitudes. The stars were out, but beyond the harbour mouth the western sky was cobalt and indigo, the sea a milky blue. Fever did not mind darkness anyway. She had better night vision than most people. To her, this was a good time for sightseeing.

The city of Mayda was bowl-shaped, built on the inside of a gigantic impact crater which rose from shallow water a few miles off the bleak coast of World's End. Fever had had plenty of opportunity to look at the outside of it as the *Lyceum* and the other barges came down the coast road and crossed the causeway, but once they had passed through the fortified cleft in its eastern wall and entered the city itself she had been too busy preparing for the show to look around, and had only a confused impression of rows and rows of houses stretching up all around her towards the ragged crags that crowned the crater. Now, as she climbed alone through its steep streets, she kept stopping to look back at the fresh views of the city that revealed themselves at each level.

From a few levels up she could see that the harbour which the barges had parked beside filled most of the crater floor. Fishing boats and pleasure yachts clustered thickly in the inner part, while big, ocean-going galleys and caravels were moored in a deep-water basin near the harbour mouth, which was a natural cleft in the crater's western wall. The buildings that lined the harbourside were old and shabby and crammed close together; warehouses, chandlers' stores, the pinched homes of the Maydan poor. Higher up the crater walls the buildings were bigger; spaced well apart in their steep gardens. Bridges spanned the goyles and gulleys of the cliffs, and some of these had houses built on them too, with baskets on long dangling ropes let down to haul up groceries and visitors from below. Highest of all, way up where those weathered crags stood dark against the stars and white birds veered on wide-spread wings, Fever could see the turreted mansions of the rich perching on Mayda's heights.

An interesting city, she decided. And strangely familiar, as if she had seen it in a dream. She wondered if Auric Godshawk had ever called here on his travels.

She climbed on, walking quickly, glad when the noise from the barges and the harbourside taverns faded behind her. On the quiet, mid-level streets the night was still, the air scented pleasantly with the soft perfume of fruit trees. Garlands of blossom decked the statues of the Sea Goddess which stood at every corner and street crossing, watching Fever pass with seashell eyes. Through an archway she caught a glimpse of the

21

midnight sea, and turned towards it along a narrow footpath which led her through the crater wall and out into moonlight and the soft black shadows of pine trees on the island's outer slopes. Fallen needles underfoot; a silvery smell of resin. The path wound upwards to an outcropping of stone and another weathered statue of the Goddess. Fever stopped there, looking out at the sea and the zigzag dark line of the causeway linking Mayda to the mainland. She thought again of the way the *Lyceum* had crept along that causeway earlier that day, and of all the other journeys she had made aboard it, from town to town, settlement to tiny settlement, across the vastness of Europa.

She had never meant to come so far. When she first boarded the travelling theatre she had not intended to stay. She had planned to get off at Chunnel, and find her way home from there. She had only joined up with the Persimmon Company to buy herself a little time to think.

She had done her thinking during the two days that it took the *Lyceum* to trundle south along the packed chalk surface of the Great South Road. Sometimes when it broke down she busied herself helping the company's technomancer make repairs – his name was Fergus Bucket, and he resented her until he saw how good she was with the old engines. But mostly she sat in the sunlight on the open upper deck and watched the weald and the wild chalk hills edge by, and tried to come to terms with everything that had happened. She had recently learned that she was half Scriven and that her grandfather had been the tyrant Auric Godshawk, whose disturbing memories, implanted in Fever's brain, had only lately been erased by a blast from an electro-magnetic gun. Fading fragments of them still lingered, as ungraspable as the memories of a dream. Sometimes, superimposed upon the passing heath, she would catch glimpses of landscapes Godshawk had known; the ice-hills of the north and the far-off countries he'd sailed to in his youth aboard his schooner, the *Black Poppy*.

And if that were not enough for her to deal with, she had two children to look after. Fern and Ruan were newly orphaned. She was afraid that they might not be safe if she returned them to London, and also that they might encounter their dead father there, for he had been reanimated as a Stalker warrior in the army of London's new ruler, Quercus. They were still silent and stunned with the shock of losing him, and she did not think they could cope with the idea that his body was still up and about.

Chunnel was a trading port, built at the easternmost end of the Anglish Channel, where the shallowing waters finally petered out into marshes and saltings. It was a linear city, laid out on the remains of a gigantic tunnel which had once linked the kingdom of Uk to the Frankish shore, back in Ancient days before the North Sea drained away. There were tech-shops everywhere, ships and land-barges from all over Europa, and a babble of excited gossip about the fall of London. News had reached Chunnel far more quickly than the lumbering *Lyceum*, and Fever soon learned that the takeover had been peaceful, and that the new rulers had announced a strange plan for the city, which was to be rebuilt as a gigantic, tracked vehicle. The merchants of Chunnel were already loading land-barges with all the scrap metal and old-tech they could find, eager to go and sell it to Quercus before he came to his senses, and Fever could have scrounged passage home aboard any one of them.

But when the moment came she found that she did not want to go. She did not want to go home to Dr Crumb, who had pretended through all the years of her growing-up that he was just her guardian and not her father. She did not want to go home to Wavey Godshawk, the mother she had only just met, a beautiful, arrogant, Scriven technomancer who regarded the laws of physics as vague guidelines and normal human beings as her natural inferiors. She did not want to go home to a city that was about to be torn down and rebuilt on wheels. She knew that scheme was not really Quercus's idea; that it had been devised by Auric Godshawk, and passed on to Quercus by her mother, and that like all things connected with the Scriven it was touched with madness. She did not want to go home to see her sober, rational friends the Engineers getting caught up in the excitement.

And again, there were the children to think of. She had had no idea how to care for them, but Ambrose and Laura Persimmon knew, and so did their daughter Dymphna (who had red hair and a face like an entertaining horse and played crones, maidservants and comic parts) and Dymphna's friend Lillibet (who was plump and pretty and played the younger romantic heroines). It seemed unfair to wrench Fern and Ruan away from these irrational but kindly women when they were just beginning to trust them.

But what use would I be aboard the Lyceum? she asked herself, while she watched the company prepare their stage that day in Chunnel. She could help with the engines, but she could not act, or paint backcloths, or sew, or do any of the other things which she saw the actors doing.

But that evening, when the play began, she realized what she could do to help the company. The play itself meant nothing to her (a lot of irrational nonsense, she thought it, all about love and jealousy and magic and other things which didn't matter, or didn't exist, or both). It was performed the same way that such shows had been performed ever since mankind first started to recover from the Downsizing; by the dingy light of a few dangling lanterns and a line of oil-lamps mounted along the front of the stage. There were some crude reflectors, made from those chrome-plated dishes known as "Hobb's Caps" which were dug up by the hundred from Ancient sites, but they did little good. It wasn't just a fire risk, it was a strain on the eyes, and Fever, who had once helped Dr Stayling electrify Godshawk's Head, knew that she could make a huge improvement.

The next morning she wrote a letter to Dr Crumb, explaining that she had been offered a position aboard the *Lyceum*. AP, as everyone called Ambrose Persimmon, was delighted by her idea of electric lighting, which he said would help the *Lyceum* to stand out from all its rivals. Even Dymphna and Lillibet grew quite enthusiastic once they realized that they were not going to be electrocuted in their beds. Fergus Bucket gave the plan his grudging blessing, and that afternoon Fever went with him and a purse of AP's money to Chunnel's tech-exchange, where they started buying the wires and bulbs and switches she would need.

While she was there she gave her letter to the master of a London-bound barge. She had regretted it as soon as the barge had gone, and she had missed Dr Crumb badly for a few days afterwards, and often since. But she knew she had done the right thing. She wanted to make her own life and her own discoveries, far from the never-ending madness of London.

*

There was a rustle and a flutter and something came down through the pine branches and landed on the cliff path just behind her. She thought at first that it was just her coat-tails she had glimpsed, flapping, from the corner of her eye. Then it fluttered again and let out a sound and she turned, realizing that it was a large bird and that it had just spoken to her.

"Snacks?" it said. "Please snacks?"

Fever stared at it. It stood there in the moonlight, a pale and dirty bird the size of a big gull. Its head was too big. Its wings hung like a ragged cloak; a long tail trailed in the dust. "Please lady nice snack?" it rasped.

Fever had met talking birds before – she knew a Bargetown parrot which could swear in twenty-six different languages – but she had never heard before of seabirds being taught to mimic human speech. There was something uncanny about the way this one looked at her, its eyes shining with the reflections of the sinking moon.

"Snacks?"

A dim memory came to her; perhaps something she had read in one of the old books at Godshawk's Head, or perhaps a memory of a memory she had inherited from Godshawk himself. Anyway, she knew what these white birds were called. "Angels". *Larus sapiens*. They were a species of mutated gull left over from the time of the Downsizing. It was said that they had evolved a sort of intelligence – Pixar of Thelona, writing two hundred years before Fever's birth, had claimed they had a language of their own with more than two hundred words. But the spark was fading in them, and now they had only enough wit left to hang around human settlements, eating scraps and singing crude songs in exchange for food or liquor.

"Snacks?" said the one on the path, hopping closer, hopeful.

"Go away!" said Fever firmly. She waved her arms at it. "I don't have any snacks." But now there were more of them, ghosting down through the shadows beneath the pines all round her on outspread wings, calling out, "Snacks? Drinkey? Pleaseyplease?" and making other sounds, snatterings and rasps and chatters that sounded like words too, but words in a language she had never heard. She heard their droppings fall, spattering on the needled earth between the trees. Ten, twenty, maybe thirty of them, hopping towards her across the rooty ground, absurd and unsettling, like wind-up toys. One landed on the trunk of a tree beside her and went scrambling down it, and she saw that there were small, white, bony fingers on the leading edges of its wings. She felt them pluck at her coat as she turned and started to push back through the flock

27

towards the archway in the crater wall.

"Let me go!" she said, becoming a little alarmed. The angels disgusted her, but she also felt a queasy sense of pity for them. She too was a remnant of a mutant race that had flourished briefly and declined; another of evolution's pitiless little jokes. She wondered if these beggar-birds were capable of understanding what their ancestors had been, and what they had lost.

"I have nothing for you," she shouted, starting briskly back along the path the way she had come. The angels followed; she heard them complaining at her, wheedling; the breath of the breeze through their feathers as they spread their big wings and glided after her. A good thing they were not predators, she thought uneasily.

Something white and wide-winged came down out of the dark above her and almost hit her head, making her yelp and duck as it whisked past. It made a papery sound as it cut the air. "Go away!" she shouted, frightened now. But it was not an angel. Intrigued, she watched it glide down into the bushes by the path, then blundered through long grass and nettles to the place where it had come to rest. It was roughly bird-shaped, but no bird; it was made out of paper and glue and slender wooden struts. Smaller than it had seemed; its wingspan no more than the width of her two hands. The thin body weighted at the front with a bronze coin, the tail split like a swift's. A small kite, she thought at first, but it had no string. It was a glider.

She turned, scanning the heights of the crater above her. Lights showed in a few buildings way up there, and the moon lit up pale stone revetments at the edges of farming terraces. She could see no sign of anyone who might have launched the glider. Angels blew like blossom across the darkened slopes. She called out to them as she made her way back to the path. "What is this? Where did this come from?"

The angels had already lost interest in her. One, scuffling among the bushes near the path, glanced at the thing she held and said, "Thursday."

"Thursday? What does that mean? What about Thursday?"

"Thursday. Thursday. Try-to-fly."

"I don't understand. . ."

Far down the slope where the crater-side steepened into cliffs one of the other angels had found some carrion or the remains of a picnic. The rest clustered round it in a squabbling cloud, begging for scraps. The one Fever had been talking to lost interest in her and took flight, beating its big wings once as it went past her and sailing down to claim its share of the feast.

Fever looked uphill again. Held up the glider in case its owner was up there looking for it. "Hello?"

No answer. Only the distant bickering of the angels, the soft snore of the sea.

She looked down at the thing in her hands. It was no toy. Even by moonlight she could see how well it had been made. And that place there between the wings; was not that where a pilot would lie, if the whole thing were made twenty times bigger? Big enough to carry a human being aloft?

In her girlhood she had often heard old Dr Collihole, her fellow Engineer, describe his dreams of flight. She had even flown herself, in the balloon that he had built from scrap paper and filled with hot air on the roof of Godshawk's Head. She had listened to him recount the legends about heavier-than-air flying machines built by the Ancients, and dismiss them, sadly, as mere fairy tales, because all his experiments had led him to believe that heavier-than-air flight was impossible. But it seemed to her that someone in Mayda did not agree. Someone in this city was designing a flying machine, or at least a glider. And now a model of it had flown into the hands of one of the few people in this quarter of Europa who could understand what it was. . .

Which seemed to Fever to be such an unlikely coincidence that she did not think it could be a coincidence at all. But whoever had launched the glider, from those dark terraces above her, did not seem to want to show themselves, and it was late, and the moon was dipping behind the shoulder of the crater, and so, clutching the white glider to her chest, she went walking thoughtfully back into the city.

The angels had lost interest in her. But from the shadowed terraces above, someone watched her go.

4

AN ENGINEER CALLS

 ook," said Fern. "That house is moving!"

It was morning, and the light of the rising sun was just starting to slant into Mayda. The company did not usually rise at such an hour, but AP had decided that the backdrops and props looked weather-worn and needed to be repaired before the *Lyceum* opened its curtains again that evening. So one by one the bleary-eyed actors and actresses were rising from their beds and making their way up the companion ladders to the open upper deck, where Fever, Fern and Ruan were eating breakfast and trying to ignore the breeze which flapped their napkins about and speckled their clothes with croissant-crumbs. Cloud shadows scudded across the harbour and the bright house fronts on the western side of the city.

"Look, Fever! A moving house!"

"That is an optical illusion, Fern," said Fever patiently. She was feeling thick-headed after her late night on the cliffs, and did not have time for Fern's make-believe. "It is the shadows which are moving, not the houses. . ."

But then she turned to look where Fern was pointing and saw that the little girl was right. High up on the crater's western wall, where the ground was so steep that even the Maydans had not tried to terrace it, a large house was descending gracefully through a long,

31

vertical garden. As it went down, so the building next to it went up, windows flashing in the sunlight. Further along the cliff another pair of houses did the same, and as Fever looked quickly across the city she saw that dozens of structures were in motion.

"See?" said Fern, with great satisfaction. She couldn't recall ever proving Fever wrong before.

"The locals call them *funiculars*," announced AP, coming up on to the sun-deck in his dressing gown, a mug of coffee in his hand. "I remember them from when Mistress Persimmon and I last came to Mayda, more years ago than I care to say. Mansions, restaurants, whole hotels on the smarter levels move up and down the cliffs."

"But to what purpose?" Fever asked.

"Oh, just for the fun of it, in the case of the restaurants and hotels." AP slurped his coffee and watched the buildings rise and fall without much interest. "As for the rich men's mansions, well, their masters like to rise each evening into sunlight and clear air, then descend again at dawn into the city's heart where they do their business."

Fever shook her head. Mobile theatres, mobile mansions, mobile fortresses. . . Why were the people of her era not content to live in places which just stood still? Was it the same urge that drove the nomad empires on their ceaseless travels, and had made her grandfather dream of fitting wheels to London? Was it a leftover from the Downsizing, when plagues and earth-storms had kept the ragged remnants of Mankind forever on the move? Maybe, deep down, people just didn't feel *safe* if their home

32

was anchored to the earth. It was deeply irrational.

And yet the Maydan funiculars *were* fascinating. She sat and watched as more and more started to move, whole neighbourhoods sliding up and down the crater walls like the shuttles of some enormous, pointless loom. She wondered what it would be like to ride in a funicular, and thought again of the glider which she had brought back from her midnight walk. She had imagined that Mayda would be a backward place, but so far it seemed full of wonders. . .

"Fever," said Ruan, nudging her. "There's someone calling for you."

Fever looked at him, and realized that the annoying noise which had been intruding on her thoughts for the last half-minute was a human voice, and that it was shouting, "Miss Crumb!"

AP went to look over the handrail at the edge of the deck. Fever joined him. Below, on the cobbled harbourside, she saw a man in travel-stained blue robes and a broad-brimmed hat looking up at her. "Miss Crumb?" he called when she appeared. "Miss Fever Crumb? Of London?"

"That man was at Master Squinter's stall aboard the *Stone* last night!" said Ruan.

"'Ere, Fever," said Lillibet, coming to join the growing crowd at the handrail, "that chap was 'ere last night after the show, asking after you. Dead good-looking he is. I told him he should call again today."

"Oh, you didn't?" said Fever. Lillibet and Dymphna were always trying to find her a boyfriend, and never believed her when she told them that she simply didn't want one. She frowned down at the stranger, wondering how she could get rid of him. But just then he pulled off his hat. He *was* good-looking, which of course meant nothing to Fever, but his head was as bald as a sea-stone, and that did. She had grown up surrounded by men who looked like that. She had looked like that herself until she came to live aboard the *Lyceum* and let her hair grow.

"Miss Crumb?" the stranger called. By his accent she guessed he came originally from one of the Scottish city states; a refugee, perhaps, from ice-drowned Edinburgh or Aberdeen.

"May I speak with you?" he asked. "I am Dr Avery Teal, of London. I arrived just yesterday, aboard the *Rolling Stone*. I'm on official business. I was delighted to learn that I am not the only Engineer in Mayda."

An Engineer? Here? *He's lying*, thought Fever. She had grown up amongst the Order of Engineers in Godshawk's Head and she was certain that she had never seen Dr Teal before. Then she recalled that Godshawk's Head had burned, and that two years had passed since she fled London.

"Wait here," she said to Fern and Ruan, and she hurried down the barge's winding companionways and out through the stage-left hatch.

The stranger stood waiting for her. He did not try to shake her hand (an irrational, insanitary greeting) but made a small and Engineerish bow. "You don't know me, Miss Crumb," he said. "I am a recent member. Quercus needs all the Engineers and men of science he can get to help him transform London. And what true scientist or Engineer could resist the chance to help set a whole city moving?"

I did, for one, thought Fever, and then wondered if that was what Dr Teal had meant; that because she'd turned her back on London she could not be a true Engineer. She blushed, and felt suddenly ashamed of her hair and the odd cut of her coat. But Dr Teal was smiling kindly at her, and she saw that he was not rationally dressed himself. No doubt he had travelled far, and had learned, like Fever, that an Engineer's standards sometimes had to be adjusted, out here in the world.

"I watched the play last night," he said. "Enjoyed it hugely."

"It is a foolish story," said Fever. "The moon is 240,000 miles away; it's most unlikely that the Ancients could have flown there. And if they did, I'm sure they did not find the goddess Selene waiting for them."

"Nevertheless, it makes a good play, and your lighting was ingenious. The smoke and flames when that chariot took flight. . .!"

Fever thanked him, and glanced up at the curious faces of her friends, which were ranged along the handrail above her, waiting to see whether she would hit it off with her gentleman caller. For a moment she thought of asking him aboard, but she felt suddenly wary. How would Fern and Ruan react to this reminder of London and all that they had lost? And what would Dr Teal make of the chaos and clutter backstage, of the shrine to Rada, dusty with the ash of incense-sticks?

The Engineer seemed to sense her unease. "Perhaps you would like to walk down to the harbour with me?" he suggested. "There is a place nearby which serves fine African coffee. Or boiled water, if you prefer."

It was unsettling for Fever to meet a fellow Londoner, having turned her back on London so decisively. On the other hand, it was not often that she had a chance of talking with someone truly rational. She waved up to her friends and called, "I'll be half an hour. . ."

"Take all morning if you like," urged AP. "But make sure you are back in time to run through the lighting arrangements for tonight. I am making some changes to Act 2, Scene III. And my soliloquy just before the first-act curtain could use a little more illumination. . ."

Dr Teal was already turning away, putting his hat back on to shield his shaven scalp from the sun. Fever did not take the arm he proffered, but walked beside him away from the *Lyceum*. Each time she glanced up at him she found him watching her with a look of faint amusement, so after a little way she stopped glancing up and kept her eyes on the cobbles instead. Crumpled programmes from last night's production blew about underfoot, and beneath a nearby barge a pair of angels was squabbling over a dropped pie.

"Are you to be long in Mayda?" he asked.

"Only two more nights; then we are to travel south to Meriam, where there is some sort of festival. We shall return to Mayda for a longer stay after that."

"Ah, Meriam!" said Dr Teal. "Yes, they celebrate the Summer Tides in great style down there. More of a carnival than a festival. . ."

Carnival or festival, it didn't seem to Fever like the sort of thing two Engineers should be discussing, so she said, "I hope that all is well in London?"

"Oh aye," agreed Dr Teal. "At least, it's some

months since I left, but everything was proceeding according to plan when I last looked. You'd scarce recognize the place, Miss Crumb. Everything south of Ludgate Hill has been cleared to make way for the new forges, the rolling sheds, the furnaces. Night and day the new factories roar and rumble, belching out their smoke. While I was waiting to take ship at Brighton harbour I could see the glow of London lighting up the sky from fifty miles away! And all the roads in that part of the world are crammed with land-hoys carting materials Londonward, and the sleepy south-coast ports like Brighton and Chunnel have come alive again with cargo ships. Quercus has had to construct steam-powered warships to keep the convoys safe from pirates. It will be some years yet before the city moves, but already he has transformed the world."

Fever said nothing. She did not like thinking about London's transformation.

"Your father is well," Teal went on. "He is busy, as we all are. Doing good work. He speaks of you often. I wish I had known that I was going to run into you; I would have offered to carry a letter. . ."

"And what of the other Engineers?"

"All well. We are a Guild now, not just an Order; you can imagine how that pleases them."

"And my mother?" asked Fever.

"Wavey? Oh, *she's* well enough." There was something odd about the way he said it, and she saw something knowing in his expression that she did not quite like, but didn't understand. Confused, she looked away again. They were passing a barge called the *Travelling Museatorium*, decorated with gaudy

37

paintings of freaks and monsters. She thought how tawdry Bargetown must look to Dr Teal, and how foolish he must think her, squandering her skills aboard a theatre. All the excuses she made to herself, her vision of herself as a scientific missionary spreading the light of reason among the fairground crowds, seemed foolish and threadbare now. She was no better really than an out-country technomancer, and she was sure that Dr Teal must despise her.

"I expect you are wondering what brings me to Mayda-at-the-World's-End?" he asked.

She hadn't been, but he told her anyway, while they walked together along the harbourside. "I am on a mission for the Guild. The new London will be a city much like this. Convex rather than concave, but a vertical city; a city of tiers. Quercus wants me to see how the Maydans manage it. In particular, he is intrigued by their moving houses. In the new London the different levels will be linked by elevators, and the Guild believes we may have much to learn from these funiculars. I must make some drawings. I'll be sending regular reports back to London. If you have any message for Dr Crumb or Wavey Godshawk just let me have it. I'm staying with London's representative here, a merchant called Hazell."

"Thank you," said Fever. "Perhaps you could let them know that I am well."

"Only that? No word of when you might be coming home?"

Fever shook her head.

They reached the café that Dr Teal had spoken of and sat down at a table under a fluttering umbrella. He ordered coffee for himself. Fever said truthfully that she had only just finished breakfast. "I slept late. . ."

"You must have been late to bed. The play, and then the party afterwards. . ."

"I did not attend the party. I went for a walk on the cliffs and. . ."

"You needed some time alone, I'm sure. It must be difficult to think, cooped up in a clattering barge with that bunch of actors?"

"It is, sometimes," agreed Fever, and felt as if she were betraying her friends. She had been about to tell Dr Teal of the white glider that had come to her on the night wind. But his coffee arrived, and watching him thank the waitress and add cream and sugar to his cup (all most un-Engineer-like things to do) she changed her mind. He would think even less of her if she started babbling about moonlit walks and flying machines.

Instead she said, "Are there men of reason in Mayda? Scientists who might have some knowledge to share with the Order . . . I mean, the Guild?"

Dr Teal laughed softly. "Hardly. You know how it is in these southern cities. They worship some nature goddess who forbids them from using technology. The Downsizing casts a long shadow. Even now, all these millennia afterwards, superstitious people still reckon that the Ancients must have been punished for all the machines they built, and that anyone who tries to copy them will be punished too. When Maydans come across some scrap of old-tech they do not try to learn from it, like rational men. They hand it to the priests at the Temple of the Sea and it is flung into a sacred tide-pool to rust."

"But what about the funiculars? How are they driven?"

"Och, simple weight-and-counterweight, water-powered, and built to a design which hasn't changed in centuries. No, Miss Crumb, you'll find no scientific minds in Mayda." He sipped his coffee, arched an eyebrow. "Not unless you count Thursday."

"Thursday?" said Fever. That was the word the angel had croaked at her in the moonlight on the cliff path. It had not occurred to her that it might be someone's name.

"Arlo Thursday," said Dr Teal. "He's the grandson of Daniel Thursday, who was once the greatest shipbuilder in Mayda. Arlo's the last of his line. Quite batty by all accounts."

"Have you spoken to him?" asked Fever.

"I couldn't even if I wanted to," Dr Teal said carelessly. "He's a complete recluse. Lives all alone in his family's old funicular up at Casas Elevado on the western wall. Sees no one, speaks to no one, just tinkers with his crazy contraptions." He chuckled. "They say that he's trying to *fly*. . ."

5

THAT OLD-TIME RELIGION

A small brown boy went running out along the arm of one of the ramshackle wooden cranes which lined the harbour side and stepped off the end into empty air. Ruan paused in his work and shielded his eyes against the sun to watch as the boy went falling over and over until he vanished in a bright burst of spray between the moored boats. He surfaced quickly, sleek as a seal, laughing, waving at his friends on the dock. Already another boy was scaling the crane to take his turn. . .

Ruan watched for just a moment more, feeling a little wistful. He would have liked to be like those boys, carefree and fearless, playing games in the sunlight that was now tilting into Mayda crater. But he had work to do. Usually the afternoons were the time when the company performed comic sketches, or AP recited poetry, to bring a little extra money in and advertise the evening's performance. But during these few days in Mayda there were to be no such matinees; instead, the *Lyceum*'s crew were busy sprucing up their sets and costumes, which always began to look a bit tattered at this end of the season.

So Ruan and Fergus were busy with paint and brushes, freshening up the shabby backcloths from *Niall Strong-Arm,* which had been spread out on the ground beside the barge. Up on stage, some of the actors were rehearsing an extra scene that AP had

41

written, while Max slapped a fresh coat of silver paint on Apollo's chariot. Ruan could see Fern watching from the wings. People on their way to visit the other barges kept stopping to watch too, but Fergus always waved them away, saying gruffly, "Come back later. Just a rehearsal. Come back at sundown. The show starts then."

But not all the passers-by were watching the stage. Ruan kept finding that people were watching *him*. It made him feel proud and self-conscious and a little awkward, the way they pointed at his work and whispered to one another. They were admiring the way he'd used brisk dabs of white and black to give depth to the coat of arms he'd sketched in on the wall of the moon goddess's palace. "Move on, move on," growled Fergus. "The boy can't work with you lot standing 'twixt him and the sun. Come back tonight and you can see it finished." But the onlookers weren't really in Ruan's light, and he quite liked them watching. He was starting to suspect that Fergus was just envious. Nobody stopped to point at the cloths Fergus was working on; the clouds and mountains he had done looked gaudy and unreal, and Ruan knew that he could have done them better, even though he was only ten.

He finished the coat of arms and started work on the stones of the wall. A line of white along the upper edge of each and down one side, a line of grey-black along the bottom and up the other. A few cracks, black for the shadow, white for the lit edge. He added some moon-ivy growing up the wall, green leaves with black shadows, a white highlight on each. He didn't know if there was really ivy on the moon, but it felt right to him, and when he paused and stood back he saw that the dull old wall had come alive; it looked as if each of those painted stones and leaves was real. It would be better, he thought, if Fergus had let him use blue or purple instead of black, but Fergus hadn't liked that idea. Black was cheaper, and using other colours smacked of arty-fartiness. "You always use black for shadows, boy," Fergus had said. "No one'll notice anyway, not from out in the audience. They'll be watching the actors, not your pretty painting."

Ruan started work on the garden. It had hedges trimmed into the shapes of fish and griffins, and two stone nymphs. He amused himself by giving Fever's face to each of them. He was just finishing when a shadow fell across the canvas and AP was standing over him.

"Ruan, is Fever back yet?"

Ruan shook his head.

AP sighed. "Well, I'm sure she and Dr Teal have much to talk about – but I need to talk to her myself before curtain-up."

Ruan could not think of anything to say. He didn't like the way that Fever had gone off so eagerly with that London man. As if some baldy Engineer meant more to her than Fern and him and all her friends. He wondered what they had been talking about all this time. Maybe Dr Teal would persuade her to start shaving her hair off again. That thought sparked others, more worrying: maybe he would want her to go back to London with him. Maybe he'd want to marry her, which would be a disaster, as Ruan had always imagined he would marry her himself as soon as he was old enough. He felt small and powerless and intensely jealous. But he could not explain that to AP.

AP peered at the backcloth and smiled. "Well, this is splendid, Ruan. Keep up the good work. And when Fever comes back, please tell her that I need to. . ."

"Fools! Blind fools! Spoiled children!" someone bellowed, and Master Persimmon stopped, astonished to find his own voice drowned out by one even more thunderous. The actors on the stage stopped too, all looking to see what the disturbance was.

An odd procession was winding its way between the parked barges, dressed in costumes as fanciful as anything that Alisoun Froy had ever run up. Flowing taffeta robes, stiff tabards, gold-embroidered copes, weird caps and headscarves, and all of it blue, or green, or blue-green. There were perhaps twenty people there, men, women and children, some banging drums and jingling rusty bells. They were led by a large elderly woman, and it was she who was doing the shouting, directing her words at all the barges and all the visitors who were milling around them. A few of the barge-folk shouted back at her, but she ignored them. When she saw the Persimmon Company watching her she wheeled and strode closer, pointing a sapphire-bejewelled forefinger at the *Lyceum*.

"Sinners against the Sea! How dare you bring your trinkets and technologies to Mayda to bewitch the young and ensnare the foolish? Do you not know that this is the island of Our Mother Below? Do you not fear the wrath of She who once raised up the oceans to sweep away the cities of the Ancients and cleanse the world of their corruption? Then you shall be *made* to fear Her! The waves of Her Holy Sea will swallow down all your workings, and Her children the fish will devour you! Her sacred waters will wash away your sin-black carbon footprints. . ."

She was just about to make a footprint of her own, in the fresh paint on the edge of the cloth that Ruan had been working on, but Master Persimmon had recovered himself and he stepped into her path, holding up a hand to halt her. They confronted one another; the actor-manager in his dowdy rehearsal clothes, the priestess in her extraordinary vestments. She was a big woman, and the wide-shouldered blue robes hung right to the ground with her fierce, red face poking out of the top so that she looked as if she were tucked up in a bed which someone had tipped on end. On her head she wore a turquoise mitre shaped like the body of a squid, with the long tentacles draped down over her shoulders. Each sucker was a gold ring, and inside each was a little sunshiny silver mirror. All the other metal about her – the necklaces and pendants, the flying-fish brooch on her gown, the settings of her sapphire rings – was rusted old iron, corroded and blessed by the sea.

"I am Ambrose Persimmon, and I am at your service, ma'am," said AP, bowing low.

"I am Orca Mo," said the woman, "and I am not at yours. I serve only the Goddess."

"Well, you and your goddess are very welcome here," replied Master Persimmon, with that charming smile which had melted the hearts of so many matinee audiences. "My company and I have travelled widely, and we have nothing but respect for the gods and goddesses of all lands. Yours is the Sea Goddess, I presume?"

"There is no other!" roared Orca Mo. "All other so-called gods and goddesses are false; there is only the Sea, and the Goddess beneath it: the *Mãe Abaixo*; our Mother Below. All life came from Her, and the lands of the earth are dry only by Her grace. How dare you profane them with your machines? Your barges and your engines and your filthy elec-trickery?"

Technoclasts! thought Ruan. *Machine-breakers!* Fever had told him about people like this; religious fanatics who believed that all machinery was evil and that the Downsizing had been the gods' way of punishing the Ancients for polluting the world with their technology. He set down his paintbrush and waited to see how AP would deal with them.

"My dear lady," said AP, "we are but simple actors. Our engines and machines are only there to aid us as we bring pleasure to the masses. Perhaps if you were to come and see our play for yourself you might feel more kindly disposed towards us. May I present you and your friends with some free tickets for tonight's performance?"

The priestess turned her back on him so quickly that the tentacles of her squid-hat swung out around her head like the ribbons of a maypole. "Listen to him!" she shouted at her followers. "Listen to that honeyed voice, which tries to tempt us from the ways of our Mother Below! Are we tempted to come and watch his sin-lit mummery? Would we throw away the love of the Goddess to see him strut and mumble on a stage illumined by the wicked technologies of the old ones?"

"Mumble?" cried Persimmon indignantly, but the priestess ignored him, and her followers were all too busy shouting "No!" to hear. One little girl forgot to shout, being too busy staring at Fern, but when Fern waved at her and she waved back the girl's mother noticed and whacked her sharply across the back of the head with a tambourine.

Orca Mo glared over her shoulder at AP, and at Mistress Persimmon, who had come down off the stage to stand beside him. "The Goddess does not want you here. If you try to perform, disaster will befall you. I warn you for your own good; bow to the will of the *Mãe Abaixo*; make sacrifice to her, and pray that she will wash clean your inky souls."

Her followers all raised their flags and tambours, shouting "Hear her! Hear her!" And through the midst of them came Fever Crumb.

Despite the noise they were making she did not really notice them till she was among them. She was thinking, and if she had heard the rattle of the sea-worshipper's tambourines at all, she had dismissed it as just another of the sounds of Bargetown. Now, looking up, she found strange hats and fervent eyes all round her.

"You, child!" shouted Orca Mo, pointing at her. "Do you too ride aboard this chariot of sin? Will you not pray with us and let the Mother Below into your heart?"

Fever blinked at the priestess's perspiring face and flaky finery. Religious people disgusted her, and they

47

seemed even more disgusting today, when she was fresh from talking about rational things with a rational man.

The priestess beamed, taking Fever's silence for sympathy. She had always found that the young were the easiest to convert; their minds were so open. She laid one plump hand on Fever's shoulder and said, "Kneel down. Pay your respects to the Goddess."

Fever flinched backwards, but found the faithful hemming her in behind. She felt herself blushing with anger and embarrassment. "All right," she said. "I'll kneel down and worship your goddess if you'll kneel down and worship my giant hen."

Orca Mo was startled. For a moment she did not understand that Fever was making fun of her. "What giant hen?" she asked.

"This one here." Fever gestured to the empty space beside her.

The priestess's face darkened. "There is no hen here. . ."

"Of course not," said Fever. "I made her up. She's imaginary. So she's worthy of exactly as much respect as your goddess."

She slid nimbly between two of the indignant sea-worshippers and walked quickly towards the *Lyceum*, ignoring the shouts behind her, the rattling tambourines. Fergus and Ruan had overheard everything and they were both grinning. Cosmo Lightely was saying, "An invisible hen, ha ha ha!" to the actors up on stage, who hadn't heard it for themselves. Fever felt rather pleased with herself. She would never have had the nerve to confront unreason in such a way two years ago. She wished Dr Teal had been there to see her stand up for her disbelief.

But Master Persimmon looked concerned as he came to greet her. The priestess and her fishy flock appeared to given up on the *Lyceum*'s crew as irredeemable and were rattling away along the harbourside in search of fresh sinners to harangue, but he watched them worriedly as they went. "Really, Fever, that was not quite polite."

"Nor was she," said Fever.

"Even so, we have to respect other people's beliefs. . ."

"No, we don't. Not if the things they believe in are stupid."

"I simply mean. . ."

Not for the first time Master Persimmon found himself feeling slightly helpless in the face of Fever's stubbornness. Not that he did not respect her for it. The more gods the better as far as he was concerned, but he knew that Fever was convinced that there were none at all, and he rather admired the way she stood up for herself. An invisible hen, indeed! He started to put a fatherly arm around her, then recalled that she disliked being touched and scratched his ear instead. "We are visitors in Mayda," he reminded her. "And that was not diplomatic. But let's not worry; that insufferable woman has already caused us enough delay. Now about the lighting in this new scene. . ."

6

THE SHIPWRIGHT'S CURSE

r Teal had given Fever much to think about. Not just the news he had brought from London, but his talk of the inventor Thursday, whom Fever felt sure must be responsible for the glider she had found. All the way from the quay where they had parted she had been turning over in her mind the things he'd said, wondering if she should have told him after all about the glider. Was it possible that here, in this irrational and superstitious city, someone had solved the mysteries of flight?

But the irrationality and superstition of Orca Mo had distracted her, and afterwards there was no time to think about anything but her work. Lamps had to be rearranged, bulbs checked, batteries charged, AP's new scene rehearsed and lit. Then a quick meal, and by the time the washing-up was done the sun was already dipping towards lost America and it was time for the performers to change into their stage clothes and for Fever to scramble down into her den beneath the stage. Sometimes, as the audience gathered outside, she found herself thinking of the glider, which lay like a fallen dream under the hammock in her cabin, but she pushed the thoughts away. She had work to do.

After the visit from Orca Mo, AP was afraid that the sea-worshippers might stage a protest. He had warned Max and Fergus to be on the lookout for troublemakers among the crowd and he had written himself an extra speech, in which Niall Strong-Arm described how, on his journey to the moon, he had looked down on Mayda:

"Finest of cities, fair and fortress-strong,
Set in that stony bowl whose noble walls
Her all-wise goddess raised from out the main
As sea-girt haven to the Maydan race. . ."

A little flattery like that never went amiss, and there was warm applause when he spoke the lines. But Orca Mo and her followers were not there to hear them, and if the rest of the audience knew how Persimmon's technomancer had insulted the priestess, they did not let it spoil their enjoyment of the play. Maydans loved a spectacle, and word of the electric theatre had spread. They sighed at the love scenes between Strong-Arm and Selene; they gasped at the moon-monster (a terrifying leather serpent which reared up and hissed when Max Froy worked a bellows offstage), and they adored Fern, for they were fond of children. When Selene's littlest handmaiden said "Yes, my lady!" they all clapped, which made her blush, which made them laugh and clap again until, at Dymphna's prompting, she had to say the line once more. When the story was ended and the cast came on to take their curtain call, the applause rolled against the stage like surf.

Beneath their feet, Fever lay back in her hot, stuffy lair and closed her eyes and let the image of the glider form again in her mind.

*

The company dined that night at a taverna called the Curious Squid, not far away along the harbourside. They had been invited there by a wealthy Maydan who had seen the play the night before and enjoyed it so much that he wanted to meet them all. Senhor Belkin was his name. "But just call me Fat Jago!" he said cheerfully, patting his enormous stomach. "Everyone else does. I grew up a little barefoot bony urchin on the harbour-side. I always thought fatness was a sign of success."

"Ooh, you must be *ever* so successful!" said Fern, gawping up at the splendid acreage of Fat Jago's embroidered waistcoat. He looked like a well-dressed planet.

There were other Maydans at the table too; Fat Jago's beautiful wife, and another merchant, Senhor Barçelo. They all wore sea-blue somewhere about their persons, and Senhora Belkin had a rusty brooch in the shape of a flying fish on the shoulder of her dress. But they were no friends of Orca Mo and her crazy followers. "It is time that we Maydans shook off our mistrust of the old technologies," said Fat Jago. "Orca Mo's brand of sea-worship is only for the ignorant. Most of us in Mayda nowadays believe we can be faithful to the Mother Below without turning our backs on all the pleasures and conveniences that the modern world has to offer. We are delighted you are here. We thoroughly enjoyed your performance, didn't we, Thirza, my dove?"

"Oh yes," agreed his wife, smiling shyly, lifting her sea-green eyes for a moment to look round at all the company. She was very beautiful, with milky skin and thick, curly, dark-red hair. When Fever looked at her she felt a splinter of Godshawk stir deep down in her mind. Her grandfather had always had an eye for good-looking women. And good-looking men, too, come to that. . .

"Are you staying long, Persimmon?" asked Senhor Barçelo, becoming businesslike over the starters.

"Just a few days, alas. Then we go south to the fiesta at Meriam. But it will only be for a week or so, and we shall call here again on the way back north."

"Then we shall come and see you again when you do," said Fat Jago, glancing at his wife, "and we'll bring all our friends, won't we, Thirza, my sweet?"

"I remember the last time you visited Mayda," said Senhor Barçelo. "Mistress Persimmon's performance as St Kylie is with me still. . ."

"Oh, but I was only a girl then. . .!" cried Laura Persimmon. "Of course, in those days, we acted by candlelight; we did not have Fever Crumb to electrify us."

"Hear hear!" said Fat Jago, raising his glass of blood-red Maydan wine. "To the brilliant Fever Crumb, and the light which she has brought us! I hope that you will allow Fat Jago Belkin to be your guide, Miss Crumb, to the many wonders of Mayda. I have long admired of the achievements of London's Engineers, but until now I have never met one for myself."

Fever thanked him, feeling embarrassed. He really was immensely fat, and although he had shaved his head in a rational manner he had spoiled the effect by painting a red diamond on the top of it. His clothes glittered with gold thread and there were jewels on his fingers and in his ear lobes. He did not seem like the sort of person who would even have heard of the Order of Engineers, let alone admired them. But he was still smiling at her, and she felt that she had to say something, so she asked, "Have you heard of a man named Arlo Thursday?"

Senhora Belkin gave a little gasp. Her husband looked at Fever so warily that she added, "A colleague of mine spoke of him. He sounded interesting. . ."

Senhor Barçelo snorted. "That's good. Yes, *interesting*. That's a good word. The whole family was *interesting*. Though *demented* might be a better one."

It was a little shocking to hear him speak so savagely. He had seemed so kindly, and had talked very nicely to the children, congratulating Fern on her performance and Ruan on his painting. He saw the surprise on their faces now and said, "You must understand, my dears, that the Thursday family has a strange reputation. People say they are – what is your word? *Witches*. . ."

"Witches?" asked Lillibet, from further down the table. The talk there was fading out as everyone turned to hear what the Maydans were telling Fever.

Fat Jago laughed. "Perhaps not *actual* witches. But nevertheless there has always been something strange there." He looked round at his fellow diners, his round red face filling with pleasure at the chance to entertain these entertainers. Nudging his wife he said, "You know the story, don't you, Thirza, my dear?"

Thirza Belkin had scarcely spoken until then. She had just sat there eating and drinking neatly, smiling pleasantly at other people's jokes, as if she were a mannequin on which her husband could display these diamond necklaces and earrings, this gold-embroidered

54

gown. "Arlo's grandfather was Daniel Thursday," she said. "He was a builder of fishing boats. But one day a stranger came to Mayda, a foreigner of some kind, a man named Açora. He wanted a ship built."

"The Mother alone knows why he went to Dan Thursday instead of consulting one of the big shipyards, like Milliades's or Blaizey's. . ." muttered Fat Jago, topping up everybody's glasses.

"That was just the beginning," said his wife. "Daniel Thursday and the stranger became firm friends. After the stranger left, Daniel went on building ships. And they were better than anyone else's. Better than Blaizey's, or Milliades's, or anyone's. They went like the wind. They cut through the sea like knives."

Senhor Barçelo said, "Some people claimed that this stranger was the Devil himself, and that Dan Thursday had sold his soul in exchange for success."

"Thursday grew rich, and old, and his son took over the business," Senhora Belkin went on. "And it was more successful than ever. The other shipbuilders were jealous. They sent spies to try and pry into the Thursdays' secrets, and even assassins to kill them, but none ever returned. It was said that the Thursdays had a familiar, a tame demon which killed anyone who threatened them. It was seen sometimes in the alleys off the harbourside, or creeping around their shipyard out in the Ragged Isles. It was called the Aranha, and it took the form of a giant spider, or sometimes a grasshopper, and it *ticked*: tick, tick, tick, like a pocket watch."

"But that's all nonsense," said Fat Jago, waving

away her words. "Have you tasted the drink in those harbourside grog-shops? Enough to make anyone see monsters! You must excuse my wife; she's a shipwright's daughter herself, and still sets store by these old superstitions. . ."

"And then the Goddess grew angry at the House of Thursday, just as everyone had said she would," Senhora Belkin went on, slapping her husband playfully on the wrist to punish him for interrupting her story. "One night she stirred the sea into a monstrous wave. It rushed over the Ragged Isles, smashing the Thursdays' house and their shipyards, splintering the ships in their basins, washing away all the sheds and workshops, tearing down the mansion which Daniel Thursday had built on the shore there and sucking the wreckage into the sea, along with him and all his family. . ."

"All except his grandson, this boy Arlo," her husband said. "All the rest of the family were swept away; all their servants and their workers too. Arlo was the only survivor. No wonder it turned him mad!"

"Not mad," said his wife. "It's just. . . He lived alone out there on Thursday Island for a whole winter before they found him."

"Imagine that!" said Senhor Barçelo. "Months and months alone on that bleak rock with only the angels and the ghosts for company. Poor thing! It is little wonder that when he was finally rescued and brought back to the city he was . . . *odd*, to say the least. A recluse. He became an apprentice to Senhora Belkin's father, old Augusto Blaizey, but as soon as he reached manhood he gave up shipbuilding and went to live all alone in the Thursday's old funicular on Casas Elevado. He makes little birds."

"Birds?" asked Laura Persimmon, thinking she had misheard him.

"Paper birds." Senhor Barçelo spread his hands out about twelve inches apart to show how big the things had been. "It was as if, when the Goddess took his family, Arlo turned his back on the sea and started dreaming of the sky instead. The white angels are forever flapping around that house of his. And these toy birds he makes used to be forever soaring over the city, though I haven't seen one for a while now. People used to say that he was planning to make one big enough that he could fly away on it."

"Nonsense," said Fat Jago. "Ridiculous."

"Well, the Ancients had flying machines. . ." said Fever.

"Fairy tales!" protested Fat Jago. "Like your play; Niall Strong-Arm flying to the moon. A pretty story, but it never really happened. Surely a scientific young woman like yourself pays no heed to those old legends?"

His wife agreed. "Only the *Mãe Abaixo* can make flying things, Senhorita Crumb," she said earnestly, fingering her brooch. "It is not for us mortals. You must have heard the old saying: *If the Goddess had meant us to fly, she would have given us wings*. It is small wonder that ill-luck pursued Arlo Thursday. . ."

"Why would your sea goddess care what goes on in the air?" asked Fever.

"She is not just the Goddess of the Sea," said Senhor Barçelo helpfully. "Her symbol is the winged fish that swims both in the sea and the sky. Her *home* is the sea, and She has lived there since all things were water, but the whole world is Hers. It is She who raised up the dry lands and lit the stars and made birds and beasts and people."

"But—" Fever started to say.

"Fascinating story!" said AP hurriedly. He didn't want Fever to offend these friendly Maydans with her outrageous ideas, the same way she had Orca Mo. "It would make a good play. *The Shipwright's Curse!* A pact with the Devil . . . murders . . . secrets . . . a storm scene. . . I would play Daniel Thursday as a tragic hero, of course, with Mistress P as his long-suffering wife, trying to turn him back from the path of evil which he has chosen. . . Dymph, Fern and Lillibet could all be mermaids. . ."

"What about me, AP?" called Cosmo Lightely from the far end of the table.

"Why Cosmo," said Mistress Persimmon, raising her glass to him, "you would play the Devil, of course."

"And I'll be the demon spider!" shouted Max Froy. "*Tick, tick tick!*"

Everyone laughed, and the talk veered back to plays. Fern tugged at Fever's coat-cuff and said, "Fever, is there *really* a demon?" and Fever told her firmly that there were no such things, except in stories and in the imaginations of stupid people. But she was barely listening. Her eyes had been drawn upwards to the lamplit windows of the funiculars on the southern heights. She kept remembering the words the angel had croaked at her that first night on the cliffs, *Thursday, Thursday try-to-fly* and the glider that had come to her on the night wind. It had been a signal, a sign; she felt certain of that. Fat Jago wasn't the only Maydan who had heard that an Engineer lived aboard the *Lyceum*. Clearly Arlo Thursday had heard it too, and he had followed her, and sent the glider to her to see if she could understand it. He wanted her to go to him. Perhaps he needed her help.

7

THE MYSTERIES OF FLIGHT

hat night in her dreams, Fever *flew*. The shock of it half woke her and she rolled over in her hammock, blaming the rich Maydan food. She almost never dreamed; she did not *approve* of dreaming. But then sleep took her again and she was back in the sky.

She was not flying in a balloon, like the clumsy thing that had lifted her clear from Godshawk's Head the day it burned. She flew like a bird; like an angel; arms stretched wide, fingers spread like flight-feathers, soaring around the castles and cliffs of cloud that formed the base of a colossal thunderhead. Below her the sea burned with sunlight, gold and blue. She was so high that she could clearly see the blue arc of the horizon, and she thought to herself, *There, that* proves *that the Earth is a sphere, that will show those superstitious people who claim it's flat.* But somehow she could not hold on to the thought; it was swept away from her by the wild, singing joy of flight as the wind tore past her and lifted her spiralling up and up and up again.

She woke with a jolt and lay there tingling, feeling the vivid sensations of the dream slowly fade. A rim of grey light showed around the porthole shutter, but it was not yet day. When she took out the wax earplugs which she wore at night she could hear Max Froy snoring in the neighbouring cabin and beyond that nothing; only the silence of the theatre and the silence of the other barges around it and around them the wider silence of the sleeping city.

Quiet as a ghost she swung down out of the hammock, pulled off her nightshirt and washed quickly in cold water from the pail she kept in the corner of the cabin. Then she dressed and put the model glider into a canvas shoulder bag and went with it out of her cabin and out of the barge into the clear, cool, empty morning.

The sky above Mayda was blue by then, but it would be some time yet before the sun rose high enough to peek above the crater rim. Sunk in lilac shadows and utterly still, the city looked like a picture painted by someone who was good at buildings but didn't do people. Not even the gulls, not even the angels were awake yet.

She walked between the barges down to the harbourside with only the sounds of her footsteps for company. Dew had formed on the yards and rigging of the ships moored there. A thin cat appeared and ran soundlessly ahead of her as she went on along the quays, stepping over mooring cables and coils of tarred rope, writhing her way past old iron bollards and rusty winches.

She found herself at the foot of the Southern Stair and started up it. The climb was long and steep and the city was waking by the time she came to the street called Casas Elevado. It curved around the southern side of the crater several hundred feet above the harbour. On its right-hand side there was just a metal handrail and a dizzy view of the rooftops and chimneys of the houses below, from which smoke and smells of fresh-baked bread were beginning to rise. On the left, long stripes of garden stretched almost vertically up the crater wall. Up the length of each garden ran two pairs of metal rails, a house at the top of one, a blank-walled counterweight at the foot of the other. One of the counterweights had just started to move, rumbling slowly up the cliff while its house descended.

Fever watched for a few seconds until she understood how they worked. Beneath their broad verandas, where an ordinary house might have a cellar, the funiculars had water tanks. When the occupants wished to descend, the tank was filled with water pumped from reservoirs up among the crags. Then the funicular's own weight would pull it down the rails, dragging its counterweight up past it until the two had swapped places. When the house needed to go back up it emptied its tanks while the tanks of the counterweight were filled, and the process was repeated. Some of the counterweights were little more than boxes on wheels, but most had been decorated to match their houses, and some were houses in their own right.

Fever was not sure how she was going to find the Thursday house, and there was nobody in that empty, early-morning street whom she could ask. But it turned out that she did not need to, for halfway along the street she passed a high wall, and then an ornate arched gateway, its portico carved with scenes of ships and dolphins and the word *Thursday* in curly lettering.

Fever pushed hopefully at the heavy gate, but it was locked. She put her face against the rusty railings and looked through into the garden. A turreted counterweight, like an ornate tomb, rested against its buffers in a grove of tall, dark trees. Following the rails up through the ragged foliage, Fever saw the house itself, a spiky, pointy-roofed construction, perched at the top of its tracks.

"Go away!" croaked a harsh voice from somewhere above her.

She stepped back from the gate and looked up. An angel was perched on the top of the gateway. It flapped its wings and opened its beak to display a pointy grey tongue. "Go away! No visitors."

"I just want to talk to Senhor Thursday," said Fever.

The angel put its too-big head on one side and studied her. Then, with a rattle of wings, it was gone. She looked through the gate again and saw it glide away between the trees and go soaring up the sunlit garden to vanish among the ramshackle spires of the house. It was the first angel she had met that had not asked her for snacks, and she wondered for a moment if it could be Arlo Thursday's gatekeeper, carrying a description of her to its master. But that was fanciful; the angels surely hadn't enough intelligence to be employed as servants.

She was just turning away when a noise from the garden made her stop and look back. The counterweight was shifting. Creaks and clanks came from beneath it, then soft tearing sounds as it broke free of the weeds which had grown thickly around its wheels and chassis. Cables glinted and twanged taut between each pair of rails as the counterweight started to climb and the house started to descend. A wide, low house with broad verandas, dusty windows, that complicated roof of spires and turrets, all built from wood gone grey with age and weather.

It reached the bottom, clunking heavily into its resting place against the bottom set of buffers. For a moment there was silence. Then another sharp, mechanical noise and the gate swung squeakily open. Wary, Fever stepped through into the garden. The gate swung shut behind her, and she heard bolts grating as they slid back into their holes, shutting her in. She tried to ignore her feelings of unease and concentrate instead on how that had been done. Not with water-power, surely. There was old-tech at work here, and she looked at the waiting house with fresh respect.

No one came out to greet her. The door stayed shut, and no face showed behind the dusty windows. Feeling nervous, yet telling herself not to be so irrational, Fever went along the mossy path between the trees and stepped on to the veranda that ran all round the house. It did not rock or give beneath her weight, as she had half expected. It felt as firm as any ordinary house. Beneath the veranda she could hear water gurgling and slopping into a drain as the ballast which had carried it down the cliffside emptied away.

She knocked at the big front door. No one answered. Yet Fever had the feeling that she was being watched, and not just by the angels which perched on the roof.

"Senhor Thursday?" she called.

The wind stirred the trees. Angel claws scritch-scratched across the shingles.

Fever was starting to grow impatient. Why would

Arlo Thursday have brought his house down to street level and let her into his garden if he did not mean to talk with her? She walked round the house, following the sagging veranda. Across every window, pale, sun-faded blinds were drawn. At the back the veranda was broader and covered by a wooden canopy, in the shade of which a white-painted wicker table and two matching chairs had been set out. From the canopy hung baskets of dry earth and dead flowers, and between them, twirling in the faint breeze, winged white shapes.

Fever reached up and touched one, stilling it. The size of a small gull, it had been made with great care from paper and thin ribs of balsa wood. Its wings were bat-like and there were four in all, two large ones mounted one above the other, two small ones front and rear. Between them, lying flat, a child's doll had been mounted, its crude wooden hands outstretched as if to grip tiny control levers.

Something hard and cold jabbed against the flesh beneath Fever's right ear. She heard the creak and clack of a pistol being cocked, and a voice that said, "Turn around."

She turned, not even breathing, just stretching her hands out slowly on either side of her to show that she was not armed. The pistol's muzzle wavered an inch from her face. A large-bore pistol, long in the barrel, with an old-fashioned wheel-lock mechanism in which a slow-match was clamped. The match dribbled a thin braid of blue smoke into the air. If the pistol's owner chose to pull the firing lever the lit end of the match would be pressed into the tray of gunpowder in front of it, sparking an explosion which would drive a slug of lead through Fever's face.

The closeness of the gun reminded her queasily of the time in London when the Skinner had cornered her and Kit Solent had been forced to shoot him. It was difficult for her to look away from the weapon. But she controlled herself, and looked, and saw her captor.

He was a young man, barefoot, and dressed shabbily in clothes which had once been white. His face was mostly hidden by his hair, which was dark, tousled and much too long. Fever could just see one greenish eye.

"Who are you?" they both said at the same instant.

"I've got the gun," said the stranger, after a second more. "That means you have to go first."

"I'm Fever Crumb," said Fever.

"And who has sent you here, Fever Crumb? Was it Flynn? Or the Oktopous Cartel? Or those clowns from the Quadrado Del Mar?"

Fever, not knowing what any of those names meant and wanting only for the pistol to be pointed somewhere else, said, "I came here yesterday on a land-barge. *Persimmon's Ambulatory Lyceum*. I am looking for Arlo Thursday."

"Well that's a new twist! A *theatre*?"

The green eye watched her unblinkingly for a long moment. Then the stranger lowered his pistol and took a step backwards, shoving his hair away from his face with his free hand. His face was pleasant, and made more pleasant to Fever's eyes by the freckles that were scattered over it. Dark against his sallow skin, they reminded her powerfully of the markings of her mother's people; for a shivery instant she thought that he too was Scriven.

"You've found me," he said. "I'm Thursday."

He was younger than Fever had expected. Twenty? Twenty-two? No older. He tilted his head quickly on one side and studied Fever. (It was a movement she would have called bird-like if that had not suggested fragility and hollow bones and a lightness not in keeping with his height and his broad shoulders.) "You don't *look* like an actress," he said.

"I operate the lights and stage effects," said Fever.

Arlo Thursday smiled. "It's a long time since I saw a play. Perhaps you have brought me a free ticket? Is *that* why you climbed all the way up here, Fever Crumb?"

Fever sensed sarcasm in the question, but she wasn't good at sarcasm and had no idea how she should respond. "I am not here on theatre business," she said. She opened her bag and pulled out the glider she had found on the cliff. "I've brought this back."

Arlo Thursday's eyes went down to the model, then back up to Fever's face. There were shadows and questions in them, and something that looked a little like fear. He didn't sound at all sarcastic when he said, "How did you come by that?"

"On the cliff path, the night before last," said Fever patiently. She knew it must have been Thursday himself who sent the model glider to her. She assumed that this was some sort of test. "It flew past me. Landed in the bushes."

Arlo Thursday watched her. There was something odd and secretive about him; his quick movements and the way he hid behind his hair. Suddenly he snatched the model from her and set it down on the table. "This was an early version. It does not fly well."

"Well enough," said Fever. "It made me want to find out more."

"Ah," said Arlo Thursday, and looked up for a moment at the other miniature gliders swaying on their strings. He put down the gun, then reached up and unhooked the largest of the models, a boxy thing with four wings. "Weasel!" he called. His voice echoed against the cliffs, and before the echo faded there was a fluttering of wings and an angel landed on the veranda, tilting its head, its blue eye glinting greedily. "Snacksies?" it croaked.

Arlo Thursday did not answer, unless that odd little quirk of his head was an answer. He was moving some part of the model which he held in his hands, winding and winding a carved shape like a double-ended spoon which was set in the centre of it. After a few seconds he walked to the edge of the veranda, held the machine above his head and threw it as far and as hard as he could.

"No!" gasped Fever, afraid that the beautiful thing would be snatched by the rising wind and dashed to pieces against the rocks of the garden. But instead of falling the model rushed busily upwards, its paper wings dazzling white in the sunlight, the spoon-thing chirring as it whirled. *A paddle-wheel; a propeller. . .* When it was almost out of sight, way up in the sky above the crater, it lost momentum and began to spiral downwind, but the angel called Weasel kicked into the sky with one big beat of his scruffy wings, soared easily after it and snatched it in his beak. Another wingbeat carried him back to the veranda, where Arlo took the model from him and laid it down carefully on the table. Arlo sat down on one of the wicker chairs, or rather he perched on it, pulling his knees up to his chin and wrapping his bare toes around the edge of the seat.

"It's just a model. But if it were built full size, with an engine – a lightweight engine – then a person could ride on it. He could fly."

He looked at her, daring her to disagree. She said, "Dr Collihole thought that it was impossible. He's an Engineer I know, in London. He says that if we are ever to fly then we must concentrate on making balloons. I went up in the balloon he built."

"Gas or hot air?" asked Arlo, as if balloons were commonplace things.

"Hot air. There was a brazier on board."

"How far did you fly?"

Fever wasn't sure. She had been terrified and exhausted and she had slept through most of that historic flight. "It must have travelled twenty miles."

Arlo Thursday bobbed his head like a pigeon. "Balloons are no use. Clumsy. Easy to get up, but hard to steer, and impossible to bring down where you want them. They make you a slave to the wind. Heavier-than-air is the answer. *Aëroplanes*, like the Ancients used."

Fever nodded eagerly to show that she too knew something about the Ancients. "Dr Collihole studied one. Well, the remains of one. It wasn't much more than a stain in the earth, but you could see how big it had been, and the shape, like a giant bird. But he could never understand how they got the wings to flap."

"They don't need to." Arlo Thursday peeked at her through his overgrown hair. She had the feeling that he didn't really want to talk to her but couldn't stop himself. He said, "When I was a boy I used to watch the angels and long to fly like they did. Look at them. . ." He pointed out into the sky where dozens of the grubby creatures wheeled, keeping watch for dropped snacks in the streets below. "They hardly move their wings at all. You saw Weasel just now. He flapped once to lift himself, again to change direction, but most of it was just gliding. That's the way I made my first models. The angels were happy enough to let me draw and measure them. They aren't quite as bird-brained as most people think. I learned everything from them."

Fever picked up the model aircraft. She turned it in her hands, running her fingers over the leading edges of the wings, feeling the roundness there, the way they tapered. There was something about that shape that must help the machine rise, and keep it in the air.

"What about the engine? Could you make one light enough for the machine to carry?"

Arlo Thursday shrugged. "I know nothing about engines. I'm Maydan; we don't have them here, except for a couple of weeks each year when you travelling folk bring your barges over. But I had a friend in Thelona, a man called Edgar Saraband; he wrote to me about flying machines. I made some models for him; some designs. He was clever with engines. He thought he could build one small enough to fly with. . ."

"Did he succeed?"

"Yes. From what I've heard, his machine flew. But then. . ."

He paused. Fever waited for more, but no more came. She dimly remembered that name, Saraband. Remembered AP flapping his newspaper at her somewhere in the rust-country, sometime early in the summer, saying, "Here, Fever; this will interest you; 'tis most scientific. . ." There had been a story about a rich Thelonan who had built a "flying machine", only it had not so much flown as fallen. She'd paid no attention at the time. Newspapers were full of stories like that.

"Are you planning to make a full-scale machine?" she asked.

Thursday's face changed. It was as if blinds had been lowered behind his eyes. "No," he said.

"Why not?"

"Too dangerous."

"Edgar Saraband didn't think so."

"Edgar Saraband is dead." He stood up, reaching for the pistol. He didn't point it at Fever, just let it hang there by his side while he said, "You're leaving now."

"But there are so many things I want to ask you!"

"Well you can't. I'm tired. Or busy. Or something."

He followed Fever back around the veranda. Angels, who had gathered along the eaves, burst into the sky with clattering wingbeats. Arlo Thursday said, "I want you to promise me something, Fever Crumb. You'll not speak of me to anyone."

"Very well," said Fever meekly. "But you should try to make a full-size machine. I could help you. I know a bit about engines."

"No," said Arlo Thursday.

71

"But you must need my help. Why else would you have sent the glider to me?"

"I didn't."

"Then who?"

"I don't know," he said. "I've lost models before. Crosswinds catch them, up among those crags. Maybe some kid found it. Thanks for returning it. Goodbye."

Fever went back along the path to the gate. Halfway there she stopped and looked back and Arlo Thursday was no longer watching her. But just before she reached the gate the lock clacked and it swung open to let her out on to Casas Elevado. It closed again as before when she had stepped through. From behind her she heard the house give a long sigh, and then the squeak and rumble of its wheels as it climbed away from her.

8

THE SECRET POOL

s soon as she had gone Arlo Thursday went back inside his house and operated the levers which opened valves high above, filling the tanks of the counterweight. As the building began its long climb he went through the big front room, squeezing his way past the thing that filled it, and looked out of the window to see if he could see Fever Crumb. He could not.

How stupid he had been to let her in! He should have kept the house up high and the gate locked. But when Weasel came flying to tell him that there was a visitor he hadn't been able to resist the temptation to talk to someone. Especially when he looked through his telescope and saw her waiting there; not that busybody Flynn or some thug from the local branch of the Oktopous Cartel but a pretty girl. He felt embarrassed now that her prettiness had influenced him. Was he that shallow? And when he'd seen her close to she had just reminded him how much he was in love with someone else.

Still, she had seemed a sweet girl. And she had seemed honest. She hadn't shown a flicker of recognition when he mentioned poor Edgar Saraband, and yet. . . That glider. . . Was it a message?

He went out on to the veranda again and picked it up from the table. He had often lost models among the crags, as he had told Fever Crumb. But this was not one of them. This was a model he had made for Edgar Saraband, and sent to Saraband's workshop in Thelona. How had it found its way back to Mayda, and into the hands of that girl?

When the house reached the top of its rails he set the brakes and stepped down into the garden, squinting in the sunshine and the brisk, dusty breeze that blew his hair across his face. His angels wheeled about the house. He called Weasel down to him and held out his arm so that the angel could perch on his wrist. "Follow the girl," he told him. He did not say it with words but with squawks and clicks and quick movements of his head, the language of angels. "Watch all that she does."

Weasel took off, and Arlo climbed away from the house, up through the last steep section of garden above the buffers to where the crags began. Small birds flew away chattering through the overgrown clumps of lavender and lemongrass. The sun was hot on his back and the crushed leaves scented the air. He stopped and shaded his eyes and watched Weasel, a white speck dwindling against the hugeness of the city. He hoped the old angel would not get distracted and forget the mission he had been entrusted with.

The wave which had sluiced young Arlo's family away spent most of its fury on the Ragged Isles. By the time it came to Mayda it was a lesser thing, and half exhausted. It still did damage, all the same, to the harbour and the shipping there. It would be the best part of a year before the city's salvagemen had ships and time to go and see if anything remained of Thursday's Shipyard.

When they brought Arlo back with them people said that he had left his mind behind him on the island. It was no surprise, after his loss and all those months he'd been out there alone. That must be why he wouldn't speak and why, when the doctors put him in a comfortable room, he would not sleep in the bed like natural, Goddess-fearing folk but used bedding, chairs and firewood to build himself a nest. He had gone lonely-mad, they said, and could remember nothing of what had happened.

But Arlo remembered all of it, and he had not been lonely. He had had the angels to comfort and to care for him. They had understood his grief, because they had so many griefs of their own; there was always some hatchling fallen from a ledge or some fine young bird taken by a hawk. They had come to the stranded boy with gentlings and cooings, with blankets of white feathers. They had taken him into their flock. And if he didn't speak at first on his return to the human world, it was not because he had forgotten how, only that he'd filled his mind with angel-words, which were as likely to be small motions of his head or shuffled dance-steps as sounds. It took him a while to dig down through that new language which he'd learned and unearth his own. And if he seemed shy and afraid it was only because the city was so strange to him, with the noise of all its people and their closeness, and their roofs and walls and window frames and chimney stacks caging out the sky.

He decided, as he settled back into his human life, that he would like to go and live at his family's town house, the funicular on Casas Elevado. But he was only twelve, and the lawyers who controlled his affairs said it could not be. They leased the property to strangers, and Arlo went to live instead at Blaizey's shipyards, and be apprenticed there.

Augusto Blaizey had been the second-finest shipwright in Mayda before the wave came, and now that he was the first he felt guilty. He had often gone to kneel at the Temple of the Sea and ask the Goddess to wash Mayda clean of his great rivals, Thursday & Sons. Now, shocked at how literally the *Mãe Abaixo* had interpreted his prayers, he felt himself responsible for young Arlo.

His shipyards were outside the city in a bay on the Costa Norte, reached by climbing up and down a steep road through the crater wall. That suited Arlo better than the harbourside. He lodged in Blaizey's attic while the years went by, turning him into an able, likeable young man. He was big, but gentle with it, and always quiet; never a drinker and a racket-rouser and a chaser of girls like the other 'prentices. But if old Blaizey had hoped he'd bring some Thursday sparkle to the yard's designs, then he was disappointed. The boy's carpentry was good; he was obedient and hard working, but that was all. He seemed uninterested in boats. His apprentice piece, a small cutter built from fragments of old Thursday vessels salvaged from the breakers' yards, showed skill but no passion. The only things he made that hinted at Mad Dan Thursday's flair were the strange folded darts of scrap paper which Blaizey sometimes found beneath his window, or on the workroom floor. Unsettling things they were, like . . . petals? Leaves? Wings? Like nothing you could put a name to.

And then there was the matter of the angels. Naturally the beggar-birds came clamouring round the yard when the workers stopped to eat their noonday pasties, and again in the evening when the smell of Senhora Blaizey's cooking wafted from the kitchen windows. But there was nothing natural about the way the big birds hung around young Thursday, never pestering him for scraps the way they did the other men, just watching him work. They talked to him sometimes with little becks and flutterings and squawks and fannings of their tails, and Arlo seemed to understand them. Sometimes he seemed to reply.

When Weasel was out of sight Arlo shook his memories aside and scrambled on, up to a small opening in the cliff behind his house. A rusty iron grating covered it, but he had the key, and he opened it and went inside, into cool shadows and the smell of water.

The builders of his funicular had dug a cistern into the crater wall to collect and store the water which was needed to move the house and counterhouse up and down. It was a large, dark space, with only the glimmer of sunlight from the entrance to show the curved rock roof and the pillars reaching down into the deep pool which filled the heart of it. Rain that fell on the heights above came creeping down through fissures and faults, and although it was several weeks since any had fallen Arlo could still hear water plopping, and see the ripples spreading as drops fell into the pool. There was a smell of moss and dim, growing things that did not love the light.

"I'm going to be needing you," he said. "I think Vishniak is here."

The echoes came back at him flatly out of the darkness. He looked across the water, his eyes adjusting to the lack of light. A ledge ran right around the pool, raised a few inches above the level of the water. Something moved on it, right at the far side where the shadows were deepest. Something lifted, rising to its feet. A small light came on, and then another and then more, packed close together like a battery of glowing eyes, lighting reflections in the water. They shifted suddenly, and the faint noise of the thing and the echoes of it sounded across the water as it came padding along the ledge to meet its master. *Tick, tick, tick.*

9

A LEAVE OF ABSENCE

ayda was waking up as Fever walked thoughtfully back down the Southern Stair. The parasols which shaded the tables of the pavement cafés had opened like daisies in the sunlight, and the bright air was full of the sounds of footsteps, voices, the distant bangs and clangs and clatterings of the shipyards around the harbour.

One of the voices belonged to Dr Teal. It cut through Fever's thoughts as she was crossing the Rua Círculo, and she looked round to see the Engineer standing beside the buffers of a big funicular hotel. A portable theodolite stood beside him on its spindly tripod like a gigantic pet insect. He seemed to have been measuring the angle of the hotel's rails.

"Miss Crumb!" he called again, snapping shut the notebook in which he had been jotting down his findings. "Out for a morning stroll, I see! How are you liking Mayda?"

Fever looked away from his smiling face. She wanted to tell him about what she had just witnessed up at Casas Elevado, but for some reason she could not bring herself to break the irrational promise she had made to Arlo Thursday.

Luckily Dr Teal seemed not to notice her hesitation. "So," he said cheerfully, turning to wave at the hotel he had been studying. "What do you make of the funiculars now that you have had a chance to see them for yourself? Impressive, aren't they?"

"They are rather ... frivolous," said Fever. "And they must waste a great deal of water every time they empty their tanks." She disapproved of waste and frivolity, and she was surprised that Dr Teal did not.

"Och, there is no shortage of water in Mayda," the Engineer replied. "The prevailing westerlies bring plenty of rain. Anyway, most of the ballast which the funiculars dump is not wasted: it finds its way through pipes and leats into the reservoirs of the lower city. But you make a good point, Fever; a very good point. In London, of course, we shall use engines to pump the waste-water from our funicular elevators back up, so that it may be used again and again. Breakfast?"

"What?" Fever had been only half listening and the sudden change of subject took her by surprise.

"Shall we have some breakfast? You can tell me your other observations of Mayda; all fascinating, I'm sure. .."

Fever shook her head. She needed to be alone with her thoughts. "I have to get back to the theatre," she said, and started to turn away before he could protest. "The children will be wondering where I am. .."

Mornings were the time when Fern and Ruan had their lessons. Fever had been shocked when she first took charge of the children to discover that they knew nothing of science and almost nothing of mathematics. At Miss Wernicke's school in London they had learned poems, read stories, and memorized a rather romantic version of history, but Fever didn't see how any of that would help to turn them into useful and rational adults.

So for an hour each day she did her best to teach them fractions and long division and the rudiments of calculus, and explain the laws of motion and the recently rediscovered theory of evolution.

They were not the most attentive pupils. Calculus and motion did not hold much attraction for them compared with the things that surrounded them on the *Lyceum*, where painted canvas could become a castle or a forest, and people could turn themselves into someone else. They had both decided already what their lives would be, and neither of them saw mathematics playing much of a part: Ruan was to be a painter, and Fern would be the finest actress of her generation. But they did not tell Fever that. They knew she would just say that they were being irrational, and make them study harder.

That morning, though, she had as much trouble concentrating on the lessons as they did. Her thoughts kept drifting up to Casas Elevado. Sometimes she would forget Fern and Ruan altogether and start studying the angels which circled overhead, trying to puzzle out equations that would describe their aimless courses. She was starting to understand the curved shapes of the wings of the models that Arlo had shown her. The air flowing over the upper surface would be travelling further, moving faster than that flowing underneath, which would mean that the pressure above the wing was lower than the pressure below. Would that pressure differential be enough to lift a whole machine into the air? Not on its own, no, of course not, but perhaps if it were combined with the thrust provided by Saraband's engine. . .

The children looked at one another, wondering what was distracting her, but not wanting to ask in case she set them back to work. It was a lovely, sunny morning and they didn't want to spoil it with sums.

That afternoon they took a walk along the harbourside to see the ships that were tied up at the quays. Fever said it would be educational, and for once the children agreed. They ran from one berth to the next, calling out excitedly. "This one's huge!" "Oh! This one's even bigger!" There was a tiger-striped caravel from the Thousand Islands, a cog from the Seamark with its prow carved as a snarling dragon, and a six-masted oil tanker just arrived from the Bight of Benin, bringing fuel for Bargetown's engines. There was also a long, lean, blood-red war-galley with a wicked-looking ram jutting from its prow and a plaque on its stern-castle announcing that it had been provided for Mayda's defence by Senhor J. Belkin. It impressed Fern and Ruan greatly to think that they had sat at dinner with a man so rich that he could buy whole warships. But Fever just kept looking past the ships, up towards the heights of the western wall. When Ruan asked her what was wrong she said, "Nothing," and then pointed out a shabby funicular, just visible among the overgrown bushes at the top of its ragged garden.

"That is Arlo Thursday's house."

"The mad lunatic Senhora Belkin told us about?"

"The man with the spider-demon?"

"He does not have a spider-demon," said Fever. "And I don't believe that he is half so mad as superstitious people like Thirza Belkin like to claim.

It is possible that his odd behaviour masks a rational, scientific mind; perhaps the only one in Mayda. How lonely he must be, hidden in that peculiar house with his inventions. . ."

"That bird is following us," said Fern, who had not been listening. An angel perched on one leg on a nearby capstan-head. It looked like a filthy feather duster on a pink stick. Fern said, "It was at the *Lyceum* while we were having lunch, and it has followed us all the way here."

"How can you tell it's the same one, silly?" Ruan asked. "They all look alike."

"It is probably just hoping that we have snacks for it," said Fever, and flapped her arms at the bird. "Shoo! Be gone!"

The angel spread its white wings lazily and flapped away, but it did not go far, just up on to a tarpaulin-covered deckhouse near the bows of Jago Belkin's warship, where it watched Fever and the children as they walked on.

Right out along the harbour mole they went, passing through the shadows of the bridge that spanned the harbour mouth and emerging into the sunlight again and the stiff salt breeze. Far out to westward a scattering of islands bristled up like splinters from the ocean's rim. "They are called the Ragged Isles," said Fever educationally, and she let the children take turns to look at them through AP's telescope, which she had brought along from the *Lyceum* for the purpose. Not that they were very much to look at. Just stubs of black rock, with the white surf coming and going round their feet and the white angel-spatter shining on their crags and the white of angel-wings speckling the sky all round them. "They look like sad, weepy, lonely sorts of places," said Fern, and Fever thought again of Arlo Thursday, who had been marooned there when he was no older than Ruan.

The angel called Weasel perched on a buoy in the middle of the harbour. Others of his flock had perched there before him; they had left their droppings, and a fish-head. He ate it thoughtfully, watching Fever with his strange little blue-bead eyes.

It was the *Lyceum's* last night in Mayda for a while. The next morning the Persimmon Company was due to leave for the fiesta at Meriam. AP was determined to give a good performance, so that word would go on spreading while they were gone and eager audiences would be waiting for them when they returned to Mayda. But whatever it was that had set Fever daydreaming seemed only to get worse when the sun went down and the play started. She kept forgetting lighting cues, and often Ruan would peek into the periscope and see that the scenery he'd worked so hard to paint was lost in shadow. If he had not hissed a reminder at her she would have forgotten to turn on the spotlight for AP's famous soliloquy in scene four (the one that began, "*'Tis but one small step for a man / Yet for Mankind it is a Mighty Leap!*"). And she missed the big blackout at the end of Act I completely, so that the curtains had to be closed on a fully lit stage.

The audience had not noticed, but AP had. "What's wrong with Fever tonight?" he asked, when Ruan went scrambling up to help with the big scene-change in the interval. "Is she in love or something?"

"Oh *no*, AP," said Ruan. Luckily he was so hot and red from his time below that his blush did not show. He could sense that if Fern or Dymphna or Lillibet ever found out about his feelings for Fever Crumb the teasing would be more than he could bear.

"Well, she's certainly daydreaming about *something*," grumbled AP. "Remind her about the spotlight in Act II, would you, Ru? I don't fancy delivering any more speeches in the dark. . ."

When Ruan found his way back downstairs into Fever's domain, the cramped space felt as hot as a smithy. She was busy fiddling with some wiring, and she had forgotten to drink anything, as usual.

"Are you all right?" he asked, handing her a mug of water.

Fever stopped drinking just long enough to nod.

"You seem a bit. . ."

"I am perfectly well, thank you," she said, rather sharply.

Ruan felt hurt. Fever had never been exactly warm, but he had never seen her this distant, this distracted. Watching her gulp the water down he remembered Dr Teal, and wondered. Was AP right? Was Fever in love with that London Engineer?

"Everybody is saying that the lighting is rubbish tonight," he said spitefully, wanting suddenly to hurt her feelings. "AP told me to say be sure you don't forget his spotlight again."

Things went a little better in the second half, and there were no more disasters. But as soon as the play was over and all the lights were shut down, Fever grabbed her coat and scrambled out of the barge.

"Where are you going?" Ruan asked.

"I need some air. I won't be long. You can put Fern to bed if I'm not back in time, can't you, Ru?"

The boy did not reply. Fern had had to grow up fast after what happened in London, but she was still only seven, and she liked Fever to be there to tuck her in. Ruan wondered what Fever had to do that could be more important than Fern's bedtime. He followed her to the offstage hatch and watched her walk away through the Bargetown crowds, wishing that he and Fern and the *Lyceum* were as interesting to her as whatever it was that she had found in Mayda.

The city grew busy after dark. People stayed in their homes during the heat of the afternoon and then came out in the cool of the night to stroll about the streets and meet their friends and eat in the open air feasteries and tavernas. Fever found the harbourside streets crammed with people. Rowdy bands of sailors barged past her, bound for the nightclubs on the Rua Círculo. They called out saucily to Fever, telling her she was beautiful and asking her to come dancing with them, but she wasn't listening. She just strode along with her head down until she reached the Southern Stair and then turned up it and started to climb. On Rua Círculo the clubs and restaurants leaked light and music into the night; she crossed it and kept on climbing, the crowds thinning as she went higher and higher.

Casas Elevado was quieter than the streets below. There were no angels roosting on the gateway of the

Thursday House. She tugged on the bell pull, waited, tugged again. She waited some more, but the gate did not open, the house did not move. When she peered through the bars she could just make it out, squatting up there among the toes of the crags, the amber oblong of a window coming and going as wind-blown foliage moved in front of it. Arlo Thursday was working late. She wondered what he was doing. Building more model gliders? Or something larger?

She rang the bell again, willing him to open the gate and let her in. She would be gone tomorrow, and she had to talk to him again before she left. She needed to know more about his ideas. But his gate stayed stubbornly shut. She considered climbing the wall, but it was high, and Casas Elevado was not entirely deserted; one of the passers-by might mistake her for a burglar.

The trees in the garden, black as puddled ink, rustled as the breeze blew on them, and she thought she heard something else rustle too, a noise that seemed independent of the wind, as if some large creature were moving towards her through the shadows and the shrubs. A fox? A deer? Fever did not know enough about the fauna of Mayda to guess. A spider-demon? There were no such things, but there was something menacing about the noise; so stealthy and so purposeful.

"Senhor Thursday?" she said hopefully. After a moment the movements ceased. She had the odd feeling of being watched. It made her shiver. She realized how irrational she was being, standing here in the dark, imagining things. It had been irrational to come up here in the first place. What had she been hoping for?

She stepped back from the gate and turned away. A tall, thin scarecrow of a man was leaning against the railings on the far side of the street, his eyes glinting in the shadows under his hat-brim. Something about the way he stood made Fever think he'd been there for a while, but when he saw her look at him he turned, pulled down his hat and walked away.

She shook herself. He had not been watching her. He had just been pausing there against the railings to admire the view down over all the moonlit rooftops to the harbour, that was all. She was letting her imagination play tricks on her.

She walked quickly along the street to the Southern Stair, forcing herself not to look back at the Thursday house.

Behind her, unheard, in the dark of the garden, something softly ticked.

The party was still going on when she reached the *Lyceum*. Fever climbed aboard the barge and went down to the children's cabin to check on them. Fern and Ruan were asleep, and she felt guilty suddenly that she had not been there to say goodnight to them. But doubtless someone else had done so.

She climbed up on to the stage, thinking how tawdry and primitive the old barge looked; the ropes and cogs and mechanisms that lowered the backdrops were like things a caveman might have made. Even her electrical machines downstairs seemed crude and kludged together. It was hard to feel proud of what she had achieved here when she compared it with what Arlo Thursday was doing.

"Fever!" called AP, breaking free of a knot of friends and admirers to come and greet her. "We don't often have the pleasure of your company at these little gatherings of ours. It's good to see you. . ."

"AP," she said, coming straight to the point as always, "I do not want to leave Mayda."

"Eh?" The old actor was not used to people who came straight to the point. He blinked at her for a moment. "But we are setting out for Meriam in the morning. . ."

"I should like to stay here," said Fever. "Ruan and Fergus are quite capable of working the electrics now, and I would only be absent for a week or two. I will come back aboard when you return."

AP looked concerned. "Are you not happy with us, Fever?"

Fever hesitated. She knew it would upset him if she said "Yes," but she hated telling lies.

"Ah!" said AP, starting to smile. "Say no more! There is a certain gentleman in Mayda, a *scientific* gentleman, and you would like to stay here and help him with his work!"

How does he know? Fever wondered. Then she realized that he was not talking about Arlo Thursday.

AP had drunk several glasses of fine Maydan wine, and it made him forget that Fever hated being touched. He put his hands on her thin shoulders and smiled his most fatherly smile. "I am sure Dr Teal will be very glad of such an able helper as he struggles to comprehend the mysteries of Mayda's moving houses," the actor went on. "And if anyone has earned a holiday, Fever, it is you, after all the tireless work you've done for us these two years past. I was only thinking during the performance tonight, 'Miss Crumb is tired; she works too hard; she needs a break.'"

He was about to tell her that she must be careful, as a young person alone in such a large and colourful city, but he could not find the right way to phrase it. Fever was more sensible than anyone he had ever met. He might be old, but inside he knew he had not really changed since he was eleven or twelve. Fever, although she was just sixteen, was definitely a grown-up. It would be impertinent to lecture her.

So he just said, "We shall all miss you most fearfully, of course. Meriam will not be the same without you. But yes, you have earned your leave of absence, and I'm sure Ruan and Fergus can manage the machines. You shall remain in Mayda my dear, while we console ourselves with the knowledge that we shall see you again on our return. . ."

10

THE BLESSING OF THE SUMMER TIDES

e shall miss you fearfully, AP had said, and all the others had found time to say it too, while they were busy packing the stage and scenery away and making the old barge ready to depart. But as Fever stood at the causeway head next day to watch them go she did not really think they would. They were all too excited about the trip to Meriam, and Fern and Ruan had the added excitement of two weeks without any lessons, for the rest of the company were all far too kind-hearted to make them spend half the morning learning things. It made her feel a little sad as she stood there waving after the departing barge. She was sure that she was cleverer than anyone else on board, but she lacked something, something that even Fern and Ruan had, that made them all part of a family and not just individuals. Strangely, she felt less lonely standing there alone than she did when she was surrounded by all her friends.

The *Lyceum* pulled away from her, with Max Froy in the driver's kiosk steering it carefully along the zigzags of the causeway. A half-dozen other barges were making for Meriam too, and the dust and smoke of their going hung over the sea and made it hard for Fever to make out the faces of the actors who clustered on the sun-deck to wave goodbye to her. She waved back until she could no longer see anyone at all, then turned and picked up her bag and walked back through the shadow of Mayda's gate-forts into the city.

Whatever sadness she had felt at being left behind soon vanished. It felt good and grown-up to be alone, with no one to answer to but herself. It was a feeling she had had briefly once before, when she first left Godshawk's Head to go to work for Kit Solent in London. That had not worked out very well – she had ended up being chased through the city by a crazed mob – but she was older and more rational now, and Mayda was not London; she looked forward to living here alone.

She had some money in the leather pouch on her belt. AP had always been scrupulous about sharing out the *Lyceum*'s profits, and although Fever's share was only small she seldom spent it on anything, so she had amassed quite a lot in two years. She found her way to a respectable hotel that AP had told her of on the Rua Bodrugan, and took a room. It was a narrow room, high up in the old building, with a window that looked out on nothing but roof tiles and chimney pots, but it was ten times as large as her cabin on the Lyceum, and for the next few days at least it was all hers. She arranged her things neatly in the wardrobe and along the bedside shelf, counted what was left of her cash, and went out into the city. She planned to find Dr Teal and let him know that she had not left for Meriam with the others. But first she would climb to Casas Elevado and try again to speak with Arlo Thursday.

Surely, when he saw how persistent she was being, he would open his gate to her?

Despite the afternoon heat the streets below Rua

Bodrugan were busy, and when Fever reached the harbourside she found out why. A religious procession was making its way across the lock-gates, amid much tooting of shawms and battering of driftwood glockenspiels. Irritated, Fever tried to shove her way through the crowds of Maydans who had stopped to watch. But the crowds were too dense, and anyway, she needed to cross the lock-gates herself; it would add an hour to her walk if she avoided them by going right round the harbour. So she stopped to watch as the priests and priestesses marched slowly towards her, some holding up big blue windsock banners shaped like winged fish, others helping to support a sort of litter on which a gaudy statue of the *Mãe Abaixo* perched. Every now and again they would all stop while someone declaimed a prayer and handfuls of petals and coins were scattered into the harbour.

"Senhorita Crumb?" said a voice in Fever's ear, and she looked round into Thirza Belkin's dizzying smile. "You have come to see our festival. . ."

"I'm just waiting to cross the harbour," said Fever.

"Then wait with us!" said Thirza, and she took Fever's arm and guided her to a clear place at the front of the crowd where Fat Jago was waiting with a servant holding up a parasol to shade him and two more carrying trays of iced drinks. Thirza passed a glass to Fever, and Fat Jago said, "A pleasure to see you, Miss Crumb! I thought your barge had pulled out this morning. Nothing amiss, I hope?"

"The *Lyceum* has gone," said Fever, "but I decided to stay."

Fat Jago nodded understandingly. "I hear there is

93

another member of your Guild in Mayda. No doubt you will be working with him?"

"Not exactly. . ." Condensation from the outside of the glass trickled coolly between Fever's fingers. The drink was fruit juice, iced and spiced, and as she sipped it she felt a thrill of pleasure that these rich and kindly people should want her company.

"You must think us very primitive, to have turned out to watch such a silly display," Fat Jago said, nodding towards the priests, who had stopped to pray again.

"It is the Blessing of the Summer Tides," said his wife.

"Of course, we don't believe it," Fat Jago went on. "We know the tides would still rise and fall and the fish would still swim into Maydan nets without all this pretty flummery. But it is a ritual; a ceremony; a tradition that links us with our ancestors and our city's past. I do hope you understand."

"I have come to watch the procession every year since I was a little girl," said Thirza, who looked as excited as a little girl still, her eyes shining and a laugh bubbling behind every word. "Do you see the statue on the litter there? That is the holy likeness of the *Mãe*, which is taken out of its tank at the Temple of the Sea for just this one day out of all the year. It was discovered in the long, long ago, washed up on the shore after a storm."

"There are educated men who claim it's not the *Mãe Abaixo* at all but a likeness of some other goddess who used to be worshipped in these parts," said Fat Jago.

"Well, educated men do not know everything,"

94

retorted Thirza, who seemed to take the old religion more seriously than her husband did. She shaded her eyes against the sunlight to watch as the procession reached the end of the lock-gates and stepped down on to the harbourside. Pretty young acolytes came hurrying through the crowd with fishing nets, into which people dropped fish-shaped Maydan coins. A dropped orange rolled in the dust underfoot until a small, tow-haired boy ran out of the crowd and picked it up.

"There was a time," said Thirza Belkin, "when the *Mãe Abaixo* used to appear to people. She would rise up out of the depths to speak with shipwrecked sailors and drowning fishermen. She would save them and carry them to the shore, and She gave them revelations; messages that let us know how we could best please Her. I used to love those stories when I was little. . . I used to hope that I might see Her for myself one day. But it doesn't happen nowadays. I wonder why?"

"Because people are less gullible than they used to be," said Fat Jago. "I bet Orca Mo would love a good revelation. Look at her; she knows she's turning into a mere party decoration! She'd love to announce some new appearance by the *Mãe Abaixo* to strengthen people's faith and restore her own power. But she knows that hardly anybody would believe it."

The priestess passed them, with all the tentacles of her squid hat trailing in the wind. She did look a little self-conscious, thought Fever. Perhaps Fat Jago was right. Perhaps even Orca Mo knew that her religion was losing its meaning.

"So what has kept you in Mayda?" Fat Jago asked,

raising his voice above the jingle of tambourines as the statue on its litter passed them. "Would it be young Thursday, by any chance?"

Fever looked at him in surprise. How did he know that she had been planning to see Arlo Thursday?

Thirza laughed and touched Fever lightly on the wrist. "There is nothing that happens in Mayda that Jago doesn't find out about. He's incorrigibly nosey."

"I'm a businessman," her husband protested. "I keep my ear to the ground, that's all. And from the way Miss Crumb asked after Thursday the other evening, I could tell he interested her." He looked serious for a moment, leaning close to Fever. "Be careful, my dear. What I said about Arlo Thursday was quite true. He really is mad."

"I did not think so," said Fever. It unsettled her that Fat Jago knew her business, but she was not sure why. And why did she feel this sudden need to defend Arlo? "He is certainly eccentric, but he seemed perfectly rational to me."

"You've actually spoken with him then?" Fat Jago's forehead crinkled like a Roman blind as he raised both eyebrows. "I didn't think he saw anyone nowadays."

"Only his angels," said Thirza softly, watching the statue go by. There was a sadness in her eyes, and Fever wondered if it was because of the Goddess or because of Arlo Thursday.

"Thirza used to have a thing for young Thursday," said her husband, turning jocular again.

"Oh Jago!" laughed his wife. "Don't be silly! He worked for a while at my father's shipyard, that is all. We were friends. . ."

"Childhood sweethearts!"

"Not at all! Anyway, imagine if I'd married him; I would be called Thirza Thursday. Have you ever heard such a silly name, Fever?"

"If you'd married Thursday," said her husband, "your silly name would be the least of your worries. It's true that I may not be as young and good-looking as him. It's true that I haven't seen my toes for thirty years, and I don't expect ever to see them again, but at least I can provide for you. . ."

"Of course you can," said Thirza, reaching across Fever to take his hand.

"Nevertheless, Fever," said Fat Jago, "I would ask you, as a friend, not to call on Arlo Thursday any more. Who knows what he gets up to, up in that old house? I would fear for your safety if you went there again."

Fever felt herself bristle. What gave Fat Jago the right to tell her what she should do and who she should see? He claimed to be rational, but he was as blinded as the rest of Mayda by those foolish stories about the Thursday family. He clearly meant his warning kindly, though, so she thanked him as politely as she could. But still she wondered how he had known that she'd been calling on Arlo.

The procession had passed. The crowd of onlookers started to break up, some following the statue of the *Mãe Abaixo* back towards Her temple, others drifting away along the harbourside or across the lock-gates. The Belkins were keen that Fever should go and have lunch with them, but she said no. The afternoon was wearing on, and she had the long climb to Casas Elevado ahead of her. She agreed to visit them at their villa the next day, then set out across the lock-gates alone.

11

AËROPLANE

t the Thursday house the gate was still locked, and there were no angels waiting. Fever tugged at the rusty bell pull again without much hope and wondered what else she could do with the remainder of the afternoon. But to her surprise the gate swung open, and as she stepped through it she heard the house rumbling down to meet her.

"Miss Crumb," said Arlo Thursday, opening the front door to her as the building came to rest against its buffers. "I thought you'd gone away."

"The *Lyceum* has gone. I decided to stay."

"Oh."

"I've been thinking about what you told me," she said. "About flight."

"That can be dangerous," he said. He was looking past her, scanning the garden, as if wanting to make sure that no one else had slipped in with her. "Even thinking about flight can be dangerous."

They stood there on the veranda watching each other. The wind blew in through the open front door and stirred the litter that lay on the floor of the hallway; angel feathers and delicate curls of wood that looked like bits of pasta and rustled like paper as they rolled across the floorboards.

"You shouldn't have stayed," Arlo Thursday said. Then he shrugged. "You'd better come in."

He led her through the shady, cluttered house to its kitchen and started making coffee before she found the nerve to tell him that she really only drank boiled water. The smell from the coffee-pot filled the large, low-ceilinged room, and to Fever, whose Scriven senses lent every scent a colour, it smelled as golden as the sunlight which washed in through the dirty windows when Arlo raised the blinds.

"Once a week I bring the house down here and a delivery boy drops off the stuff I need and picks up payment," he said. "I've got some money left out of what Edgar paid me for designing his flyer. Not much, but enough for bread and cheese and coffee. That's all I need."

Fever gave a sceptical sniff. Bread and cheese and coffee hardly constituted a balanced diet, and she could also think of several other things that Arlo Thursday needed, such as some soap, and a broom, and a feather duster. The faint blue odour of his unwashed body reached her clear across the kitchen, and mingled unattractively with the scent of days-old food mouldering on the plates piled up on the table. Books and papers were heaped up there too, and splashes of bird-lime crusted on shelves and chair-backs suggested that the angels were allowed indoors. The place offended Fever's sense of order as well her sense of smell, but she did her best to ignore it and concentrate on the model flying machines which swayed above her, hanging on their barely visible threads from the kitchen ceiling.

He handed her a tin cup filled with coffee. She looked down at it and saw her reflection gawping up at her from its umber surface. It was definitely too late now to tell him that she didn't approve of coffee, and she wondered what she was going to do with the stuff.

"I've got something to show you," said Arlo Thursday. "Come on."

They went back through the house, past an open doorway which gave Fever an unattractive glimpse of Arlo's unmade bed and a bedroom strewn with cast-off clothes. He led her to another door, around which the floor was heaped with more of those curls of pale wood she'd noticed earlier. Sawdust lay thickly there, and mice had left wandering trails through the drifts, like the footprints of lost explorers in a desert, vanishing in the draught as Arlo swung the door open.

He stood back to let her go past him into a big, curtained space which she supposed had once been the old funicular's dining room. There was rich paper on the walls, though it was old and peeling and the mice had nibbled it. There was an expensive-looking antique dining table which seemed to have been turned into a workbench, its surface completely hidden beneath heaps of tools and piles of papers. Fever barely noticed it. There was only one other thing in the room, but it occupied her whole attention.

It was a flying machine.

It was only half finished, the fine blond wooden bones of its wings and body not yet covered with paper, but already it had the grace which Fever had recognized in the models. There was a sense of imminence about it; of some flying thing at rest, readying itself to spring into the air. It looked caged, filling the room, the tips of those skeleton wings touching the walls.

She looked back at Arlo. He was watching her. She could see the machine mirrored in his eyes. "It is based on the designs I made for Edgar Saraband," he said, "but I've made some improvements."

She circled the machine, ducking under the broad wings, running her fingers over the smooth, planed struts. Again she noticed the shape of the wings in cross section; that rounded leading edge and the unmatching curves of the top and bottom surfaces. Still watching her, Arlo said suddenly, "There's a bit of ancient maths, the Navier-Stokes equations. . ."

"They describe the movement of objects in water," said Fever, startled, for she had never imagined that anyone outside the Engineers would know of the equations. They had been one of the Order's treasures, unearthed in an old library.

"The equations work for air, too," said Arlo. "For any fluid medium. My grandfather was a shipbuilder. He used them to work out the best shape for oars and keels and rudders. That's what made me think of applying them to wings. Once you know how the air flows round a wing you can shape it to provide more lift. . ."

Fever looked at him out of his web of struts and cables. This strange young man had made a leap of reasoning worthy of an Engineer. She touched the propeller, mounted in the heart of the structure, pointing backwards. Still crude, waiting to be planed and sanded, but already roughly shaped and moving easily on its axle.

She said, "How is it to be powered?"

Arlo pointed at something among the debris on the table; a dark metal thing like a warrior's helmet, hinged open to expose crude pistons. She went closer. It was an engine; a *Saraband MkI Aëro-Engine*, according to the brass plate on its side.

"Edgar sent that to me just before he died. He sent instructions on how it should be mounted; how it's linked to the propeller. I'll launch from a cliff top. The engine will thrust me forward while the wings provide lift."

"A cliff top?" asked Fever. "How will you even get your machine out of the house?"

"In sections. It comes to pieces, and it is quite light. I have a place in mind where I can test it."

"I could help you," she said.

"It's dangerous."

"I don't care."

"You would if you understood. In his last letters to me, Edgar was frightened. And then he was killed. His machine crashed."

"An accident. We'll be more careful."

"Not an accident. I'm sure of it. The machine should have flown. I read reports. It climbed, but then it fell. Someone must have tampered with it. Saraband was murdered."

"By whom?"

103

"There was a man called Lothar Vishniak. Edgar wrote to me about him. A stranger who hung around his workshop. Edgar said at first what a good fellow he was, but later, I think he was afraid. I think that's why he sent the spare engine to me. So that I could continue his work if he was murdered. . ."

Fever saw very clearly in her mind's eye that tall man who had stood watching her the previous night while she had loitered at Arlo's gate. Then she shook her head. This was just paranoia. Saraband had been involved in dangerous research, so it was natural that he would have been apprehensive. There was no rational reason to think that he'd been murdered.

She came right round the machine and back to where Arlo stood waiting by the door. "Senhor Thursday. . ."

"Arlo."

"Arlo, I could help you. You needn't do all this work alone. There is another Engineer in Mayda; Dr Teal. I'm sure that if I told him about you, he could put you in touch with our Guild in London. . ."

It was the wrong thing to say. Those blinds came down again behind Thursday's eyes. "I *knew* you were working for someone!" he said angrily.

"I'm not working for anyone. . ."

He let out a laugh so bitter that it barely sounded like a laugh at all. "Oh, Fever Crumb," he said, "I almost believed in you the first time you told me that. But you're just another spy, aren't you? That's why you're still here even though your theatre's gone. You're working for this Londoner, and he sent you to me because he thought I'd be more likely to talk to a pretty girl than an ugly old Engineer."

"That isn't true. . ."

"Well, you can tell your London Engineer that I'm not interested."

"But he'd want to help, I'm sure," said Fever, flustered by his sudden show of emotion. "All scientific progress is of interest to the Engineers. They will want to hear all about your discoveries. Dr Collihole will be fascinated to see your machines, and to share his own designs with you. That is the way of true scientists, isn't it? To share our work, so that our colleagues can point out the flaws in our theories and build upon our discoveries. . ."

"Get out!" shouted Arlo Thursday. He snatched a wrench from the table, knocking other tools to the floor. Fever backed away, alarmed by the anger in his eyes. Maybe Dr Teal and Fat Jago had been right about him after all. Maybe, for all his brilliance, he was crazy.

She hurried to the door, and out into the hallway. "Out!" shouted Thursday behind her. She heard his footsteps and thought he was coming after her, but when she looked back she saw he had turned the other way, into a small room packed with levers, dials and gauges. She felt the house lurch, and heard water splashing beneath the floor as the tanks emptied. The tanks of the counterweight must already have been filled, for by the time she opened the front door the building was in motion, rising slowly away from its buffers. Fever hesitated, then jumped from the moving veranda, landing awkwardly in the long grass beside the track and falling over.

As she went shakily back through the overgrown garden she sensed something moving through the bushes by the path, and thought for a moment that she heard a noise; a stern ticking, like an angry grandfather clock. But when she stopped to listen, the noise stopped too, and she dismissed it. She went to the gate, and it opened to let her out and closed again behind her with a clang that sounded final this time.

"Arlo Thursday is deranged," she told herself, as she stood in his gateway, slowly calming down. "I was wrong to seek him out."

But just because he had been unreasonable did not mean that she should abandon reason too. She recited perfect numbers to herself until she felt calmer, then thought about Arlo and his strange past. She had been unfair to him, she decided. Unlike her, he had never had the benefit of an upbringing among Engineers. Indeed, he'd been partly brought up by birds. Clearly it had left him with a deep mistrust of other people. That must be why he lived all alone, with only that gaggle of angels for company. That must be why his only friendship had been conducted by letter, with a man he had never even met. He was frightened of people. That was why he imagined enemies everywhere, and fancied that Saraband's death must have been murder.

He needed help. He needed to be protected from his own irrational fears. He might not know it, but he needed Fever Crumb. She straightened her clothes, smoothed back her hair and set off. Whether Arlo wished her to or not, she had a duty to take the news of his discoveries to Dr Teal.

She was so busy with her own thoughts that she did not notice the tall, shabby man who leaned against the railings on the far side of Casas Elevado and watched her go.

12

THE FOUNTAIN

 onathan Hazell, London's representative in Mayda, was a small man, a quiet man, and in many ways a dull one. He had moved to the city in his youth with vague ideas of romance and adventure, but he wasn't cut out for those things, and in his rambling house on the Rua Penhasco he lived alone, leading the same small, quiet, dull life that he might have lived in London. Not that he was unhappy. He enjoyed his daily routine: visiting the harbourside exchange each morning to trade and drink coffee with the other merchants, walking briskly home in the middle afternoon to sit in his courtyard garden. On days when the sea was calm he sometimes took his little boat out fishing in the shallow waters between Mayda and the mainland. And he enjoyed his role as London's official representative in Mayda, which meant that visiting London traders would seek him out, bringing news from home.

At least, he had enjoyed it until Dr Teal arrived. Dr Teal, who had turned up very late two nights before, striding in his muddy boots across Jonathan Hazell's polished floors, and announcing that he would be staying. Saying breezily that he meant to make the house his "base of operations" (whatever that might mean!) "for the foreseeable future" (however long that was!). Insisting that

Jonathan Hazell send a message off to London, by expensive express courier, with no mention made of compensation.

Jonathan Hazell had half a mind to throw the impertinent fellow out. But Jonathan Hazell was not the sort of man who threw people out of places. And, angry though he was, he realized that it might not be a good idea to upset this envoy from London, who carried papers signed by the Chief Engineer and by London's new ruler, the barbarian warlord Quercus. So, eager to show how loyal he was to the new regime, he had let Dr Teal take over his lovely, comfortable bedroom up at the top of the house, and had removed himself to the guest room. Since he had never had any guests he had not realized how lumpy and uncomfortable the guest-room bed was until he slept in it himself – or failed to sleep. For two nights now he had lain awake, listening to the grumble of nearby funiculars going up and down the crater walls.

He had been too tired and upset to go to the exchange that morning. He had decided to stay at home and catch up on his sleep, and let his Maydan clerks handle business. But no sooner had he dropped off for his afternoon nap than he was woken by a jangling at the doorbell.

He waited for the servants to answer it. But of course, at this hour the servants were all out. So he got out of the horrible bed and wrestled his dressing gown on and went stalking downstairs, past the breakfast room littered with Dr Teal's papers, to the door.

A girl of some sort stood on the step. A tall girl in an odd white coat, with severe hair. Jonathan Hazell supposed that was the fashion among girls nowadays. She had strange eyes. Indeed, she had a strange sort of face altogether. She reminded him faintly of the Scriven, who had ruled London when he was young. Some old, submissive instinct kicked in and stopped him telling her to go away.

"I am Fever Crumb. I am here to see Dr Teal," she said primly.

Well, of course she was. Jonathan Hazell drew himself up to his full height, though it didn't do him much good as it only brought his nose to the level of Fever Crumb's sternum. He said, "Well, he isn't! Isn't *here*, I mean. To see you. He's out. He's gone out to make drawings, for some reason."

"Do you know when he will be back?"

"I am not Dr Teal's social secretary!" said Jonathan Hazell sharply. But he wasn't much good at being sharp with people. This girl was very pretty really, despite her Scrivenish looks, and she seemed so disappointed to find Teal gone that he at once felt guilty for speaking in that hasty way. He remembered something that the Engineer had said at breakfast, while he sat reading Jonathan Hazell's newspaper and eating rather a lot of Jonathan Hazell's marmalade.

"I think he told me that he was going up to the Plaza Del Cielo," he mumbled. "You will probably be able to find him there. The second stairway on your left at the end of the street will take you to it."

"Thank you," said Fever Crumb, and she walked

away along the street through the sunlight and the shadows of the lemon trees, while Jonathan Hazell stood on his front doorstep and watched her go, wondering why such an attractive young person would be seeking out the bumptious Dr Teal.

The Engineer was sitting cross-legged on the wall of a fountain in the corner of the Plaza Del Cielo. There was a statue in the middle of the fountain which showed the *Mãe Abaixo* in her sky-goddess aspect, surrounded by leaping stone flying fish and fat stone rainclouds. Water from holes in the bases of the clouds fell prettily into the fountain all around the goddess, and sometimes, when the warm breeze gusted, it fell on Dr Teal as well.

The Engineer had a large notebook open on his lap and he was making a careful drawing in it of a nearby funicular, a house much larger than Arlo Thursday's, with six sets of rails stretching up the landscaped crater wall behind it. The little crowd of Maydan children who had gathered to watch him work were as quiet as he, absorbed in the strange foreigner and the picture he was making. But they drew aside when Fever came striding up. Dr Teal left off his drawing, snapped his notebook shut and looked up at her, beaming.

"Miss Crumb! I thought you had gone south with your theatre. . ."

Fever couldn't be bothered to explain again, so she just shook her head. "I have spoken with Arlo Thursday," she said.

"Really? And what did you make of him?"

Fever sat down beside him. The ledge around the fountain was damp, brushed by the drifting spray. She said, "He is very peculiar. Unkempt and agitated. Not at all like an Engineer. Yet I think he has a great deal of knowledge. Have you heard of Edgar Saraband?"

"Yes. A Thelonan nobleman who killed himself trying to fly some sort of contraption off the cliffs there a few months back. . ."

"I believe Saraband's flying machine was nine-tenths Arlo's invention. Saraband built the engine, but Arlo designed the wings and body, and he has intriguing ideas about..." She cut herself short. She was babbling. "Dr Teal, I think he has unlocked the secret of flight. . ."

She repeated, as quickly as she could, the things that Arlo Thursday had told her.

When she had finished Dr Teal rubbed his chin and said, "So the Thursday boy is an inventor. . ."

"Can the Guild help him?" asked Fever. "He is afraid. He mentioned a man named Vishniak."

Dr Teal shrugged. "The name means nothing to me. Who is he?"

"Arlo thinks he murdered Edgar Saraband."

Dr Teal looked sharply at her, and then started to laugh. "Murdered? Miss Crumb, your time aboard the theatre has left you with a vivid imagination!"

Fever felt herself blush at the insult, but pressed on. "I know it sounds irrational, but. . . There *was* a man hanging around outside Arlo's house yesterday evening."

"What manner of man?"

112

"Tall. Shabby. A hat like yours, and a long coat. Rather a long face, unshaven. . ."

Dr Teal looked thoughtful. "That sounds like Flynn. I didn't know *he* had dragged himself to Mayda. . ."

"You know him?"

"I've met him once or twice on my travels. Midas Flynn. He's a shady small-time technomancer, out of ideas and not above stealing them from better men."

"Do you think *he* might have killed Edgar Saraband?"

"No, no. . . Flynn's shifty, but he's not the murdering type. Anyway, poor Saraband didn't need any help killing himself. That fool engine of his exploded. He was blown to bits."

"So the fault was with the engine, not with Arlo's machine!" said Fever eagerly. "If we could only find him somewhere where he could work in peace, and help him to make a better engine. . ."

"You think his invention would be in London's interests?" asked Dr Teal.

"Of course it would! It would be in everybody's interests! If we could fly like the Ancients did. . . Think of the possibilities for trade, for exploration. . . Above all, it would put an end to this mad notion of setting London moving. Why would a city need to move if there were flying machines which could move faster and more safely?"

"Why indeed?" said Dr Teal, raising an eyebrow.

"We Engineers should not be helping Quercus to put London on wheels; we should be advising him on how to lay the city out harmoniously on solid ground and surround it with the take-off stations for Arlo Thursday's air machines. Can you not take him under your protection? I know that Dr Collihole would be fascinated by his discoveries. . ."

Dr Teal winced. "Dr Collihole. . . Fever, I should have told you, I completely forgot. . ."

"What?"

"Dr Collihole is dead."

"Dead? How?"

"I'm not sure. It happened shortly before I joined the Guild."

"But he was so well!"

"They just found him dead one morning. It was a heart attack, I think."

"I mean, he was old, but he was well. . ."

"He was an old man. There are so many things that kill old men."

A gust of wind blew spray from the fountain into Fever's face and she was glad of it, because it gave her a chance to wipe her eyes before Dr Teal could see that she was weeping.

He put his hand on her shoulder, surprising her. Engineers did not usually touch one another. He said, "I'll have Hazell send word to London about the Thursday boy. If Flynn is after him, who knows? He may have stumbled upon something after all."

"He has," insisted Fever.

It was frustrating. She knew that Dr Teal still doubted her. He was blinded by the stories about Arlo Thursday being mad. But there was nothing more that she could say to convince him, and she knew that there was no point in dragging him back across the city with her to see Arlo Thursday's work for himself. Arlo would never let him in.

Dr Teal looked thoughtfully at her, and said, "I'm pleased you decided not to go down to Meriam with your friends. I would have worried that I might lose you again. I have sent word north about you, you know. Master Hazell's courier should reach London in a day or two. Your mother and father will be relieved to hear that you are found."

"I was not lost," said Fever. It annoyed her that he had written to her parents. "I am not a child."

"Clearly Ambrose Persimmon does not think so, if he has let you remain here in Mayda all alone," said Dr Teal. He opened his book and studied his drawing of the big funicular. "Where are you lodging? A hotel? You would be better off at Jonathan Hazell's place. I shall have him prepare a room for you. . ."

"No," said Fever.

He looked up at that, surprised, perhaps a little angered.

"I am quite capable of looking after myself, Dr Teal," Fever said. She stood up. "Please do not forget what I have told you about Arlo Thursday. Please send word to London quickly."

"Now hang on. . ." the Engineer started to say, but she had already turned away.

She strode back down the stairways towards Rua Penhasco and her hotel, wondering where she would eat that night, trying to forget the patronizing Dr Teal and the sad news about Dr Collihole and regain that feeling of freedom and independence that she had felt earlier. The sun was low and red in the west now, and Mayda was filling with shadows. In the busy streets beside the harbour a sedan chair pulled out in front of her, going in the same direction. She followed it, glad of the path it cut for her through the crowd, remembering how, in London, she had always thought sedan chairs a most unreasonable mode of transport. Here in Mayda, with all these stairways, they made more sense. She guessed that this one was on its way to Bargetown, and wondered if its rich passengers would be disappointed to find the *Lyceum* gone. . .

But suddenly the two men carrying the chair set it down, blocking her way, and turned to meet her. One stuck out a beefy hand and seized her by the arm as she tried to step around him. "Senhorita Crumb?"

His friend opened the door of the chair. It was empty.

"Get in," said the first man. "Someone wants to meet you."

"Get off!" Fever was struggling to free herself, but the man was immensely strong, as you'd expect of someone in his line of work, and she could not help noticing that there was a big knife stuck through his belt. She wondered if she should shout for help, but there was so much noise all around her that she didn't think anyone would hear. While she was trying to decide, the man pushed her at his friend, who shoved her inside the chair and closed the door. She tried to open it, but it was bolted.

A sedan chair that could be locked from outside?

Fever could not see the point of that, unless these bullocks made a habit of such abductions. Worried, but uncertain what she could do to help herself, she sat down on the plush leather-covered seat and peeked out of the window as the bearers picked the chair up and hurried off with it.

They were not heading for Bargetown after all.

13

THE RED HERRING

he street called Rua Cĩrculo ran all round Mayda, about halfway up the crater wall, even spanning the harbour mouth on a vertiginous bridge. Some stretches of this street were smart and others shabby. The stretch where Fever's abductors finally set her down was on a boundary between the two; fine mansions with sea views to the west, to the east long rows of run-down town houses like rotting teeth. Between them a buttress of the cliff rose almost sheer, and ten or more big funiculars had been built on it. Most of these were restaurants or nightclubs, and they shuttled ceaselessly up and down their tracks, entrancing their guests with an ever-changing view, filling the night air with the grumbling song of their wheels and cables. It was a restless part of town.

The chair door opened, and the two men reached in to pull Fever out, grabbing an arm each. They did not hurt her, and to anyone watching it would have looked as if they were helping her, but their big, sturdy hands gripped like manacles and she knew that there was no hope of escape.

The chair men led her up some steps and along a pathway covered by a red awning to the door of one of the funiculars. It was a nightclub of some kind, she thought. Four storeys high, all wood, with painted carvings over the doors and ground-floor windows, the higher parts neglected, peeling. A sign shaped like a bright red fish was bolted to the wall high up on one corner, lit from within by gas. Across the portico was a name: *The Red Herring*. Fever guessed that the building was preparing to move up the cliff because she could hear the tanks beneath it emptying into some cistern beneath the street. People were queuing at the big front door, waiting to go in. Wealthy looking couples; men in leopard-print or sharkskin robes, their women much younger, with bright teeth and huge hair and gowns slit down the back and up the side. The chair men bustled her quickly past, the burly guards in the doorway ordering customers aside to make way.

A young woman who had been standing just inside the club's big doors came out and smiled a large white smile at Fever and said, "You're expected."

"By who?" asked Fever, but the woman just kept smiling and turned away.

Fever's captors let go of her and gestured at her to follow the woman. She could think of nothing else to do. One of the men walked behind her as she went after the woman past an open inner door and up a long wind of stairs, the walls and the treads of the stairs all painted black, the reedy music of flutes and drums echoing from the low and flaking ceiling. They passed through another door at the top of the stairs into a tight, unhealthy-feeling warren of corridors somewhere at the back of the building. This place was a bit like the *Lyceum*, Fever thought; there must be a gaudy, spectacular-looking bit downstairs that the public saw but all was clutter and confusion behind the scenes.

The woman opened a door, looked in, said something that Fever didn't catch, then stood back and ushered Fever past her into a room with a big desk, a couple of chairs, stripes of red light coming through a blind on the window. A man sat writing at the desk but he looked up when Fever entered and gestured with his angel-quill pen towards an empty chair.

Fever knew him. He was the same man who had watched her the previous night as she left Arlo Thursday's house. *Midas Flynn*. She recognized his deep-set eyes and that long, bluish jaw. His hat was off, baring a steep, domed head with five strands of black hair greased carefully across his scalp.

"Miss Crumb," he said, still pointing with the quill. He had a high, breathy voice; a hard-to-place accent.

Fever did not sit down.

Behind her, the man who had helped to kidnap her fidgeted as he waited in the open doorway. "Want me to stay?" he asked.

"Thank you, Senhor Vigo," said Midas Flynn. "I think I can manage. You may wait downstairs. Make sure nobody comes up."

The man grunted and turned away, closing the door with a soft click. Fever heard him say something to the woman as they walked off along the corridor.

"It is easy to hire thugs and assassins in Mayda," said Midas Flynn casually, blinking his big eyes moistly at Fever. "There are whole guilds of them. The Shadow Men, for instance, who dedicate all their murders to the Mother Below. The Lords of Pain, who specialize in torture, the Songbirds, who will murder or maim your enemy while singing him a message of your choice. . . Vigo and his friends are Shadow Men. I would not usually employ such violent fellows, but my business in Mayda places me in a certain amount of danger, and their Guild had a special offer on. They will protect me from anyone who might wish me harm, and if anyone does harm me Senhor Vigo and his chums will hunt down and kill them for no extra charge."

Was that a threat? Fever wondered. In case she was tempted to harm him herself, with the little clasp knife in her inner pocket?

"You look afraid," said Midas Flynn. "There is no reason to be."

"I'm not," said Fever, although she was, a little. "Why did your men—"

"Kidnap you? I am sorry for that, it was necessary. Please believe me, you are in no danger. We need to talk, and it might be dangerous for you if you were seen speaking to me."

"You could have just—"

"Invited you?" Midas Flynn seemed to have a nervous habit of finishing her questions for her. "You look far too sensible to accept invitations to cheap hotels from strangers, Miss Crumb."

Fever looked around the room. It seemed very ordinary. Shabby, like its occupant. There was a bed in one corner behind a curtain, clothes strewn on an armchair. The music from the club downstairs came up faintly through the floorboards. "Do you . . . ?"

". . . live here? No, I am in Mayda on business," said Flynn. "The rooms here are very reasonably priced, perhaps because of the noise. You were at Arlo

Thursday's funicular this afternoon, I believe? *Please* sit down."

Fever spread her coat-skirts and sat down carefully on the chair's greasy edge. Midas Flynn blinked at her. *Shifty, but not the murdering type*, Dr Teal had said. She hoped he had been right as she watched Flynn's long hands go spidering across the desk to a carafe of blood-coloured Maydan wine. He filled two glasses and slid one towards Fever, who did not take it.

"Now, Miss Crumb," he said, "you must not think of me as your enemy. I am a scientist, like you. I worked for many years on the secret of flight. Perhaps you have heard of the Flynn Ornithopter? No? Well, that is not surprising. It never flew, and with every crash it took a little more of my money with it. But I am still determined to solve the problem! So I go hither and thither to speak with others working in the same field. And this past year I have started to find many of them dead."

Fever said, "I know Edgar Saraband was . . ."

". . . killed, yes." (He pronounced it *kheeled*.) "Poor Saraband was just the latest victim." Midas Flynn took a long drink of wine. "Before that it was Ugo Carax, who hanged himself in his studio, having burned all the plans for the dirigible balloon he had been working on. Most out of character. Before him, Caspar Delabole, crushed under his own experimental glider. . ." He paused, watching for Fever's reaction, as if wondering whether she had heard these names before. She hadn't, and he went on with his list, counting off dead aviators on his fingers. "Branscombe Dekkers's motorized box-kite broke up on its first flight; Mindy Van Der

Waal's steam-powered triplane exploded in mid-air; Dr Preston Collihole allegedly died of heart failure. . ."

"Dr Collihole?" said Fever, startled. "What do you mean, 'allegedly'?"

"Only that it seems rather an unlikely coincidence, don't you think?" asked Flynn with a nervous smile. "So many philosophers, all working on the same problem, and all dying within a few months of each other?"

Fever tried to come up with a reply, but all she could think of was Dr Teal saying, *"There are so many things that old men die of. . ."* Frail as he was, it would have been simple for someone to murder Dr Collihole and pretend his death was natural.

"Somebody is killing them all, Miss Crumb," said Midas Flynn. "Whenever a scientist starts to work on the problem of flight this killer gets to hear of him, and stretches out a hand, right across Europa, and snuffs him out."

"Who? Why?"

"The *why* I do not know. As for *who*, I have only a name. Lothar Vishniak."

Fever tried to hide her little start of recognition, but he noted it, and nodded. "Who he works for, I don't know, but I'm certain he was in Nice when Carax died, and in Thelona a few months ago when young Saraband was killed. It would be a shame if Arlo Thursday turned out to be next on his list."

"Why do you care?" asked Fever.

"Because I believe that Thursday is on the right track. He is building an *aëroplane*, isn't he? Come, Miss Crumb, I know you talk to him. He will not open

123

his gate to me, I can only keep watch on him from a distance, but you, you've been up to the house; I've seen you. He has shown you the machine, hasn't he?"

He was leaning towards Fever across the narrow desk, his eyes bulging slightly in his eagerness to know. She said nothing.

"Miss Crumb," said Flynn, "Vishniak is in Mayda! I have seen him! Your friend Thursday must be made to understand how much danger he is in. I have tried. I have sent letters, posted notes, rung at his bell, but he takes no notice. He thinks I am a bad man, an enemy. But you, you talk to him. You must go and warn him. And you must take me with you. If I am with you, perhaps he'll listen to me. Perhaps he will let me protect him and his invention!"

That's what he's really after, Fever thought. *He doesn't care about Arlo at all. This story of murders he's spun me is probably all lies. Perhaps he's told the same lies to Arlo in his notes and letters and that's where Arlo got the notion from. He's just after the machine. Maybe he invented Vishniak just to scare Arlo into sharing his secrets. . .*

"Well?" said Midas Flynn, still watching her. His steep forehead was covered with beads of moisture, like warm cheese. "We can go now. Tonight. This building will climb to the second level soon. It's not far from there to Casas Elevado. Will you introduce me to Senhor Thursday, Miss Crumb? Will you vouch for me?"

Fever wondered what she should say. She had no intention of taking him to Arlo, but if she told him that, he might become unpleasant. She was alone here, at Flynn's mercy. Those hired thugs of his were still downstairs. It would be more rational to lie and pretend she would go along with him, then find some way to escape once they were outside. But she hated lies, and knew she was no good at telling them. She needed to calm herself and prepare, but it was impossible with Flynn's eager eyes fixed on her. She looked away. A door in the corner of the room stood ajar. She could hear water trickling in there; a toilet cistern filling. To buy time she said, "May I use your. . ."

"Of course," said Midas Flynn. "I am a patient man, Miss Crumb. But we may not have much time. . ." His eyes followed her all the way to the door.

She closed it behind her. The room she had stepped into was bigger than she'd expected. It contained not just a toilet but a bath too, left over from days when the Red Herring had been some Maydan merchant's high class villa. The bolt did not work. She closed the door and leant against it and wondered what to do. She went to the washbasin and stared at herself in the mirror, her face lit by the red glow of the big gas-lit sign bolted to the wall outside the frosted window. Rain was patting at the glass. She wondered if it was raining in Meriam, too. The *Lyceum* would have to raise its awnings to keep the audience dry. . .

The room lurched suddenly like a land-barge going over rough ground. Midas Flynn's greyish toothbrush jiggled in a glass mug on the side of the bath. The Red Herring was on the move. Fever heard a bang from Flynn's office, a startled shout. She thought he had dropped something. But that seemed strange; he

125

must be used to the club's movements. He had told her himself that it was about to set off, so it should not have caught him by surprise. . .

"Great gods!" she heard him say, his voice sounding strange and muffled through the door. And then, "Vishniak!"

A second bang, just like the first. The thud and scuffle of something heavy falling.

She held her breath, standing there in the half dark, in the blood-red glow from the window. The building quaked and rumbled as it was dragged up the cliffside. On the other side of the door she could hear someone moving about; opening and closing drawers, dropping things. She bent down and peered through the keyhole, which showed her a corner of Flynn's desk and a swift glimpse of a wet weatherproof cloak as someone walked past.

It wasn't Flynn.

She straightened up quickly and the floor creaked under her heel. The movements outside stopped suddenly and she knew that whoever it was out there had heard. In the next instant there was another gunshot. A hole appeared in the bathroom door and a tile shattered on the wall behind her, dust and splinters pattering to the floor. The bullet must have missed Fever by inches. She froze; made a statue of herself, not even moving her eyes, which stayed fixed on the hole in the door, on the rod of yellow light which poked through it from the room beyond.

Footsteps came to the door. The hole darkened. She could hear someone breathing, just the other side of the thin wood.

Slowly, silently, the doorknob began to turn.

Fever waited until the door started to open, then stepped as noiselessly as she could into the angle behind it, flattening herself against the wall. Light came into the bathroom, and with it a silvery smell of gunpowder. A shadow fell across the chessboard tiles on the floor. Someone in a cloak and a hat. Someone with a pistol in his hand.

Vishniak, she thought.

The hand holding the pistol came into view around the edge of the door. A man's hand, the cuff of a wet sleeve, the pistol itself of northern workmanship, blond wood and steel, the long barrel decorated with a snarling wolf's head.

She needed to breathe and she dared not. If the gunman so much as touched the open door it would press against her and he would feel the resistance and know that she was there. If he took just another step into the bathroom. . .

The cistern trickled again; a long trill of falling water and then a series of single, musical drips. The sound was a semitone higher than the noise the loose board had made, but to the man with the gun it must have sounded the same. He let out a sigh that was half a snort, turned, and was gone. Fever waited until she heard the outer door close before she let her own breath out. The moving building rumbled on. The toothbrush jiggled.

When she went back into the main room she could not see Midas Flynn at first. Then she spotted his feet poking out from behind the desk, tangled with the fallen chair. The patterns of hobnails on the soles of his boots glinted in the red light from the window like the eyes of spiders.

Fever stood in the bathroom doorway and watched the boots. They didn't move. She listened, and heard the whisper of the rain, the drip of the cistern, her own raggedy breathing.

14

BUILDINGS IN MOTION

"aster Flynn?" she said cautiously.

She didn't expect an answer, and she didn't get one. She went to the desk and looked over into the narrow gap between the desk and the wall. Midas Flynn was lying there, and the carpet under him glistened wetly in the red light. He was dead. You could tell he was dead because of the expressionless way his eyes watched the ceiling and because of the two big holes in the front of his tunic. There was blood on the wall too, and on the desk, which Fever didn't notice until she put her hand down in it; it was thick and slightly warm. One of the drawers of the desk was half open and she could see the handle of a gun in there. She pulled it out, wondering if it were loaded, remembering how she'd loaded Kit Solent's pistols for him in that sedan chair back in London.

"Midas?" said a voice, the door opening. She looked round. The girl who'd shown her up was coming into the room, a faint frown between her perfect eyebrows. Fever held up a hand to halt her. The girl stared at it; stared at the blood on it, at the pistol in Fever's other hand, stared at the splashes on the wall, stared at Midas Flynn's dead legs sticking out from behind the desk.

"He's been shot," said Fever.

The girl started to scream. It was a shrill, awful sound, like a klaxon, and Fever started to go towards her, wondering how to make her stop, but the girl backed away from her and slammed the door on her way out. "No!" shouted Fever, dropping the pistol and running to the door, but by the time she opened it the corridor outside was empty. She could hear the girl running away from her down the stairs, her fading shrieks mingling with the distant music. In a few moments she would be back, probably bringing Flynn's hired thugs. They'd hear the girl's story and they'd come up here and find her and find Flynn dead and there'd be nothing she could tell them that would make them believe she wasn't the killer. She imagined trying to reason with them, but she knew too well that when people get panicky, reason is the first thing they abandon. They'd probably shoot her before she could get two words out. How had Vishniak come in and out without them seeing him? she wondered. He must have found a way in over the roof. . .

That gave her an idea. She went back into the room and closed the door, turning the key in the lock. She crossed the room and got in between the blind and the window to force the casement open. The night air smelled of rain and metal as she scrambled on to the shuddering, rain-slithery wooden window ledge. Above her a flaking cornice jutted out, spattered with the droppings of pigeons and angels. Raindrops fell from it and plunged past her through the red light from the fish-shaped sign and down into the steep ragged strip of cliff garden which separated The Red Herring from the rails of its counterweight. The rails glistened wetly in the light from the club. Fever looked up the slope and saw the counterweight coming down; a big white restaurant, stately as a ship. Beyond it, all along the cliff-side, buildings were going up or coming down, lights gleaming through the rain.

Back in the room she could hear fists pounding on the door and muffled voices shouting at her to open it. She glanced up the line again. The counterweight restaurant was still a hundred yards away, but it was coming quickly closer. She estimated The Red Herring's speed to be a brisk walking pace; say four miles per hour. The counterweight must be moving at the same rate, which gave a combined speed of eight miles per hour. They would both reach the track's halfway point at the same moment, and at that speed they might take twenty seconds to pass each other. That should be time enough. . .

The door burst open and the room started filling with men. They carried knives and swords; one held a pistol. Fever peeked in at them through the streaming windows, watching between the slats of the blind. She saw the one called Vigo giving orders to the others. He pointed to the half-open door of the bathroom and two of the others went in to check it. He stooped over Midas Flynn and she saw him shake his head. Then he raised it and looked straight at her through the blind.

She started to edge along the ledge. The wood was wet, slippery, rotten. A chunk fell off under her weight and dropped, turning over and over in the red light. She dug her nails into the wet boards of the wall to save herself from going with it.

"There she is!" Vigo was leaning out of the window, pointing her out to another man; the one with the pistol, who stretched it out towards her, holding one hand over the firing mechanism to keep the rain off it.

"It wasn't me!" she shouted. "There was someone else! Vishniak, I think. . ."

"Don't give me that!" he shouted back. "You killed Flynn!"

He was being as unreasonable as Fever had feared. She looked away from him. The descending restaurant was only a few yards uphill now, but it was veering away from her. In the spill of light from its verandas she saw that the rails curved here to allow the two buildings to pass each other with a few yards to spare.

Could she jump those few yards?

There was a flash and a hissy bang and a pistol ball sang past her nose and thudded into the cornice above her, spraying her with scales of old paint and splinters of rotted wood. She looked round. The gunman was already reloading, while one of his mates scrambled warily out on to the ledge with a knife in his hand.

It was either jump or die.

The restaurant was passing, filling the air with noise, splashing pale light up the walls of The Red Herring.

There was only one rational choice.

Desperate and ungainly, flapping her long limbs as if she were trying to fly, she flung herself across the yawning space between the buildings. Caught a whirling glimpse of the canyon between them, the lighted windows and the falling rain. Then she slammed against roof-tiles and slithered down, grabbing for a handhold, gasping, fetching up in a guttering. A pistol ball shattered a tile a few feet away. She turned her head and saw The Red

Herring go grinding past, the Shadow Men watching her furiously from the window of Flynn's room.

Just before it parted from its counterweight two of them made the same leap Fever had. She heard them land with thumps and grunts and curses a little further along the roof.

A second before they landed she had felt as if she'd never move again; a second afterwards she was up and running, knowing that her only hope was to outpace them. The restaurant roof formed a strange landscape; steep hillocks tiled with green copper dragon's-scales; flat plains of asphalt where the rain had pooled. She splashed through the puddles, hearing shouts and heavy footfalls behind her. Chimney stacks towered up around her. Ventilators with visored cowls like the helms of evil knights exhaled smells of cooking from the kitchens below. Twice she scared up roosting angels, flinching from the applause of their wings as they took off into the rain.

Then she was at the far side of the restaurant, and a neighbouring building was climbing past it, and she hesitated on a sagging corner of the roof and heard the Shadow Men come blundering across the tiles towards her and threw herself forward just as the first of them reached for her.

This time the distance was even greater and she almost missed; her hands caught hold of a guttering which tilted and nearly gave way, drenching her in dirty water. Dangling there, she looked back, and there were her two pursuers standing uselessly between the restaurant's chimneys as it carried them down to Rua Círculo.

Fever's hands slipped on the wet lead of the guttering. She screamed, fell, landed with a jarring thump on the pierced metal landing of a fire-escape which switchbacked down the wall below her.

There she lay, listening to the sounds of music and laughter from inside, letting the building take her with it as it glided up the cliff. By the time it reached its railhead she had managed to stop herself trembling. She pulled herself upright, brushed the dirt from her clothes and went down the metal stairs to mingle with some raucous customers who were spilling out of the building's exits into one of the labyrinths of little streets near the top of South Stair.

She turned downhill, feeling immensely tired and wanting nothing more than to be in her neat little bed in her neat little room at the hotel. But after she had gone a few yards she stopped. Vishniak would have left The Red Herring by now, unnoticed amid the confusion. And if Flynn had been right, he would be making for Casas Elevado. He might be there already.

She shivered, recalling the sound of his breathing, the shadow he'd thrown on the floor of Flynn's bathroom. *Lothar Vishniak.* Even his *name* sounded scary. The locks on Arlo's gate would not stop a man like that.

She went a few more steps, thinking that she must go and find Dr Teal. But Dr Teal was on the far side of Mayda; it might take her an hour to reach and rouse him. Maybe Fat Jago Belkin and his beautiful wife could help her ... but she didn't even know where their home was.

She looked about for someone she could ask for

134

help, but these streets were rough and disreputable; she saw only drunk sailors shambling from bar to bar and irrationally dressed women calling down to them from balconies. In an alleyway a man was being kicked and beaten by a quartet of brawny thugs in straw hats and stripy coats who were singing, *"That's for squealing on Louie, you double-crossing fink,"* in a catchy four-part harmony.

Realizing that no one would help her but herself, she turned back up the hill, running as fast as she could towards Casas Elevado.

15

AT THE THURSDAY HOUSE

asas Elevado was almost deserted in the dark, and what few passers-by there were, were hurrying along with their heads down against the strengthening rain. No one seemed to notice Fever as she ran to Arlo Thursday's gate. No one even glanced up when the gate swung slackly open at her touch and she cried out.

She stood there in the shelter of the gateway, with the warm rain hissing on the road behind her and rattling on the wet leaves of the garden in front of her and the gate with its broken lock swinging wider, squeaking on its rusty hinges.

She was too late. Vishniak had beaten her here, or else he'd come here before he called in on Midas Flynn. She stepped through the gate and went a little way along the path between the trees. The house was right up at the top of the gardens, no lights in its windows. Among the bushes in the garden something rustled, scaring her, but at her answering movement it took sudden flight, white wings between the wet boughs, and she saw that it was just an angel.

She started to climb without really knowing why. For all she knew, Vishniak was up there, and she did not imagine him to be the type of man who liked being disturbed when he was working. But she had to know if Arlo Thursday was alive or dead. Alive seemed unlikely, given the broken gate and what had befallen

Midas Flynn. But dead seemed impossible. All his ideas, all his knowledge, gone. . . Maybe, if she was quick and careful, she might be able to salvage something; his notes, or one of his models.

A long flight of concrete steps ran straight up the middle of the garden, between the tracks for the house and the tracks for its counterweight. Fever supposed they had been put there so that the tracks could be maintained, and maybe as a means of escape in case the house stuck halfway down. She went up them, breathless, her thighs aching with each step, looking up all the time at the house. Nothing moved there. No lights showed.

She reached the top of the stairs and stepped on to the veranda, walking round to the back of the house where she had first met Arlo. The air was full of the smell of crushed herbs: lavender, lemongrass. The models which had hung from the veranda roof were gone, but that might not mean anything; Arlo might have taken them in because of the rain. Fever tried the back door. It was unlocked. She opened it a crack, but dared not go in. She put her face to the kitchen window and peered hard. Things in there looked much as they had that afternoon. She tried to imagine that Arlo Thursday was asleep behind the drawn blinds in one of those other rooms, or ignoring her the way he had before. Not dead on the floor somewhere like Midas Flynn.

She knew that it was stupidly dangerous to go into the house. What if Vishniak was inside? What if he had seen her light as she climbed the stairs? What if he was waiting for her? She couldn't prove that he was not.

But she had no evidence that he was. She waited for a while and there was no sound from inside the house. "Senhor Thursday?" she called softly at last. "Arlo! It's Fever Crumb!"

Echoes of her voice came flatly back at her off the wet cliffs at the top of the garden. That was all the answer she got.

She opened the door wider and stepped through. Went past the empty kitchen, padding along the hall with her breath held, her eyes adjusting to the dark. Rain rattled at the windows and a guttering somewhere dripped steadily. In the doorway of the former dining room the sawdust and wood-shavings made pale patterns on the floor. She pushed open the door. The room was empty. The flying machine was gone. Even the battered table was bare, cleared of tools and drawings as well as the Saraband engine. If it were not for the dust and the shavings Fever could have believed the machine had been nothing but a dream.

She moved on through the house, afraid of what she expected to find. But all she found were empty rooms. Most barely furnished, what furniture there was tiger-striped by the dim rainy light which pierced the blinds. In the bedroom something lay on the floor, but when she fumbled her torch out and switched it on it revealed only a heap of Arlo Thursday's clothes.

She swung the torch beam on to the wall behind the bed. A painting hung there in a driftwood frame. It was the sort of painting that proud Maydan shipowners commissioned to mark the launching of a new vessel. Two young men in the clothes of half a century ago, standing on a quayside with an elegant ship behind them. The man on the right was black-haired, and his freckled face was so like Arlo's that it seemed logical to assume that he was Arlo's grandfather, the notorious Daniel Thursday. But the other. . .

Fever went closer, kicking aside the drift of abandoned clothes without noticing them as she stared at the double portrait. Staring at a confident-looking man with a long jaw, grey eyes set slightly wider apart than the eyes of *Homo sapiens*, a lion's mane of dark-gold hair. Over his cheekbones, across his brow were clusters of dark markings, like messages scribbled in an unknown alphabet. The artist had captured something arrogant and playful in his smile.

She knew that smile, that face, that noble head. She ought to. She'd lived inside a statue of it for fourteen years.

She wished she still had hold of Godshawk's memories. That way, she might have been able to understand what the Scriven super-brain and sometime king of London had been doing in Mayda fifty years ago, posing for his portrait with a Maydan shipwright. As it was, she could only make a guess, based on the tale she'd heard at supper the other night; the stranger from the north who had befriended Daniel Thursday. *What did you give him for the ship he built you, Grandfather? Was it* you *who taught him those Navier-Stokes equations? Helped him become Mayda's finest shipwright?*

Her eyes switched their focus, some instinct in her sensing movement long before her conscious brain. When Godshawk posed for that portrait all those years ago he had chosen to wear a dark, plum-coloured tunic.

That dark portion of the picture with the glass over it made a passable mirror, and reflected in it, just above his breast pocket, she saw her own long face with its echoes of his, and the candlelight reflecting in her eyes and also in the eyes of someone else who was creeping into the room behind her.

She spun round, ready to run, but there was nowhere to run to. The man, who must have entered the house silently while she was searching it, barred the doorway. She thought at first that he was Vishniak, then that he must be one of Flynn's men who had followed her up here, but he was a stranger: a big man wearing a sleeveless leather tunic. A tattooed octopus on his bicep seemed to flex its tentacles as he strode quickly towards her and put an arm around her neck. There was a knife in his other hand, which he lifted up for her to see. Light from her dropped torch rolled down its blade like liquid. "Come," he said, and she went numbly without trying to argue, tripping over her own feet in her hurry to keep up while he walked her out of the house with his thick arm still locked round her throat.

There was another man on the veranda. Another sleeveless tunic, another octopus tattoo. Who were they? They didn't speak, but marched back down the stairs with Fever between them. At the bottom, in the shadow of the trees, a third man waited, pacing to and fro with a lantern. When they drew near she saw with immense relief that he was Jago Belkin, and realized that these other two must be his servants. If she had had any gods she would have thanked them. She could not guess what had brought Fat Jago there, but she was

140

glad to see his round, amiable face.

"Thursday's cleared out," said one of the men. "There was just the girl."

Fat Jago looked at Fever. She thought he would tell the man to let her go but all he said was, "You know where he is?"

Fever shook her head. The man holding her said, "Don't reckon she does, Fat Jago. She was calling his name like she was looking for him."

Fat Jago sighed. He handed the lantern to one of the men. Rain had beaded on the red diamond of make-up on the top of his head. "You're a difficult young woman, Miss Crumb," he said. "Didn't I tell you not to come here again? Didn't I tell you it was dangerous? Yet you were here this afternoon and now you're back again—"

"Arlo's gone!" said Fever, trying to twist herself free of the man's arm. "Vishniak's here! He killed Midas Flynn! You've got to—"

Fat Jago slapped her suddenly across the face, so hard that her head jerked sideways and she bit her tongue. She was so shocked that for a moment she couldn't breathe. She tasted blood, thought, *He's not here to help at all. He's here for something else.* She could guess what it was. Like Midas Flynn, the fat man was after Arlo's *aëroplane. . .*

"So Flynn's dead?" he said. "Well, Flynn was a loser. I didn't care if *Flynn* was poking about. You're different. Thursday *talked* to you. Don't deny it. I've had my own people watching this place. Who are you working for? The Londoner, is it? Dr Teal? He set you to win Thursday's trust, did he?"

"I'm not working for anyone," said Fever. Her voice sounded tiny and trembly. She was very afraid that Fat Jago would hit her again. She said, "Please listen, there is a man called Vishniak. Midas Flynn said that he's killing everyone who tries to fly, and then he killed Flynn too and I came here to warn Arlo!"

"Or to kill him yourself and steal his secrets," said the fat man. "I've heard tales about this Vishniak. You know what I think? I don't believe there's any such person. Vishniak doesn't exist. He's nothing but a bogey man; a scare story. But you're real enough, and so's your boss, that Engineer."

"Dr Teal's only here to study the funiculars," said Fever, wishing there was something she could say that would turn him back into the friendly, jovial Jago she had known before. "And I don't work for him anyway; I work at Master Persimmon's theatre."

"But the theatre's gone, and you're still here, and so is Dr Teal." Fat Jago grinned. "So London wants the Thursday machine as well. And I'd thought they were too busy sticking wheels on their city! Where is Thursday?"

"I don't know."

He considered her. "No, I don't believe you. But I'll find him." His eyes went up and down her. "It's a pity. Thirza had taken a fancy to you; she was looking forward to you coming for lunch tomorrow. Now I'll have to tell her you can't make it after all."

The man holding Fever moved his knife. It splashed reflections of the lantern into her eyes. "What are we going to do with her, Fat Jago?" he asked.

Fat Jago held up a hand, shook his head. His eyes

lingered thoughtfully on Fever for a moment. "Nothing crude," he decided. "Something *theatrical*. Something to show her London masters what happens to people who pick a fight with Fat Jago Belkin."

16

MOBILE HOME

o they took her a little way back up the steps and one man tied her tightly across one of the rails while his comrade hurried on up to the house. The rain was heavy now. Jago Belkin held an umbrella over his bald head while he watched his men tug the knots tight on Fever's wrists and ankles and gag her with a grimy handkerchief. Fever thought about his adorable wife, and wondered if she knew that he got up to this sort of thing. Probably not, she decided. Probably he kept this life quite separate from the other one, the one where he enjoyed the theatre and invited actors out to dinner.

"Well, Miss Crumb," he said, when she was securely bound. "You'll appreciate that I can't hang around here to watch the show. I'm a busy man and you've already taken up too much of my time as it is. But don't worry; I'll leave Murtinho and Splint here to keep an eye on you."

He gave her a friendly little wave and went away. Soon afterwards, Fever felt the rails start to vibrate, and she knew that the man who had gone up the steps had operated the house's controls and that it was beginning its descent.

She started to struggle then, although reason told her that it was useless. The cords on her wrists and ankles were tied so tight that they were cutting

144

into her flesh. She gave a few sobbing screams, but they were muffled by the gag. The man who had set the house moving came running back down the steps to join his friend and they sat down side by side and took swigs from a flask which they passed between them while they watched her. They kept chuckling, and after a while she realized that they were enjoying her struggles, so she stopped and lay still. If she turned her head she could see the greasy cable moving down in the shadowy gully between the rails. If she turned it the other way she could see the house coming down at her.

"She's fainted, Splint," said one of the men.

"No, she's just resting," said the other. "She'll wriggle hard enough when that house goes over her."

They were mocking her. They had to shout to make themselves heard, because by that time the counterweight was trundling past, wheels grating and squealing against its own set of rails as the weight of the descending house dragged it up the cliff. Fever did a quick calculation and worked out that she had five minutes left before the wheels of the house rolled over her. Except they wouldn't roll over her; they would roll *through* her, shearing her slowly in half.

When she realized that, she started to struggle again, and this time she couldn't stop herself.

"There you go, Murtinho. What did I tell you?"

There was a scuffling sound and a shrill, small voice close by her ear said, "Snacksie?"

Twisting her head round, she got a faceful of an angel's fishy breath. It was perching on the rail beside her, peering at her with its head on one side.

"Snacksies?" said the angel again, ever hopeful.

"Help me," said Fever, through the gag. "Fetch help!"

"Snacksies!" said the angel once more. Then one of the men on the steps threw a stone and a curse at it and it spread its wings and heaved itself clumsily into the air. "Snacksies!" Fever heard it call, and a white splash of excrement broke on the rocks a few yards away. She listened to the wingbeats till they faded, wondering if it had understood her, if it was flying to find help. Maybe the patrons of some mid-levels taverna were listening to its garbled story even now and going, *"What's that, boy? Someone's in trouble? Up on the cliff?"*

The rails were shuddering steadily now, and she could hear the mumble of metal on metal, the squeak of individual bearings in the house's undercarriage as it came closer. *I'm going to die*, she thought, but she couldn't seem to make it mean anything, she couldn't really believe that in a few minutes more she would be nothing. That was why people believed in gods and afterlives, she supposed, because it was so hard to imagine yourself just gone. But she was an Engineer; she wasn't going to seek comfort in fairy tales and make-believe, not even now. This here and now was all there was, so she had to use every last instant of it. She braced herself and strained against the cords and against the pain of the cords and screamed as loudly as she could behind the gag.

"She's screaming again," said one of the men on the steps.

"I like it when they do that. It's satisfying. Gives you the feeling of a job well done."

146

Twisting her head around, Fever looked down the gleaming rails towards Casas Elevado, hoping to see some passer-by who might have heard her muffled shout. There was nobody. She looked upwards instead, but the other funiculars were perched peacefully at the tops of their tracks, and if any of the householders wondered why the Thursday house was trundling downhill in the middle of the night they did not bother coming out to investigate.

She was just readying herself to shout again when she saw a movement high above her, up where Arlo Thursday's garden petered out into scrub-oak and scree and the steep blackness of the crags. Metal was glinting as something pushed through the bushes there. A man, she thought at first, but then she wasn't sure.

It emerged from the scrub and came crabwise down the steep slope past the descending house, moving quickly, with a weird hopping motion. Crooklegged. Headless. Shiny as a gun.

Her eyes must have widened in surprise. "What's *she* looking at?" asked the man named Murtinho.

The other turned to see. He jumped up, pulling out his knife. *"Mãe Abaixo!"* Fever heard him mutter, as the thing came hopping into the pool of light cast by the lantern.

And she still couldn't tell what it was.

It was man-high and crab-shape and it had two legs, but the legs bent the wrong way, jagging up to sharp elbows above its moon-shiny shell, then down to the flat, clawed feet which gripped the edge of the stairway. It looked as if someone had pulled six legs off a vast spider and given it armour in exchange. It had no face, but as it swung its gleaming body towards her she saw a battery of small lamps at the front glint like eyes and she felt sure that it had seen her.

"*Mãe Abaixo!*" said the man with the knife again. His voice rose suddenly to a scream. "*Aranha!*"

There was a sudden flickering of winter light beneath the thing's body and a rapid stuttering noise, like someone ripping a page out of a spiral-bound notebook. The knife came out of the man's hand. He somersaulted backwards and went tumbling downhill, a smell of lavender bursting over Fever as he slid past her through the shrubs. The lantern went out with a chink of smashed glass. "Splint?" said the second man. He started to stand up too and then stopped. Caught in a second fluttering of light and sound, he folded like a pocket knife and toppled into the gully between the rails.

The thing lost interest in him. It turned towards the house, which was about twenty feet away. The light flared under its body again, but this time Fever couldn't hear the ripping sound because it was drowned out by an immense rattling, as if hailstones were hammering against the metal wall of the tank under the veranda. The metal seemed to jolt and shimmer. It made a deep, unhappy, gonging noise, and suddenly the whole front of the tank gave way and a whiteness burst from it that Fever did not quite realize was water until it crashed coldly over her and rushed around and past her, and went churning and gurgling away down the gully between the rails.

She gasped and spluttered, drenched, half drowned. Above her the funicular was starting to slow. *The tank is empty*, she thought. *It's no heavier than the counterweight now. The drag of the counterweight will stop it. . .* And sure enough the house was shuddering, slipping, grumbling to a stop, so near to her that the light spilling down through the veranda planking from the kitchen windows striped her face.

She looked at the steps again. The thing which had stood there was gone. *It was the Aranha*, she thought, and knew she must have imagined it, because the Aranha was only a demon in the story Belkin's wife had told at supper. But *something* had stopped the house coming down on her, and in the silence, as the last of the water trickled and dripped out of the ruined tank, she thought she could hear a faint sound fading among the moonlit shrubs.

Tick, tick, tick, tick.

There seemed to be a pause then; a break in the night's momentum. Maybe she passed out for a few seconds. She had a dream or a memory, very clear, of Fern and Ruan giggling at some silly joke on the taverna terrace the night before last. Only the night before last! Then she woke, regretting it, wishing she could stay unconscious. The rain had stopped. Through gaps in the scudding clouds she could see stars; Orion's belt, and one of the Minor Moons, which some people claimed were really Ancient satellites. Her wrists hurt. Someone was plucking at the wet cords which bound them.

"Keep still," she heard a voice say.

A blade shone in the light from the house windows. She wondered if this was another of Fat Jago's servants, but then he leaned over her, sawing at the cords, and she saw the freckles on his upside-down face and his long hair hanging down.

"You shouldn't have come here," he said.

"Arlo! I wanted to warn you! Lothar Vishniak is here, in Mayda! He killed Midas Flynn! I thought he was coming for you too. . ."

Arlo grinned, dragging her away from the rails, and although Fever generally didn't like having anyone touch her it felt pleasant to have his arms about her; like being a child again, lifted up after a tumble by some grown-up who was going to make everything better.

"Do you think I didn't know that Vishniak's in town? I knew as soon as you brought me that glider. It's one of the ones I sent to Saraband. Vishniak must have brought it with him from Thelona."

"Then it was *Vishniak* who was up on the cliffs that night? Throwing the glider so I'd see it? Why?"

Arlo shrugged. Fever realized that she was pressed against him, enjoying the sea-grey smell of his damp clothes. She moved away and started smoothing her hair, trying to reclaim some of her dignity. "I thought Fat Jago would help me," she said shakily, trying to excuse the stupid predicament in which he had found her.

"Fat Jago?" Arlo laughed, which made her feel worse. "That's a good one! Don't you know who he is?"

"No. Who?"

"He's part of the Oktopous Cartel. They're a society of businessmen based in Matapan on the Middle Sea, and he looks after their interests here in Mayda. You can guess what sort of businesses they're in. Slaving. Mercenaries. Smuggling. Making profit out of other people's misery. I don't know how Fat Jago found out about my machine but he wrote a few months back asking me to work for them. I refused, but it looks as if he didn't take my 'no' for an answer. . ."

Every time he said "Fat Jago" Fever shivered, remembering the way the rails had trembled under her as the house came downhill. She said, "Then they'll come back, won't they? What will you do?"

"I'm moving out," said Arlo, watching her. "I know a place where I can finish the machine. It's already loaded aboard my boat. I was about to set sail when Weasel came and told me what was happening here. I couldn't just leave you to be squashed, could I?"

"The *Aranha*. . ."

"I sent it. It works for me. An old servant of my grandfather's." He stood up, and reached down to help Fever to her feet. "Come on."

"Come on where? Where are we going?"

"You'll have to come with me. When Fat Jago Belkin finds out you're still alive he'll want to kill you all over again. The Oktopous Cartel doesn't forgive or forget."

"I must find Dr Teal. . ." said Fever.

"You *can't*, Fever." Arlo seized her by her thin wrists as she started to turn away. He held her, staring into her face. "Be rational! Don't you understand? You can't go back into the city. You must vanish, or you'll endanger us both."

"But the children, and my friends. . ."

"We'll get word to them when they return, I

promise. But you can't stay in Mayda. Come with me. You can help me. Isn't that what you wanted? Fever, I'll teach you to fly. . ."

17

THE RAGGED ISLES

 *oat*, she thought dreamily, as the bed she lay on lifted her up and down, up and gently down. *I'm on a boat.*

She opened her eyes. She was in a cabin even smaller than her quarters on the *Lyceum,* and the reflections of sunlight came through a small porthole and patterned the low roof with ripply ribbons of light. The bed went up and down, up and gently down.

After Arlo freed her from the rails he had not led her down the garden to Casas Elevado as she'd expected, but up, towards the screes and crags at the top of the crater wall. It seemed the Thursday house had a back exit. A narrow fissure breached the crags, screened by trees, all but invisible. The path which wound through it opened on to empty cliff side on the crater's steep south-western face. There the Aranha had been waiting for them, motionless and moon-silvery, and Fever tried to tell herself it was a dream while Arlo helped her down the cliff paths and the Aranha walked behind, hopping along on its big, clawed feet, its shell all spiny like a deep-sea urchin, the joints of its legs whizzing and creaking and squeaking, the gravel of the path scrunching as it set its feet down, the sea booming in the rocky coves below. *Not a demon*, she thought. *A machine. . .*

But although she tried to order her thoughts and

observe it rationally, she couldn't. She was too shocked and exhausted by her misfortunes. She slept or fainted several times between the cliff's top and the beach and to her shame Arlo had to pick her up and carry her. He didn't seem to mind. "Light as a bird, you are," he said.

And then they were on the shore, in a tight little steep-walled secret cove where a boat rode at anchor. It was about thirty feet long, without the beak or stern-castle that boats from Mayda usually wore. Fever saw polished wood shining faintly as he carried her aboard. She heard the tick and creak of the Aranha as it withdrew itself into the bushes and the shadows on the shore.

Arlo had brought her down the cockpit steps and left her in this cabin, where she had eased herself out of her wet clothes and into this bunk with its clean, crisp covers and woolly, comforting blankets. She had snuggled down and gone to sleep as easily as Fern. . .

She sat herself up and looked out of the porthole, but there was nothing to see but sea. The water foamed white along the boat's side, and she realized that it was not at anchor any more.

So she stirred herself, despite wanting to go back to sleep. She swung her legs over the bed's edge and pushed herself upright. The swaying of the deck took a little getting used to, but it was not so different from riding the *Lyceum* over rough ground. She dressed and went to the door and opened it and climbed up the narrow ladder she found outside it, emerging into sunlight and the crying of angels.

The big birds hung all about her, riding the sea wind

154

above the boat and on either side of it. Shadows of them slid over the taut sail, a parallelogram of white canvas which reared high above Fever's head. Away from land and people the angels seemed less absurd; their wide wings were made for these empty spaces, and instead of begging for scraps they were finding their own food, stooping every so often to pluck a shining fish from the wave-tops. Fever watched them for a while, wondering if one of them was Weasel and how she could thank him for saving her.

"Fever!"

Arlo Thursday was sitting at the tiller at the stern of the boat. There was a blanket wrapped around him, and she had the impression that he had not slept. Behind him, far astern, Fever saw the unmistakable outline of Mayda silhouetted against the morning sun. She turned, and there behind a cloud of birds were the Ragged Isles, jutting from their skirts of surf a few miles ahead.

"This is one of my grandfather's ships," said Arlo, pushing the tiller over, the boat heeling. "In fact she's about seven of them; a bit from one hulk and a bit from another; I rescued them from the wrecker's yards and cobbled them back together. She's called the *Jenny Haniver*. In the Museum at Mayda there are some things which the old sea priests claimed were mermaids. They're bogus, of course, stitched together from halves of monkeys and fish. They're called Jenny Hanivers, and since my *Jenny Haniver* was stitched together from pieces too, it seemed a likely name."

Fever looked about. Brass rails, oak planking, that towering sail. "Where is the Aranha?" she said.

"It will make its own way to the place we're going."

"It can swim?"

"I suppose."

In Fever's memory the Aranha paced down the cliff path, spines agleam, its back-to-front knees glinting as it minced along. "It is a machine," she said.

"A very old machine. A gift to my grandfather from a grateful client."

Fever could guess who the grateful client had been. She had seen things a bit like the Aranha before, in pictures and in the memories which she had inherited from Auric Godshawk. When the Scriven ruled London machines like that had been unleashed in Pickled Eel Circus to slaughter their enemies. If her grandfather had kept a few for the Scrivens' army the London mobs would never have been able to overthrow him, but no, he had chosen to squander them all in bloody games with human gladiators, or give them to his friends. . .

"It has a Stalker's brain inside," said Arlo.

"It must have more than that," said Fever, thinking back to the Resurrectory aboard Quercus's traction fortress, where she had watched Fern and Ruan's father reborn. "It must have been a person once."

"Not quite."

Fever glanced at him. "An angel?"

Arlo nodded. "It is the world's one and only Stalker-angel. Armed with a swift-firing gun. It saved my grandfather and my father many times when their enemies hired the Shadow Men or the Lords of Pain to murder them."

And in return, thought Fever, his grandfather had built Godshawk a ship: the *Black Poppy*, a fast, strong ship that took him north to frozen islands on the fringes of the great whiteness, searching for more knowledge of the Stalkers. How he would have loved this voyage, she thought; the sunlight and the motion of the cutter and the blue, salt smell of the sea. It was almost as if he were still there, just beneath the surface of her conscious mind.

The *Jenny Haniver* ran on into the west with her escort of angels all about her and the sunlit water foaming down her flanks, and soon she began to pass among the Ragged Isles.

Twenty miles to the west of Mayda there had once been a second crater, even bigger, and perhaps created by the same Ancient weapon. But perhaps because it lay in deeper water, or was made from different rocks, the wall of this western crater had crumbled to form a loose ring of spiky islands and treacherous shoals. Seeing them from Mayda, Fever had taken them to be barren, and certainly they looked sheer-sided and inaccessible. But as the *Jenny Haniver* sailed between them Fever saw that there were mats of grass on the tops of some, pine trees and dwarf oak jutting at angles from the cliffs, and on one of the largest, a scatter of ruins.

Arlo moved the tiller and the cutter swung her nose towards it, passing through narrow straits between high jagged rocks. Other rocks, almost submerged, broke the sea's surface like black teeth. It felt dangerous, but Arlo seemed sure of himself.

Fever started to suspect that the angels who flew ahead of the *Jenny Haniver* were not just weaving random paths but were guiding Arlo through those choppy channels; they kept looping back, swooping over the cutter's helm with raking cries, which the young inventor seemed to understand and respond to, adjusting his course between those slabs and knives of rock.

He saw her watching and laughed. "They are really quite intelligent, if you know how to speak to them."

Some of the looming rocks had been splashed with angel-guano in patterns that Fever realized were not as random as they seemed. They lined up with one another to form waymarks, blazing a safe trail through the maze for anyone who knew how to read them.

"There is a good, clear, deep water channel further north, beyond those stacks," said Arlo. "Fishing boats from Mayda pass there sometimes. But Thursday Island itself is bad luck; nobody comes near it now."

Young trees clustered among the tall, rocky crags on the island's summit. Lower down Fever could see the ruins which she had glimpsed earlier. Roofless sheds, dead warehouses, the broken stub of a lighthouse on a harbour wall. She remembered the story that Thirza Belkin had told, of the wave that had destroyed the Thursdays and their shipyard. It had come from the west, the shock wave from some almighty earth-storm in lost America, rolling clear across the Atlantic before breaking over Thursday Island. It had smashed down buildings, and sunk the ships whose dead masts could still be seen jutting sadly from the water in the harbour. Close in against the shore there were concrete basins, like the pens of a fish farm, where yachts and schooners must once have been dry-docked. The sea had filled them, and all that was left were crumbled, weedy walls that barely showed above the waves.

Here, among these ruins, young Arlo had lived for months after all his family were drowned, with no one to care for him but the angels. She would have thought it must hold horrible memories for him, but when she glanced at him she saw that he looked happier than he had ever looked in Mayda. This was a homecoming for him. But not for her. This place made her uneasy.

Smiling, Arlo steered the *Jenny Haniver* into one of the abandoned pens, a shady cave-like space between two roofless warehouses so overgrown with weeds and small trees that they looked more like cliffs than buildings. A shiver ran through the cutter as her fenders grazed against the rotting concrete, the sail came rattling down, and for a moment Fever thought that they had run aground, but no, it was all deliberate, and there was Arlo springing forward to make fast to a rusty bollard on the pen wall.

"Welcome, Fever Crumb," he said, turning, and held out a hand to help Fever ashore. Sand had drifted thickly between the dead buildings. When Fever looked down at it she saw that it was partly composed of thousands upon thousands of tiny white shells. She imagined the great wave scooping them up off the sea floor as it rolled eastwards, depositing them here like payment for the lives and ships it washed away.

Arlo pointed inland, up a cobbled hill. "The shipyard

buildings are all in ruins, but the old watchtower was here before them, and it's still sound, I think. . ."

A metal ladder, orange and scaly with rust, stitched its way up the cliff face behind the abandoned harbour. Three-quarters of the way up a platform was bolted to the rock, like a landing. From there another ladder rose to the cliff top, where a squat tower perched, dark and unwelcoming, high above the beach. It was very old; a watchtower and artillery emplacement left over from some earlier era.

"Are we going to stay there?" asked Fever.

"Why not? It's good shelter. We're castaways; we can't be choosy."

Fever's unease settled on that word "castaways". Sometimes in the plays at the *Electric Lyceum* people found themselves cast away on desert islands, and if there were two of them, and they were male and female, they might bicker for a scene or two, but they always ended up by falling in love. She hoped that Arlo Thursday would not get that sort of idea.

The sea nearby stirred into ripples, hummocked, and split to disgorge the spiny steel carapace of the Aranha. It stalked out of the water up a flight of weedy steps and stood there dripping, trailing pennants of kelp and bladderwrack, ticking patiently to itself. It looked like a living gun. Had it swum here? Or had it walked, scuttling like a weird crab across all the miles of sandy seabed between this place and Mayda?

She stood there in the sun and stared at it, torn between disgust at its strangeness and envy of her grandfather for knowing how to build such things.

"Don't be afraid of it," said Arlo, misunderstanding the look she was giving it. "It'll keep us safe. If Vishniak or Fat Jago finds us it'll see them coming, and kill them. Come on now. Let's unload."

18

THE WATCHTOWER

hey set up camp in the tower. It had one big room with lime-washed walls and arrow-slit windows and a doorway with no door that opened on to a narrow platform outside where the ladder came up through a hatchless trapdoor. There was a fireplace and some broad shelves that might have been bunks set into the walls, and some old tables and chairs covered with dust and angel-droppings. Another ladder went up through another trapdoor on to the broad, flat roof. Guns or scorpions had been mounted up there once, commanding the northern approaches to the island, but they were long gone, leaving only a few rusty metal mountings set in the stonework. There was a low parapet, crumbling in places, sprouting weeds with pink and yellow flowers that nodded and whispered thinly in the breeze.

"This is where we'll build the machine," announced Arlo, peering over the edge.

"In the open?" asked Fever.

"Of course. If we put her together inside we'll only have to take her apart again to get her up here. This is where we'll be launching her from. It's not as high as the cliffs that Edgar Saraband launched from at Thelona, but it's high enough, I think."

"You *think*?" Fever was starting to hate her own

scepticism. She knew that risks must sometimes be taken if progress is to be made. But when she went to stand with him at the parapet and looked down to the jagged rocks at the cliff's foot, she could not imagine flying, only falling.

"What if there's more rain?" she said. "What if a storm blows in?"

"The weather will hold," Arlo said. "We only need a few days."

Fever hoped that he was right. "What can I do?"

"The engine," he said. "I know nothing about engines."

"Of course." She remembered what Dr Teal had told her about Edgar Saraband's accident. "I'll strip it down and rebuild it; check every part. . ."

Arlo looked sideways at her, squinting in the sunlight. "Fever, I thought I wanted to be alone out here. But I'm glad you're here too."

"I don't approve of mating rituals," said Fever sternly.

"What?"

"Romance. Kissing. Holding hands and . . . that sort of thing. Just because we are on an island does not mean that. . . The Earth has a perfectly adequate population nowadays, so there is no need for people of reason to give in to the primitive urge to mate and reproduce. I just thought I would let you know."

Arlo Thursday stood and looked at her and she didn't know if she had offended him or disappointed him or what. Her ears felt as if they were about to catch fire.

"You needn't worry," he said, after a moment.

"There's someone else, you see. I'm in love with someone else."

"Oh. Good."

"She's called Thirza Blaizey," said Arlo. "At least, she used to be. She's Thirza Belkin, now..." He shrugged, looked away across the ruins for a moment and then, as if the conversation had never taken place, said, "We must start getting the machine ashore. I'll need your help with the bigger pieces."

How had it begun, that friendship between Arlo and the Blaizeys' eldest daughter? Even Arlo wasn't really sure. She had always been there at the Blaizey place on Costa Norte, hanging about the yards and "and Blaizey's..." slipways, or helping her mother in the house. He had scarcely noticed her at first. But slowly something about her had started to call to him, and make him think it might be time to shake off his solitary, birdish moods. It was the tallness and the grace of her, and that calm face that never let you know what she was thinking. She reminded him of the women in the paintings which the sea had stolen along with his grandfather's gallery. A maiden in a story, waiting at a castle window for the man who'd rescue her.

Thirza had no time for the jokes and boldness of Blaizey's other 'prentices, but she seemed to be amused by Arlo's conversations with the angels. Shyly, he taught her the special call that he used to draw his favourites down from the flocks that flew over the shipyards. He showed her how to hold out her arm so that Weasel could perch on her wrist, and explained the meanings of all his movements. He was delighted by how quickly she learned, and how well she spoke the angel language. Her long neck and slender hands were better suited to their dances than any part of Arlo was. Her white fingers were as delicate as angel feathers.

It was not long before Augusto Blaizey started to find notes in his daughter's room, scribbled on those dart-like, wing-like things that Arlo made. They seemed to have flown from the boy's window into hers. That made him uneasy. So did the bird-shapes that Arlo had taken to making and launching from the cliff sides on his afternoons off. Stringless kites and paper angels which an unfortunate wind might carry right over the crater-crown and down into the city, leading to awkward questions at the Shipwrights' Guild. ("That Thursday boy of yours still away with the angels, is he, Blaizey? Don't he know the *Mãe* alone makes flying things?")

It would not do, the old shipwright decided. He would have to break this link of tenderness that he saw growing between Thirza and the lad. It pained him, for they were a pretty pair, and he held his daughter very dear and wanted nothing but her happiness. But, as he told her, these youthful loves meant nothing; they were only fevers of the heart and the hotness of them cooled to clinkers after a few years of marriage and a kid or two. Most people never knew that sort of love at all, and took no harm from the lack of it. Far better for Thirza she accept the offer he'd had for her from Jago Belkin, a merchant who wasn't exactly young or exactly handsome but had grown rich from his contacts with traders in Matapan and other ports around the Middle Sea. "Love fades," he told her, "but money, if it's tended right, increases and increases, and with enough of it you *can* buy happiness, no matter what the poets say. What do poets know about money?"

Thirza bit her lip and thought hard, and a few months later she put on a blue silk gown and stood at the altar in the Temple of the Sea with half of Mayda watching while Fat Jago Belkin cast the ceremonial fishing-net over her and the High Priestess pronounced them Man and Wife.

Soon after that Arlo Thursday left Blaizey's and went back to live alone at Casas Elevado, being old enough by then to decide his own affairs. The city forgot him, except on the days when his strange, silent air-machines went sliding their shadows over the streets and rooftops. Then people would look up and shake their heads and remind each other of the rise and fall of the Thursdays.

*

It surprised Fever to find how much more capable she was than Arlo. She'd seen the things he'd built and the way he'd steered the *Jenny Haniver* and she had assumed he'd bring the same easy skill to everything, but no; it turned out that boats and aëroplanes were the limit of his practicality. She watched in astonishment as he tugged the pieces of his flying machine out of the *Jenny Haniver*'s holds and cabins and started to carry them one by one up the ladder that led into the tower. It was she who had to show him how to rig up a simple hoist, taking ropes and tackle from the cutter and rigging them over the handrail at the ladder's top.

She spent the rest of the morning making bundles of the spars and spare timber and tying them securely to the rope's end so that he could haul them up, untie them, and carry them inside the tower. Then there were big bales of paper to be lifted up, and bags of tools, and the unfinished propeller, and the clanking portions of Edgar Saraband's aëro-engine. Finally, there was a bag of provisions. When Fever looked inside it she saw that it held only a wheel of cheese, some ship's biscuits, a bag of sugared almonds and a flask of Thelonan wine.

"No flour?" she asked, not quite believing that he expected them to live here on just that. "No butter? Fruit? Water?"

"There's water on the island," Arlo said. "I'll fetch my fishing tackle from the *Jenny* to catch our meals. And I think there are berries on the western side; there used to be. Anyway, we'll be not be staying here long. We'll finish the machine, and when it's ready I shall fly it back to Mayda. It will soar over the city, and land on the lawns behind the Quadrado Del Mar."

"Orca Mo will not like that," said Fever.

"Not many Maydans think like Orca Mo nowadays," said Arlo. "My people cling to their superstitions, but they're not stupid. Once they see that flight is possible, and understand what it will mean for trade and profit, they will soon take to the idea, just as they have taken to land-barges. I'll ask for investors, and set up a company. Vishniak and Jago Belkin will not dare to try anything once I am in the public eye. I'll build a whole fleet of flyers, bigger and better models, able to carry passengers and cargoes. . ."

He held out one arm and startled Fever by letting out a piercing cry. With a flap of wings an angel settled on his wrist. *Weasel*, guessed Fever, and wondered how long she would have to spend among these birds before she learned to tell them apart as Arlo did. She couldn't even sort males from females yet.

Arlo was talking to the bird, in clucks and gestures and in words as well. "The house. . . Yes. . ."

"House," said the bird, and took flight. Fever shaded her eyes with one hand to watch him as he soared away over the sea towards the far-off, misty cone of Mayda. The angels made flying look so *easy*. You could see why Arlo, growing up among them, might start to think that he could do it too.

"Weasel will be our eyes in Mayda," said Arlo. "I've asked him to tell us what's happening at the house. If Fat Jago has found those dead thugs of his yet. Whether he's looking for us."

Fever didn't answer. She kept watching the angel until he was out of sight. She remembered Fat Jago in the rain last night saying, *"I'll find him."* She remembered Thirza telling her, *"There is nothing that happens in Mayda that Jago doesn't find out about."* And it was not just Belkin and the Oktopous Cartel they had to fear, but the faceless threat of Lothar Vishniak as well. Could they really expect one scruffy seabird to outwit both of them?

19

LITTLE BIRD

p went Weasel, high, high, spreading his wings so that the kind, warm air above the beaches lifted him. Pitying as he went the poor left-behinds below him, Arlo and Arlo's new young female, with only their feather-naked arms, no wings to loft and carry them, poor nestlings!

Carried on the gyres of the air he reached Mayda-sky with barely a wingbeat. From his height the city looked like a nest, and the harbour a blue egg laid in it. He half folded his wings and let earth-tug take him down, spreading them again as all the chimney pots lunged upwards at him. He swooped through the city's invisible awning of scents, and the smoke smells and snack smells and garbage smells reminded him that he was hungry; but he knew he mustn't stop. He was wiser than the rest of his people; he was not to be distracted by snacks and smells. Arlo wanted to know things, and Arlo was his friend.

So he went to the house; to Arlo's house, which sat in the morning sunlight empty and dead-looking at the bottom of its garden. A sharp scent of carrion drew his eyes down to the two dead men in the garden, crawling with flies in the morning heat. Others of his people were there, hopping about in the grass beside the rails. They were picking up things in their beaks and their fingers; things that flashed and glittered in the sun. Fights broke out now and then, with fierce

169

squawkings and wide-spread wings, as a new angel arrived and tried to take one of the glittery things for himself, but there were plenty to go around. Little shiny brass tubes they were, open at one end, empty inside, with a smell of fires and smoke about them. Good for decorating a nest, thought Weasel, landing, turning one of the tubes in his wing-fingers. He had to remind himself again that he was not like these others whose small heads were full of nothing but snacks and nestings. He was not here for nestings; he was here to be Arlo's eyes.

He flew to the house. The door was open. More of his flock were inside, squabbling over scraps in the kitchen.

Suddenly, from the trees at the garden's foot, a voice shouted, "Thursday? Fever?"

Angels exploded out of the house and rose from the garden like litter in a whirlwind. Their alarm calls jangled in Weasel's narrow head. His instincts dragged him into the sky, but instead of fleeing with the rest he circled there and landed on the house roof, watching as the stranger climbed towards him up the steps.

"Fever?" shouted the man again, thinking that if she was hiding somewhere she might not have heard him over the screeching of those stupid birds. "It's me! It's Dr Teal!"

There was still no answer. Dr Teal snuffed the air suspiciously, catching the same sickly scent that Weasel had noticed a few moments earlier. He stooped and picked something up from the grass. A shell-casing from some sort of old-tech gun. Going

170

to the rails, he looked down into the trench between them and saw what lay there. For a moment he was afraid that it might be what was left of Fever, but then the coverlet of blowflies lifted for a moment and he saw that the thing had been a man; bearded and brawny, with an octopus tattoo on his arm. Another just like him sprawled among the lavender bushes further down. The angels had already eaten their eyes.

"The Oktopous Cartel has been here, Dr Teal," Dr Teal said aloud, covering his nose with his handkerchief and looking at those tattoos. "The Oktopous, and someone else who does not like them and is rather more heavily armed. . ." It was not strictly rational to talk to oneself, but it was a habit that he had. He reached inside his coat and took out the pistol he had been issued with before he left London, holding it ready as he moved on up the steps. The back door of Thursday's house was open. Dr Teal went inside and moved cautiously through the empty rooms, stooping sometimes to examine a pattern of footprints in the dust and shavings on the floor.

"Och, Fever, Fever," he said. He went outside again. Best to get away from this place before someone came looking for those Oktopous thugs. He put his pistol away and ran a hand over his head, three days' worth of stubble rasping under his fingers. Just his luck. His message would have reached London by now. The Chief Engineer was sure to send envoys here to collect the Crumb girl, and Dr Teal would have to tell them that she was either missing or dead.

He went down the steps, looking back once at the sound of wingbeats as a lone angel took off from the roof of the empty house.

Weasel lifted himself easily over the trees and turned and rose, losing interest in the human, whom he did not know. He would tell Arlo later that the man had been here. For now he was hungry. The hunger was like a little voice inside him pleading for snacks. But he was not going to eat garbage-pail scraps and nasty dead men's eyes like those less-clever ones; he knew where the best snacks were, better even than Arlo's. Skimming over rooftops and the crags of the heights, he soared out of the city and slid down the kind sky to where a massive funicular sat among its gardens on the crater's sunny southern slopes.

Weasel had another friend here. He called her name as he spiralled down towards the villa's roofs. "Thirza-a-a-a! Thir-z-z-a-a-a!"

Everyone misunderstood Thirza Belkin. She knew what they said about her. That she had married for money. That she did not really love Fat Jago. That she was a bird in a gilded cage. Even her best friends said it, behind their fans, at the lavish, wonderful parties that she gave. "She cannot love him." But they had such *simple* ideas of what love was; little-girl ideas which they had cribbed from plays and stories.

Thirza was the first to admit that Jago wasn't pleasing to look on. But what on earth did that matter? He was kind and gentle (at least he was to *her*), and he was clever, and he was *very* rich, and her father had been right; those things meant much more than physical attractions. She loved his wealth, and she loved helping him to make more of it, for it is one of the great pleasures of life to be surrounded by beautiful things and to know that you have earned them.

If she ever thought of Arlo Thursday, as she lay in her bed, which was as soft as summer clouds, or strolled down her gardens to her private beach, she was far too fine a lady now to let it show. But she was still amused by the angels, and she still talked to them sometimes in the language he had taught her, and gave them things to eat when they visited her in her garden. She was always pleased to see Weasel. When she heard him calling her name that morning she looked up, and waved to let him see where she was, and said to her maidservant, "Bisa, fetch some tidbits for our visitor."

The maidservant, a little African girl whose parents had come to Mayda as refugees from the Zagwan Empire, set down the khora she had been playing and ran off into the house, while Thirza lazily stretched out her arm for Weasel to land on. He settled on the edge of an ornamental urn instead, and cocked one blue eye at her.

"Weasel!" she said. "Where have you been? It's been days and days!"

Weasel made a movement that meant "fishing", another that meant "flying", a third that might have been his birdy version of a shrug. Days meant little to him. One of the first things that Arlo had taught her about the angels was that they had almost no concept of time.

The girl Bisa came running back, barefoot like all the Belkins' servants so that her footsteps wouldn't spoil the pleasant noises of the garden, the whispering ornamental grasses and the wind-harps. She was carrying a tray of lovely snacks; little fishy pieces, and creamy things in soft pastry cases. Most people couldn't afford such dainties for their children, let alone as gifts for passing angels. Weasel hopped on to the tray's edge and counted the snacks eagerly. One, two, lots! He was very glad that Thirza was his friend.

"And how is Arlo?" she asked, while he ate the snacks one by one.

She sometimes asked him about Arlo, and he saw no reason not to tell her, because Arlo was her friend too, even though she roosted with the large one who Arlo didn't like. He bobbed and shuffled to make her understand that Arlo himself was roosting with a new female. "Fevacrum!" he said.

"Fever Crumb?" Thirza seemed pleased. Weasel thought she must be happy for her friend Arlo. He thought that she was hoping his roost would be safe and Fevacrum would give him lots of nestlings.

"Where are they?" Thirza asked him. "Where are they roosting, Arlo and Fever Crumb?"

Weasel told her. He raised his tail and slinked his head forward. That meant *Thursday Island*.

"Dear Weasel," she said, resting her fingertips on the crest of his head as he ate. "Will you come back? Come often, and tell me all that Arlo is doing on his island?"

"Snacks?" said the angel hopefully.

"Oh, lots of snacks. But don't tell Arlo, will you? Don't tell him that you talk to me? He would not understand. You promise?"

"Promise," said Weasel. He didn't understand either; the ways of Arlo's kind were often strange to him. But he knew they were clever; cleverer than him, and if Thirza didn't want him to tell, he wouldn't tell. Thirza was his friend, and her snacks were even nicer than Arlo's.

Fat Jago came home late that evening. Thirza did not need to ask him how he was, or how his day had been. She could tell from the sound of his footsteps as he crossed the atrium that he was weary and frustrated. She sent Bisa running for cold drinks, and dispatched another servant to the kitchens to tell the cooks to start preparing supper. She rang a bell to alert still more servants, and the house shivered gently and began its long descent towards the foot of the garden, so that the Belkins would have a view over their beach and the sunset sea while they dined. Then she went and settled herself beside her husband and rested her head upon his comfily upholstered shoulder.

"Bad?" she asked.

Fat Jago stroked her hair. "Bad. The girl's vanished. I blame myself. I should just have had Murtinho and Splint cut her throat for her last night, but I wanted to do something a bit showy with her: let people know not to anger the Oktopous. Now she's gone, and the lads are both dead, shot to pieces somehow. I've never seen the like. And Murtinho's got a wife and three kids. He *had* a wife and three kids, I mean."

"It's not your fault," said Thirza. "We'll look after Senhora Murtinho and her little ones, won't we?"

"Of course. But Arlo Thursday's still missing, too. Is the Londoner responsible? Teal? Some of our people saw him nosing around the Thursday place this morning. But he doesn't look hard enough to have taken out Splint and Murtinho. He's a scholar, not a shooter. I suppose I'll have to bring him in for questioning. . ."

"No," said Thirza firmly. "Teal is London's man and you mustn't risk offending London. What about all those contracts Quercus has signed with our friends in Matapan, for slaves, steel, copper? If you upset London the Oktopous will *not* be pleased with us."

This was something else that people didn't understand when they saw Thirza with her husband. She was so young and beautiful that they assumed she must have no more brains than one of the charms that dangled from his watch chain. They certainly never imagined that she knew anything of the murkier depths of his business affairs. But Thirza had a sharp mind, and Fat Jago had recognized it right at the beginning of their marriage, and shared everything with her. He had not regretted it. It had been Thirza who had first suggested that he make contact with the Oktopous Cartel and put himself forward as their agent here at the World's End.

"Anyway," she said, snuggling against him, pleased to be able give him good news here at the end of his hard day. "I don't believe this horrible Dr Teal has any idea where Arlo and the girl are. But *I* do."

"You do?"

"A little bird told me. Arlo has gone back to his island. Fever Crumb is with him. He is going to build his machine there in peace and quiet, alone. . ."

"Except for the London girl. . ."

"Maybe he wants her as his assistant; or maybe they are an item. They are certainly strange enough for one another."

"I'll send a ship to Thursday Island first thing tomorrow," said Fat Jago, all his weariness falling from him as the news sank in. "We'll kill the girl and bring Thursday back to Mayda. . ."

"No!" said Thirza again. "There is no need. Why shake the tree before the fruit has ripened? We are the only ones who know they are out there. Let them stay. Let them build their machine. My little bird will tell us when it is ready, and then you can go there and collect it."

Fat Jago looked admiringly at her. She was always surprising him.

A tiny frown crumpled her perfect forehead for a moment. "You are certain that it was Fever Crumb who shot Flynn?"

Fat Jago snorted. "She told me it was this fellow Vishniak, but I've had our people ask all over Mayda, and nobody's heard of any Vishniak arriving here. It *must* have been the Crumb girl."

Thirza shook her head and laughed. "And she seemed such a prim and proper little thing!"

"Well so did you, my dove, when I first asked old Blaizey for your hand in marriage," said her husband fondly.

Their house bumped gently against its buffers, down at the garden's foot. Outside their windows flights of angels blew across the sunset, and small waves crumpled neatly into lace and silver on the sands of their beach, while their servants entered barefoot, silent, bringing them their supper.

20

WINGS OF THE FUTURE

t felt strange, next morning, waking in that tower. Such a big space, especially to someone used to living in a land-barge cabin no larger than a wardrobe. Fever thought for a moment of her room in the hotel on Rua Penhasco, feeling sad that she had never actually got to sleep in it. It was a pity she had paid in advance. . .

But it was hard to feel sad for long, with such a soft, golden, watery light shining through those slices of window and the empty doorway. She could hear the sea breathing softly. Nothing else. When she lifted her head and looked across the room, Arlo's bunk was empty. She stood up, pulled on her shoes, checked that her hair was still tied back tidily. When she stepped outside, the air was all light and wings; a blizzard of angels tumbling past the tower and blowing along the beaches, their shadows racing over the ivied ruins by the quay.

Walking westward, Fever climbed over a spur of the cliffs and came down on to a flat expanse of grass divided by low mounds and hummocks, looking out across a beach. The sun made a mirror of the wet sand, and Arlo was standing there, naked on his own reflection. He had been swimming, or about to swim, but he had stopped halfway between Fever and the sea to talk to the angels.

The birds whirled all around him, a white vortex of wings with Arlo as the still point at their centre. He stood with his arms outstretched and the angels landed on them. Fever watched him bob his head and sway his neck in answer to their swayings and their bobs. She heard the angels softly squawking and chattering, and she guessed that if she went closer she would be able to hear Arlo making the same sounds. Then one of them saw her, and the whole flock rose in alarm, whirling away over the sea like a bashful tornado.

Arlo turned, waved, remembered that he had no clothes on and hurried awkwardly to where they lay heaped on some nearby rocks. He ran doubled-over and trying to hide various portions of himself, but Fever could not see what the fuss was about. Did he imagine that she had never studied human anatomy?

He hopped about pulling his trousers on, shrugged on his shirt and came running up the beach to her, waving two silvery shining things like trophies. "Breakfast! You wondered what we were to eat? I caught these in the old pens. . ." He stood there holding the fishes out for her to see, grinning foolishly, a little flushed. "Welcome to Casa Thursday, my old family home."

"There is no house here," said Fever, and then looked down and saw that the mounds around her, overgrown with wild flowers and grass, marked out the roots of walls, the floor plan of a vanished building.

"This is the villa my grandfather built," said Arlo, as if he were still proud of it. "Look, here was the atrium, with the entrance-hall leading out that way towards the shipyards. That was the dining room, with the bedrooms beyond. This place where we are standing was Grandfather's study."

"It was extensive," said Fever. "He must have been a very wealthy man."

"The best shipwright in Mayda. Best in the world, probably."

"Thanks to his friend Senhor Açora."

"Yes. . ." Arlo bounded off across the old walls like a proud householder giving his guest a guided tour. "Grandfather kept his pictures here. He was a great one for paintings. They're some of the things I remember best from when I was little. . ."

"I saw one in your house in Mayda," said Fever. "Of your grandfather and Açora and the *Black Poppy*."

"Yes," said Arlo again, looking slightly mystified at the way each thing she said turned back to the mysterious Açora.

"I recognized him," Fever said.

"Who? Grandfather?"

"No, Açora. And the ship too, actually. He travelled all the way to Anchorage aboard the *Black Poppy*. His real name was Auric Godshawk. He was my grandfather."

Arlo turned and came back towards her, a fish hanging stupidly from either hand. "Really? You know, you have a look of him about you. Like his picture. . ."

"He was Scriven."

"One of those northland mutants? *Homo superior*?"

"Well that's what they called themselves. They weren't really very superior."

Arlo was watching her and she couldn't guess what he was thinking. She hoped it would not unsettle him to be sharing his island with someone not-quite-human.

He grinned suddenly. "Açora means 'goshawk' in one of the old tongues of Mayda. Do you see? It's *almost* 'Godshawk'." He laughed. "Fever, this is wonderful! It's fate! A sign from the gods! Your grandfather helped mine build his ships, and now you're here to help me build my *aëroplane*. . ."

"There is no such thing as fate," said Fever sternly. "And there are *certainly* no such things as gods." But as she followed him back towards the tower she felt pleased that she had told him about her grandfather. She thought that Auric Godshawk would have been glad that she was here, on Daniel Thursday's island, helping Daniel Thursday's grandson to change the world.

For the first few days she kept expecting trouble. The memory of how Fat Jago Belkin's men had wrenched and tethered her was like a stubborn stain; however hard she tried she could not shift it. But slowly, in the sunlight and seeming safety of the island, it began to fade a little. The mysterious Lothar Vishniak did not appear, and when Weasel visited the island he had nothing much to tell them about Fat Jago. Belkin was busy "doing business" he kept telling them.

But even Weasel did not come often. "He's found some female in the city," Arlo guessed, watching him flap back towards the heights of Mayda.

Fever stopped sneaking glances from the windows quite so often. When she did she saw only the empty beaches, the *Jenny Haniver* moored under the trees at the abandoned quay, and sometimes the Aranha pacing the foreshore like a thoughtful crab, still keeping guard over the Thursdays' island and its secrets.

On the tower's roof the flying machine was taking shape again. Arlo seemed so absent-minded sometimes that Fever wondered how he could possibly make sense of the mass of disassembled struts and sections they had dragged up from the cutter. But soon the machine was looking much as it had when she first saw it, except that in the open air it seemed both smaller and more alive. She watched Arlo work at it, using a spokeshave or a rasp to skim off as much as he could from the struts and wing-bones, smoothing and shaping them until they were as light and delicate as they could be without losing the strength they would need.

Sometimes they worked together at the propeller, smoothing the rough thing he'd shaped, working oil into it with a brush before sanding again. Fine sawdust covered them, sticking to the sweat on their sunburnt faces, making them sneeze. One hot afternoon Arlo pulled off his shirt and Fever saw that his shoulders and chest were as covered with freckles as his face. He stirred deep, unexpected memories in her; of Scriven girls her grandfather had loved; their cowrie-shell shoulders and dappled throats. Was that why her grandfather had chosen Daniel Thursday to be his shipwright? Not because of his boatbuilding skills, but simply on account of all his lovely freckles?

Arlo looked up, saw her watching him, and smiled vaguely at her. Then he went back to his work, the star-charts of his speckled skin slowly fading under fresh layers of sweat and sawdust.

In the evenings the surf boomed along the island's beaches, but in the pens and basins of the old Thursday shipyard the sheltered water grew still as glass, reflecting the peach-coloured sky. A dead tree had washed up on the beach. Arlo chopped it into logs while Fever gathered dry brushwood from the cliff tops and made a fire in the tower's hearth. The fish which they caught in the pens and tide-pools they spread open like silver books and roasted on a rack that she made from an old window grille. Their oil sizzled, dripping into the hot ash below, and the smell of them was the colour of old terracotta flowerpots. When they had eaten, Fever might leaf through Arlo's scruffy notes and drawings while he explained to her the secrets he had learned from the angels. Or they would talk about the next day's work, and then of the other inventions they might make, other wonders from the Ancient World still waiting to be rediscovered. Then Fever would curl up on one of the stony bunks under a blanket brought up from the cutter and fall asleep, dreaming of flight, and of the machine that waited on the roof above her, tethered to the mountings of the old artillery-emplacement, its wings trembling in the night wind.

Days went by: days of hard work and sunlight. Soon the frame of the machine was complete. Together, she and Arlo pasted strip upon strip of paper over it, building up the wing-surface, sculpting the careful, asymmetric camber which would give the machine extra lift. As the paste dried they painted the paper with a solution, dizzyingly smelly, to strengthen and waterproof it. They attached the control cables which would lift the flaps at the wings' tips and trailing edges to steer the machine up and down, and turn the swallow-tail rudder to make it go left or right. Arlo was determined to launch from the tower's top, although Fever was sure that if he could get up enough speed he would be able to take off from a flat stretch of ground, like one of the island's beaches. But Arlo said he was not going to take the machine apart and carry it all down again, and she had to give in. It was his machine, after all. She suspected his real reason for wanting to launch from the tower was rooted in his memories of watching the angels fly, hurling themselves into the wind from their precarious roosts on the sea cliffs.

Fever was happy. Happier now, she thought, than she'd been since she was a little girl, helping Dr Crumb with his experiments in Godshawk's Head. She sometimes missed the children and the rest of the *Lyceum*'s company, but she knew they would be having a good time in Meriam, and mostly it was a relief not to have to listen to their endless chatter, and waste time thinking about ways to light the foolish plays. Here on the island there was always the feeling, giddy and intoxicating, that she was helping to build the future.

The only crack in her happiness was the engine which Arlo expected her to attach to his machine. To someone brought up among Engineers it was a crude-looking thing, an inelegant metal box full of pistons and gears, powered by the constant explosion of liquid ethanol, lubricated with castor oil. She carefully dismantled and reassembled it, and she could see no reason why it should not work, but it still seemed to her to be much too heavy, although she could see no way that she could make it lighter. Worse still, Arlo had brought with him only one small barrel of fuel. There was not enough to waste any running the engine for long before they mounted it on the frame of the machine. Its first proper test would come when Arlo took to the air. . .

21

LOST MAPS OF THE SKY

ometimes Fever still needed to be alone, and sometimes, too, she sensed that Arlo did not want her company. Then she would go off by herself along the narrow tracks which wound between the pines and dwarf oaks, into secret hollows among the rocks on the island's high spine.

It was on one of those lonely expeditions that she found the birdcastle.

At the island's western end stood the remains of a second tower. Five hundred years before, Mayda had been a target for all sorts of sea-rovers and sea-raiders: corsairs from the Islamist caliphates of old north Africa; roving pirates from Oak Island and strong-walled Dun Laoghaire. The Maydans had had a use for lots of watchtowers. This one was roofless now and tumbledown and a tangled mass of branches and debris had somehow become wedged in its top. The first few times she saw it, Fever imagined that Arlo's wave had washed right over it and left it clogged with driftwood. But this evening, when she had climbed up higher than before on to the summit of one of the rock formations, and was looking down at the tower, she started to see that there was a sort of structure to the jutting baulks and branches, and that in places they had been woven together like a wicker basket, or an enormous bird's nest.

She scrambled down off her rock and found a way to the tower through the juniper bushes and low-growing clumps of heather. There was a doorway at the base of it, nothing left of the door but rusted hinges and a scattering of nails among the nettles which grew on the threshold. She crept inside and looked up. The westering sun slid long needles of orange light through chinks in the walls, lighting up a metal staircase which spiralled through the sagging ceiling. She went up warily, feeling the treads shift as they took her weight. She could hear nothing but the wind-blown bushes outside rhubarbing like actors in a crowd scene and, far below, the lazy pulsing of the surf.

The top floor was thick with fish bones and ancient guano. The raggedy mass of old branches overhead formed a roof; a driftwood dome, tied together with rotting rags and ancient straggles of oily rope, with fisherman's floats and old bottles stitched into it here and there. It was clumsy, rank-smelling, crude, probably unsafe, yet in its way it was as impressive as any building she had ever seen, and she stood there for a long time just staring up at it; the architecture of angels.

A scuffling, a fluttering, and one of the creatures landed beside her. "Snacksies?" it asked. Fever was coming to know a few of the angels by sight now. She had often noticed this young female hanging around Arlo's tower, waiting for scraps.

"Sorry," she said, spreading her hands out so the angel could see they were empty. "No snacks. I just came to look at this place."

"Old," said the angel, hopping away from her,

picking up a fish skull with the fingers of one wing.

"How old?" asked Fever.

"Yesterday."

Older than that, thought Fever. *Years and years old.* But to the angels everything that was not happening now had happened yesterday.

She asked, "Why don't you live here today?"

The angel made no reply. It probably hadn't understood the question. Weasel seemed to be the only one with a vocabulary of more than a few words. Fever left it examining the fish bones and walked across the room to where a gap in the driftwood gave her a view of the western sea. Angels were wheeling whitely around a tall stack offshore. She could make out their nests, crammed together on rock ledges high above the surf, the cliffs beneath them drizzled with long white beards of guano like frozen waterfalls. She wanted to ask the angel what had made them stop building their birdcastles and go back to roosting on cliffs, but there was no point, and she already knew the answer. They had forgotten how, just as people had forgotten how to fly.

The sun was sinking quickly. Orange rays tracked through the tower like the beams of spotlights, revealing flurries of scratches on the ancient lime plaster of the walls. There, too, Fever could see order. There was nothing she could read, but there was a rhythm and a reason to the marks which the angels of long ago had made. There were long lines of parallel scorings which might have been tallies of numbers, and in one place a collection of rough shapes which looked oddly familiar, until she

189

recognized them as the outlines of Mayda and the Ragged Isles, just as they had looked on the maps in Master Persimmon's atlas.

"You made charts!" she said, crouching down to bring her face closer to the old drawing. It was very detailed; she could see the causeway zigzagging from Mayda to the mainland, and the double curve of the harbour wall. Stylized bird-forms marked some of the outer islands, perhaps to show which ones were home to angels. She looked to her left along the wall's curve, and there she saw another coastline, with bites and headlands scratched carefully into the paint and things that might have been fish in the sea. The fish-symbols must mark the best fishing-grounds, she thought, places way to the west of Mayda, out of reach to human fishermen but well within the range of the angels, gliding on their wide wings. But what was that other shore, so far to westward?

"Is this America?" she asked, turning to the bird behind her.

"Merica," said the angel.

"Did your ancestors, the old angels, did they sometimes fly all the way to America?"

"Merica," said the angel, with its head on one side. It had never heard the word before. It was just mimicking the sound. Then it caught some other sound, the clatter of a kicked stone down below, and took flight, filling the room for a moment with its panicky wingbeats before bursting out through a gap in the driftwood lattice overhead. A white feather came zigzagging down through the sunbeams, and settled in Arlo Thursday's hair as he walked up the stairs.

"Fever. . . I came to tell you that supper's almost ready. Oh, I see you've found the angels' atlas."

"Is that what it is?"

"That's what my grandfather called it. He used to bring me up here when I was little. He reckoned that it showed their fishing grounds, their roosts, even the currents of the upper air. You see those swirling scratches? 'The bird roads', he called those. Maybe we'll ride them too, one day."

"And this coastline. . .?" said Fever, touching the wriggly scar of it.

"You can't be sure it *is* a coastline, you know. Birds drew these maps, and they may not have shared our concepts of east and west, distance and direction. Just because they drew Mayda here and then that shore over there doesn't mean anything. That could be a map of somewhere further down the coast, or in northern Africa, or some made-up country, some birdy heaven."

"Or it could be America," said Fever.

"Well, yes. That's what Grandfather believed. Angels have been known to travel for thousands of miles. He thought that they could easily have reached the Dead Continent."

"But if the angels reached it, it can't be dead," said Fever. "Other birds must go there. They'd take seeds with them, plants would grow. Insects and spiders would blow there on the wind. And there are fish in the seas, look. . ." She pointed to the fish-shapes which angels had carved in the nooks and inlets of that unknown shore.

Arlo laughed. "Perhaps we'll fly there ourselves one

day, when the machine is ready, and find out. What do you think?"

Fever thought that she was being made fun of. It had happened often enough in the past, and she was starting to recognize the signs. She smiled to show that she did not mind, then got up and followed him back down the stairs of the tower, still contemplating lost America. "Perhaps it's just a taboo that stops people going there and exploring for themselves," she said, squinting into the red sunlight, wishing she could see over the curve of the earth. "All those old stories about America being destroyed by the gods; a wasteland; a continent of death. We've all grown up on those stories so we half believe them, even the rational ones among us."

"Old myths are very powerful," agreed Arlo. "Look at the Zagwans, burning people like you and me alive because they think technology offends their god. Or my own people. We were still sacrificing children to appease the Sea Goddess until a few hundred years ago. And as for you Londoners? Isn't this obsession with making London move just another crazy cult? And it's spreading as fast as any religion; I gather that half the towns of the near north are thinking about adding wheels and engines. . ."

"It won't catch on," said Fever firmly. "Not when people hear about your flying machine."

"Ah yes. . . The machine. . ." He looked at her and there was an odd light in his eyes; a banked-down excitement so boyish that he looked for an instant no older than Ruan. "Fever, she's ready. There's no reason to delay any longer. If the wind stays in the west and not too strong I mean to test her. . ."

"When?"

"First thing tomorrow."

They went home together along a path which Fever had always avoided before. It was more direct than the winding heather-mazes she usually walked up on the island's crown, but it skirted close to the cliff's edge, and the views of the white waves breaking all that way below made her stomach feel strange, however often she told herself she was being irrational and there was really no danger of falling. She walked carefully, keeping her eyes fixed on Arlo's back and the lights the sunset lit in his hair. She feared for him, and she dared not say so in case that made him fearful too. She knew that the machine should fly; she had checked and checked his figures. But the cliffs were so high, and his body so fragile.

"I should be the one," she said, as they drew near the tower. "I should pilot it. It is only rational. I am lighter than you. 'Light as a bird', that's what you called me. And if I crash and am killed, you would be able to build another machine."

"No!" he said, rounding on her almost angrily. "It must be me! I want to fly, Fever." Then, more kindly, "Besides, if something does go wrong, like it did for poor Edgar. . ." He reached out and quickly brushed her cheek with his rough carpenter's fingers. "I'd rather be dead than have that on my conscience."

"Yes, of course," said Fever, taken off guard by that touch. She felt giddy, sensing the edge of the cliff behind her, the long drop into the surf. But Arlo only smiled at her, and turned, and walked along the path away from her. Angels hung above him in the evening air on their big wings, almost motionless, and it was easy to imagine him up there, soaring among them, as if the sky was where he had always belonged.

22

JONATHAN HAZELL INVESTIGATES

or the first few days Jonathan Hazell thought that matters had improved. Something had taken the wind out of Dr Teal's sails, wiped the smile off his face, and generally made him far easier to live with. He was still treating the house on Rua Penhasco like a hotel, letting himself in and out at all hours, but he was no longer quite so *boisterous* about it. He no longer sat himself down at the parpsichord to tootle out Aberdonian marches at 3 a.m., or rearranged the statues on the household shrine into amusing dioramas. He didn't shout, "Morning, Hazell!" every day in that big, booming voice of his when Jonathan Hazell came creeping downstairs after another rough night in the guest-room bed. Didn't scatter his drawings of the wretched funiculars all over the house, and get ink in the rugs. Indeed, he seemed to be out most of the time, and when he was at home he scarcely spoke.

But after the first few days, his guest's gloom started to oppress Jonathan Hazell almost as much as his cheerfulness had. What was troubling the fellow? he wondered. He sensed that, as London's envoy at the World's End, it was his duty to find out. He would not want Teal sending a bad report about him back to this new mayor, Quercus.

The Engineer looked at him darkly when he asked

what was wrong, over breakfast one morning. Looked at him darkly and then shook his head. "It's a bad business, Master Hazell."

"Well, may I be of any assistance?"

"I doubt it." Teal poked half-heartedly at a kipper, then glanced up again. "You remember I had you send a courier to London the morning after my arrival?"

Jonathan Hazell remembered it well. It had cost him a small fortune, and Dr Teal showed no sign of paying him back.

"The message he was carrying concerned that girl Fever Crumb," Dr Teal continued. "She is very important to some *very* important people in London. Important enough that I felt sure it would do me no end of good if I could only persuade her to return home with me when I go. But she has vanished."

"Vanished? I thought that theatre of hers had cleared off to Meriam or somewhere. . ."

"Do you think I don't know that, Hazell? She remained behind, and she has vanished. The hotel where she was staying has no knowledge of her. When I went to the home of . . . of a man I thought she might have called on I found it empty, no sign of either of them. She has fled, or been kidnapped. I will have to confess to these important Londoners that having found Miss Crumb, I have lost her again, perhaps for good."

"Dr Teal!" said Jonathan Hazell, pushing away his own kipper half-eaten. "This is terrible!"

The Engineer nodded grimly. "Indeed it is. My career may never recover from this blow."

Jonathan Hazell frowned. He remembered Fever

Crumb standing in sunlight on his doorstep. He was afraid that he had been rather rude to her. She had struck him as a sensible young person. Sensible and very charming. Who cared a fig for Dr Teal's career when the poor girl was missing?

"We must find her!" he said, thumping the table so hard that he startled himself and made all the cutlery jiggle.

"Eh?" Teal looked up at him, surprised. "Well, what do you think I've been trying to do, these past days? I've been walking around and around this unreasonable city of yours like a fly in a toilet-bowl, looking for her high and low."

"But you haven't found her. . ." Jonathan Hazell was starting to feel strangely excited. He had thought for a long time that he needed a new hobby. He had been considering building a model of Mayda out of matchsticks, but might not a spot of investigation be just as diverting? He had always enjoyed a good puzzle.

He said, "You should have told me as soon as Miss Crumb went missing. I am London's envoy, remember, and I have a great deal of local knowledge at my, ah, fingertips. I have contacts, and things. If anyone has heard of Miss Crumb's whereabouts, I shall learn of it. I shall start at once, this morning, at the exchange. Where was she last seen, Dr Teal? What was the name of this gentleman you think she may have called on?"

Dr Teal looked doubtfully at him. He was used to working alone. He could think of no more unlikely partner than this meek little mole-like man. And yet the situation was desperate, and Hazell's suggestion was not irrational.

"His name is Arlo Thursday."

"Thursday! But there was some sort of disturbance at his funicular a few nights ago! I heard it said at the exchange that the Oktopous Cartel was involved! If *they* have kidnapped poor Miss Crumb. . .!"

Dr Teal just looked glumly at him.

Jonathan Hazell finished his cup of tea and set it down on the saucer. He stood up. "I shall look into this, Dr Teal! I shall look into this at once!"

And look into it he had. The trail led him from the rumour-mills of the exchange, through harbourside coffee-shops and low-end chandleries, up into the slums of Muro d'Oeste where the refugees from Zagwa lived. It was as he had guessed. People who had been wary of talking to a bumptious stranger like Teal were quite prepared to share what they knew with Jonathan Hazell, a familiar merchant who was known for his honesty and tact. None of them had actually *seen* Fever Crumb, it was true, but he learned much that was interesting. He started to enjoy himself. Who would have thought that he would make such a good detective?

On the same evening that Fever found the angels' map, he met with Dr Teal in a funicular bar on the Rua Círculo to report his findings.

"Honestly, Hazell," grumbled the Engineer, as Jonathan Hazell sidled up to him in a shadowy corner, "why can't we discuss this at home? We are not spies."

Jonathan Hazell looked quickly over his shoulder to make sure that no one was listening. What he was about to say could have been said just as easily at home, it was true. But he didn't get much chance to arrange clandestine meetings in bars as a general rule, and he wasn't about to let this one slip through his fingers.

"I have made progress, Dr Teal!"

"What's that? Speak up!"

"In my investigation. Firstly, the chandlers tell me that young Arlo Thursday has been placing orders for certain materials in recent months. Wood, tools, glue and great quantities of paper have been delivered to his funicular."

"And what do you deduce from this?" asked Dr Teal wearily.

"Why, Dr Teal, I deduce that Thursday has been building something. He is Daniel Thursday's grandson after all. Perhaps he has finally given up on the kites and toy birds which won him such a strange reputation, and started making something of more practical use. A new kind of ship, perhaps. It may be that your Miss Crumb, with her background as an Engineer, was helping him. And it may be that the Oktopous Cartel got wind of this and tried to steal it from him."

He paused. He was pleased to see that Dr Teal was attentive now, leaning forward slightly, his eyes watchful and oddly lightless. "Most convincing, Hazell. Do go on. . ."

"Well," said Jonathan Hazell carefully, trying not to get ahead of himself, "at first, what with those two thugs who were found at Thursday's funicular, I was afraid the Oktopous might have succeeded. If they had captured Thursday and his new ship who knows what might have become of Miss Crumb? She could have been murdered, or sold as a slave to some cruel Zagwan princeling! But I do not now believe that is the case."

"Why not?" asked Teal.

"Because when I started asking after her I was frequently told that other men had been asking the same questions a few days previously. It did not matter whether I asked at the exchange or at some grubby chandlery, the story was the same; someone had been there before me. And when I dug a little deeper, I found that these other men were employees of Fat Jago. And when I dug deeper still, I was told that it is Fat Jago who handles all the Oktopous's business here!"

"And who is Fat Jago?"

"Ssshh!" Jonathan Hazell looked about again. A man like Fat Jago could have spies anywhere. "Fat Jago Belkin!" he whispered. "Only the most important businessman in Mayda! Only the richest man west of Thelona! He has a huge villa on the southern coast, and a charming wife. It is a great shock!"

Dr Teal refused to be shocked. "And what makes you think that Fever isn't locked up in this charming villa, a prisoner of Belkin and his huge wife?"

"No, the villa is huge; the wife is charming. And the fact that Belkin has been asking after Miss Crumb tells that he does not know where she is, do you see?"

"It tells us that he *did* not know. But if he has stopped asking, perhaps he has found her. And if he doesn't have her, where is she? We're no further on than we were when you first stuck your oar in."

"Ah!" said Jonathan Hazell. "That brings me to the second strand of my investigation. I have learned something about Arlo Thursday's house. Local fishermen, who know all the ins and outs of Mayda's shores, tell me that there is a hidden cove on the south-western side of the island. When Daniel Thursday lived in that funicular, he used to keep a boat there. I believe there must be a path leading through the crater wall from Thursday's garden down to this cove. That must be the way that Thursday escaped after he gunned down those two Oktopoid gentlemen. Doubtless he took Miss Crumb with him. They have escaped by sea. If only we knew where they were making for. . ."

"What about the Ragged Isles?" asked Dr Teal. "Didn't Thursday's family have shipyards there? Could he be holed up there?"

"Oh no," said the merchant. "Those shipyards were swept away by the great wave. The Ragged Isles are dead, bare places now. Cursed, the locals say. It's far more likely that Miss Crumb and the boy would seek shelter in Meriam or Nowhere. We should send at once to those cities and see if there have been any sightings of them!"

Dr Teal said, "This is excellent work, Hazell. I could not have done better myself. Tell me, in your delvings, did you hear any mention of a man named Lothar Vishniak?"

Jonathan Hazell looked blank. "I can't say I did. Who is he?"

The Engineer shook his head. "No one. Just a name that I heard mentioned once. I merely wondered. . . But if you have not heard anything of him, perhaps we may reassure ourselves that he is not in Mayda."

23

TEST FLIGHT

rlo had always planned to call his new machine the *Thirza*. Through all the months of planning and hard work it had never once occurred to him that it should not be dedicated to her. It was as beautiful, as delicate, as precious as his Thirza, and he liked to imagine how she would look when the news reached her; not only had a miraculous device alighted on the lawns behind the Quadrado Del Mar, it was named after her. Fat Jago Belkin might have given her pearls and diamonds and fine dresses and a house the size of a small town, but Arlo would make her a present of all tomorrow's skies.

But when he woke on the morning of the first flight he knew that was not the right name after all. The picture of Thirza Blaizey that he had carried in his mind all these years had begun to fade, like a painting hung on a sunny wall. She was still there, but she seemed less real. Maybe she had never been real. How many actual words had he ever exchanged with her? A few hundred? Maybe not that many.

He rolled over in his bunk and looked across the big, bare room to where Fever Crumb lay sleeping. She always went to sleep flat on her back, which she claimed was healthier, and as far as he knew she always woke up in the same position, still with her hair tied back in that tight bun, which must be as hard as a pebble under the nape of her neck. Arlo grinned. When they had first come to the island he had sometimes thought how much he would rather have had Thirza Belkin there with him instead of this bony, stubborn, cold-natured Londoner, but now that the machine was finished he could see that Thirza would never have been able to help him as Fever had. He could not imagine debating lift-to-weight ratios and angles of attack with Thirza, nor could he see Thirza planing a propeller blade for six hours straight, or wearing without complaint the same grubby clothes day after day, and washing only in the sea. Slightly surprised at himself, he decided that Thirza did not deserve to have her name on his machine.

He rose quietly, and went up on to the roof, and by the time Fever awoke and joined him there he had already painted the new name he had chosen on the machine's nose. She frowned when she read it.

Goshawk

"It is irrational to give a name to a machine," was all she said.

Eastward, behind Mayda, the sun was coming up, but in the west the sky was still dusky, the ocean almost colourless. A cool breeze from the west, salt-smelling, hummed through the *Goshawk*'s rigging. Together, using mallets and hammers and their bare hands, they demolished the parapet on the tower's windward side. Then Arlo pulled on his goggles and tied back his long hair and clambered into the harness that was slung beneath the trembling paper wings. His hands grasped the levers which operated the wing-flaps and rudder.

"Wish me luck," he said, as Fever went round to the back to start the engine.

"Good luck," she said obediently, although she did not believe in luck, only in engineering and the laws of physics. She reached up and gripped the edges of the propeller they had made, and found that her hands were shaking, which annoyed her. Surely Arlo was the one who should be afraid, but she did not see him trembling; he just lay there in the harness as if he were a part of the machine, as if he were a new fledged angel spreading its wings on some shelf of the sea cliffs. . .

She swung the propeller as hard as she could. The clumsy engine came to life at last with a hard, throaty roar that shivered all the struts and cables. She reached up and gripped the edges of the propeller they had made and swung it as hard as she could and it whirled into a blurred disc, scattering shadows over the wings and the tower roof. Then she put both hands on the bar which Arlo had mounted below the tail and used all her weight to shove the machine forward, into the wind.

It went off the edge of the roof, seemed to hesitate for a moment, dipped its wings and plummeted. "No!" she screamed, the scream lost in the angry shout of the engine, which echoed from the cliffs and the tower wall as the *Goshawk* plunged downward. She ran to the roof's edge with that dreadful feeling of watching something fall and being helpless to save it. But the machine saved itself. Before it hit the rocks its nose lifted; the engine roared and whinnied as it scrambled up the sky and Fever was kneeling on the roof watching it fly away above the beaches, wiping the silly tears from her face and feeling glad that there was no one there to see her.

Alone in the sky, Arlo eased on the rudder lever and felt the *Goshawk* respond, veering to the right. He drew back on the wing controls and tried to make her climb. *I'm flying*, he thought, wondering how he could nail this moment into his memory. He wanted to keep all of it, everything, every last shadow in each ripple of sand on the low-tide beach below him. The noise of the engine battered at him, its echoes reflecting off the cliff faces. The curious angels whirled all round him, circling the machine, an honour guard welcoming him into the realms of the air. He saw Weasel among them, crossing and recrossing the machine's path; heard his cry above the engine roar: "A-a-a-ar-lo!"

But he was too heavy. He could feel it each time he tried to go higher. A sluggishness. The grumpy tug of gravity. That big engine mounted above him was upsetting the delicate balance of the wings and spoiling all his careful mathematics. It was a struggle to keep the *Goshawk*'s nose up. Engine fumes blew in his face, smearing his goggles, stinking of castor oil.

He had planned to circle the island and land on the long flat strand beside the quay, but he was barely halfway round and already he had dropped almost to sea level. Rocks rushed by just beneath him, exposed by the low tide, spine-breaking rocks with skirts of bladderwrack and black barnacled backs as friendly as cheese-graters. He saw sand ahead; a long stretch of wet sand under wet black cliffs, and he steered for it as best he could, already feeling a little sad that the sky did not want him after all.

The harness punched him in the breastbone, knocked all the air out of his lungs. Flung divots of sand stung his face, clogged his mouth as he gasped for breath. The machine bounced and took flight again, rushing along a few feet above its own shadow. A ripped-off wheel bounded along beside it for a way, drawing a line across the beach. He saw a rainbow hanging in the fan of spray that it threw up behind it from the wet sand. Then there was another thump, sand between his teeth, salt water, his hip banging painfully against a strut, the crunch of snapped wood, paper tearing, a line of rocks sliding towards him sideways. . .

It took her an unbelievably long time to reach the place where he had fallen. She scrambled over breakwaters and barriers of wet rock; clattered across deep drifts of pebbles, pulled off her shoes and pelted barefoot along the shining sand. The flying machine stood on its nose, surrounded by inquisitive angels. Spilled fuel slid in rainbow-coloured ribbons down the little streams and runnels of the beach towards the sea. Arlo was still dangling in the harness, caught there, upside down. He was laughing, and as she struggled to unstrap him she thought he must be delirious. Perhaps too much blood had run to his head in all the time he'd hung there waiting. But she helped him down and set him upright and slapped his face a couple of times and he went on laughing. He was just happy.

"I flew, Fever! I *flew!*"

Fever stepped away, because he showed a definite inclination to hug her, the way the *Lyceum* actors sometimes did after a good performance. She did not want to be hugged by Arlo Thursday. She did not know where it would end.

His laughter slowly wore itself out. He pulled his goggles off and wiped his eyes. There was a small cut beneath one of them.

"You were right about the engine," he said. "We shall need a lighter one."

Fever shook her head. "That isn't possible."

"You could make one," he said. He had flown; he felt all things were possible. "I bet you could make one even better than Edgar's. . ."

"Out of what?" Fever complained. "I haven't the materials or the tools. I have no idea how to make an engine that would be light enough. And even if I did, what would it run on? Half our ethanol has spilled away. You will just have to make the *Goshawk* bigger. If it had a broader wingspan perhaps it would be able to lift the engine. . ."

"No. . ." Arlo sat down on the sand, sobered. The angels swooped to and fro above him, dropping echoes of his spent laughter like bombs, *Ha ha! Hoo hoo hoo!* He traced shapes in the sand for a moment; wings; letters. "No; we haven't the time; we haven't the wood; we haven't the paste or the paper. We must have another engine."

"But I have already explained. . ."

"You don't need to build one." He looked up at her, shading his eyes with one hand, smiling so happily that she wondered if he were still delirious. "We already

208

have one. Right here, on the island."

Fever thought for a moment. "The Aranha?"

"Why not? Your grandfather's gift to mine. There's some engine inside it that doesn't seem to need fuel."

"All engines need fuel."

"Then maybe it has a limitless supply. If we can get it out and use it to drive the *Goshawk*'s propeller we'll have solved the weight problem."

"But we need the Aranha! What if Belkin finds us? Or Vishniak?"

"What if they don't?" asked Arlo. "They haven't yet. Why should they now?" He stood up, brushing sand from his clothes, shaking it from his hair. He had been in the sky, and he was not going to let his enemies stop him from returning. "Fever, we've almost done it! Powered, controlled flight! We can't let fear of Belkin and Vishniak stop us now!"

They spent the rest of the morning dismantling the *Goshawk* and moving the pieces up above the tideline before the sea returned. In the afternoon they carried it all back, piece by piece, to the tower, reassembling it on the roof while the Aranha hopped on its endless, eerie sentry duty among the overgrown quays below them.

At about the age when most children were learning nursery rhymes and how to count to ten, Fever had been taught the first and second laws of thermodynamics. Dr Crumb said that everyone should know them; they were the key to understanding so much about the universe. The name made them sound complicated, but they were really quite simple. The first law said that energy cannot be created or destroyed, it can only change its form. The second, that entropy increases in a closed system; which, Dr Crumb explained, meant that hot things, if left to their own devices, cooled down; that heat only moved from hotter places to colder ones, and that machines could never be completely efficient.

So where did that leave the Stalkers? Reanimated corpses, armoured and mechanized, powered by technology from who-knew-when, they burned no fuel as far as Fever had ever been able to see, and they had been known to keep going for centuries. So either they must be making their own energy somehow (which broke the first law), or they were charged up when they were made and the charge kept them running for ever (which broke the second).

A technomancer Fever had talked to in Bruges claimed that they drew power from the air by harvesting invisible electric fields, but she suspected he was only guessing. Her mother, chief Stalker-builder to the Movement, had mentioned something called Molecular Clockwork, but she had not been able to explain it, and it sounded like voodoo to Fever.

It was a mystery, and as she followed Arlo down to the shipyard in the evening sunlight she looked forward to learning more.

In the alleyways between the ivy-covered ruins Arlo called the machine's name softly, like someone calling for a strayed cat, and after a few moments it came to them, hopping out through a hole in a wall with the sunset winking on its spines.

"Careful," said Fever. "You should have seen what it

did to Fat Jago's thugs and the front of your house."

Arlo ignored her. He held out his hand to the Aranha. It hesitated, then seemed to understand, and came closer, swivelling its blunt body from side to side. Fever saw the gun jutting out of its underside, the metal around it darkened and made iridescent by the exhaust from the muzzle. She saw other details which she'd never noticed before, having never been so close to it in daylight: the rims of small inspection hatches set into its flanks and belly; the pistons at the joints of its legs shining sleekly with oil.

"Come here," said Arlo, as if it were a pet. It hopped close to him and he deftly popped a hatch open and drew out a glittering ribbon of brass-cased bullets, lifting it into the sunlight as carefully as a Bargetown swami handling a snake. The Aranha just stood there, patiently waiting. He took out a screwdriver and started undoing screws all around the carapace. Fever caught them in her hands as they fell. When there were twelve cupped in her palms she put them down carefully on the ground and she and Arlo between them lifted the whole top of the carapace off.

A stink of chemistry and must escaped into the air. Fever looked inside the Aranha and saw a mass of wires and ducting wound around and through the featherless carcass of a long-dead bird, all cupped in that metal shell. Mechanical tendrils sprouted from the angel's skull and from dozens of junction boxes anchored to its spine; a cat's cradle of wiring more complicated by far than the one she'd created under the *Lyceum*'s stage. Beneath it all a doughnut-shaped contraption buzzed. Cautiously, she put her hand close to it. It felt as warm as an egg.

211

"That's the power source. Look. It's wired into everything. . ."

"Behold, the Doughnut of Power," said Arlo.

"But what is it?" asked Fever. "We should be careful. If we start un-wiring it, it might explode and take us with it. It might make another crater as big as Mayda."

But Arlo was already at work, with snips and tweezers, detaching the magic doughnut from the machinery it had powered. He did not care what it was. If it could keep the Aranha on duty through three generations, it should have no difficulty carrying the *Goshawk* back into the air.

As he started to lift the doughnut free the Aranha jerked into motion, swift and startling as a spider. It took a step, turned, poked out its gun like a long black tongue. Something inside it went *snick-snick-snick* like a sewing machine.

"The power source is no use on its own," said Fever, wincing with disgust as she snatched a spanner and delved in past the threshing angel in its nest of tubes. "We'll need the drive mechanism too. . ." Together they wrenched out the doughnut, along with a fat electric motor. There were sparks, a smell of burned wire, and the Aranha jerked rigid and toppled backwards. Fever jumped out of its way just in time to stop herself going with it as it pitched off the edge of the quay. The splash rang off the ruined walls. The Aranha sank away from her into the greenish water, down into the shadows cast by the wavering weed, the darting silvery fish.

"Pity," said Arlo. "I was going to try and salvage the gun too."

Cupped in his brown hands, trailing severed cables, the weird power-ring buzzed like a maybug.

Nothing that Fever knew about power sources could help her understand the object they had taken out of the Aranha. It was high old-tech from the deep past. She didn't even know a name for the pale metal it was made from. It had no need for fuel and no visible moving parts, and yet it was clearly producing energy, and even wasting a little in the form of that beetly buzzing and a faint warmth, until she discovered a square pad on its underside which, when pressed, seemed to shut it off.

Arlo wanted to call it the doughnut, but Fever thought that sounded undignified and insisted on the torus. Fever thought they should try to prise it open and see what was going on inside, but Arlo shook his head.

"We're here to build an aircraft, not to study this contraption. Besides, what if you were right? If we start trying to get inside it, it might explode, or poison us. You hear sometimes of scavengers being poisoned by old machines; their hair falls out, or they puff up like bladders."

"If we don't know how it works," said Fever, "we'll never be able to make another."

"We won't need to," said Arlo. "The important thing for now is to get the *Goshawk* airborne, so we can show the merchants of Mayda that it really does fly. Once we have some money behind us then we'll build bigger machines, capable of carrying a real motor."

They laid the torus on the floor of the tower,

arranging its spaghetti of wires around it like the legs of a jellyfish which they were getting ready to dissect. The wires were sheathed in plastic, with little terminals of the pale metal at their ends. "It's like a battery," said Fever, wishing again that she still had some of Godshawk's memories. "Look, this red wire must be a negative pole and this black one is positive. . . Or perhaps the other way around. Either way we should be able to form a circuit. . ."

Arlo nodded encouragingly, but Fever could tell that he did not understand. She fetched Edgar Saraband's engine, which they had not bothered to mount again aboard the *Goshawk*. Opening the heavy cowling, she studied the parts inside. If they were to lose the fuel keg and all those unsightly ducts, she could house the torus there, and use its motor to turn the gears and power the reduction drive. A pity the Aranha had sunk; it would have been a useful mine for the materials she would need. But Arlo's toolboxes were well stocked, and she was an Engineer. She thought that she could do it.

She told Arlo to bring spanners and screwdrivers, and set to work dismantling the old engine.

24

DROWNED OFFERING

t the foot of the cliffs in a corner of the Belkin's beach Thirza kept a sacred tide-pool. She knew that it was silly, but the *Mãe Abaixo* had been so much a part of her childhood, and it made her feel safe and childlike again to perform the age-old rituals. So she had had a priestess from the temple come to bless the pool, and Fat Jago's architect had designed a pretty little copper-domed temple with driftwood pillars to shelter it, and each day (if she was not too busy) she came down to make an offering there.

She was kneeling at the pool's edge watching the green and purple weeds wave in its depths when Weasel found her that afternoon. He came winging low over the wave tops, and settled beside her, calling her name, full of excitement at having flown with Arlo.

*

When Thirza returned to the house she was shaking a little, and her dress was wet. She went to find Fat Jago, who was reading in the garden room. "The fruit is ripe," she said. "It's time to shake the tree."

"You're sure?"

"Arlo flew this morning. Poor Weasel told me all about it. He was very excited. There was a lot I didn't really understand, about Arlo and the Crumb girl and a big crab? But the important part was clear enough. Arlo has finished his machine, and he flew all round the island in it and landed on a beach. Flew like an angel, apparently."

Fat Jago set his book aside and levered himself up out of his chair. "Excellent. I'll cross to Thursday Island tonight. Prepare a letter for the Cartel; we'll send it as soon as I come home with the machine. What about that bird of yours?"

"Oh, I have dealt with him," said Thirza, as carelessly as she could.

Her husband came closer and saw the state she was in; the small scratches on her hands and the seawater dripping from the hem of her dress. "Poor Thirza!" he said, and held her close.

She had drowned Weasel in the tide-pool. It had been horrible. She had had to hold him under with both her hands, and it had taken much longer than she had expected for the life to go out of him. Water had splashed everywhere, and his little fingers had clutched and clawed and scrabbled at her hands. It had made her sad, but she had no further use for the angel now, and if she had let him live there was always a danger that he might fly back to the island and let Arlo know what he had told her. Anyway, he would be her gift to the Goddess. The *Mãe Abaixo* was usually content with wine or coins these days and never asked for human sacrifices any more, but at a time like this, with such important business to be conducted, it could do no harm to offer her a life.

While she changed out of her wet clothes and Bisa dabbed ointment on her scratches, Fat Jago made his preparations. He sent messengers running into the city to tell the captain and crew of his galley that they would sail on the evening tide. He took off his gold-embroidered house-robes and put on some clothes which Thirza had given him especially for this expedition; a sturdy canvas jacket with dozens of useful pockets, dark blue barragan breeches, gaitered boots. She thought he looked splendid when he emerged from his dressing room. The brass buttons that secured all the pockets glinted and winked in the evening sunlight, bright as new gold coins, and he had changed his diamond scalp-symbol from red to a nice, nautical blue. She fetched the packet of sandwiches that she had made for him and slipped it into one of the pockets.

"I wish I could come with you," she said, smoothing a crease out of his collar.

"It's no place for you, my sweet," said Fat Jago. He knew there might be violence and unpleasantness ahead, and he liked to keep Thirza free of such things, in a separate compartment of his life. He kissed her goodbye. "I'll miss you!"

"I'll miss you too."

When his sedan chair had departed for the harbourside she went back down the garden to the beach. Angels were flapping and cawing around her little temple, striping its roof with their poo, wailing over the bundle of dirty feathers that washed to and fro in the pool between the driftwood pillars. "Shoo!" shouted Thirza, flapping her arms at them. "Be off with you!"

They lifted into the sky like wind-blown newspapers, still wailing.

A half-hour later, Jonathan Hazell stepped out on to the little balcony outside his study. He had dispatched messengers to Nowhere and Meriam that morning, and Dr Teal had been pacing the drawing room ever since, waiting for them to return with news of Fever. Jonathan Hazell had busied himself with all the letters and receipts and bills of lading which he had been neglecting during the past few days while he played detective. It never ceased to astonish him, the way such paperwork heaped up. . .

Standing on the balcony, he started to notice that there was some sort of confusion going on among the angels. Alarm calls racketed across the rooftops. The big birds were flying in crazy circles over the harbour and executing wild manoeuvres between Mayda's chimney stacks. He shivered. The idea that he shared this city with intelligences that were not human had always unsettled him, no matter how dim and amiable the angels were. He could not help but find this strange behaviour ominous. He'd often heard his Maydan friends recall that the angels had been the first to raise the warning when that great wave came; the *Ondra Del Mãe*, rolling in like a judgement from the western deeps. . .

He glanced towards the harbour mouth and the open ocean beyond. There was no sign of a wave. But he saw something in the outer basin that concerned him almost as much. He stared for a moment, then ran inside the house.

"Dr Teal! Dr Teal!"

He dragged the Engineer out on to the balcony with him and pointed at the harbour.

"What are we looking at?" asked Dr Teal. "That red ship?"

"That is Fat Jago's galley, the *Desolation Row*!" said Jonathan Hazell. "She's been towed into the outer basin. She must be making ready to sail on the next tide!"

Dr Teal looked again, and this time Jonathan Hazell could see his mind working. For all his bumbling, the Engineer wasn't stupid. "He must have had word of Thursday and Fever. He's taking that ship to find them and bring back Arlo's machine."

"Of course, it may be some other matter," ventured Jonathan Hazell hopefully. "A man like Fat Jago must have many matters of business to attend to."

"Believe me," said Dr Teal, with sudden, startling earnestness, "none of them will be more important than Thursday's machine."

"Machine?"

"His boat, ship, whatever it is that he is building. We must get aboard that galley and see where Fat Jago is going to—"

"Oh, no, no, no, no!" said Jonathan Hazell. "Fat Jago's men will see us – I mean, they will see *you*—"

"But how else can we find out where they are bound, and get there first, and ensure ... ensure Fever's safety?"

"Believe me, Dr Teal, I am as concerned about Miss Crumb as you, but to try and stow away aboard the *Desolation Row* would be madness." He blinked a few times, looking from Teal to the distant harbourside, where tuns of water were being rolled into the galley's holds. "Madness," he said again, and then, "I have a little boat of my own. . . It will take a big ship like the *Desolation Row* several hours to make ready and get out of the harbour. In my boat we could leave at once."

"For where? Nowhere? Or Meriam?"

"Meriam," said Jonathan Hazell firmly. "It is most likely that Miss Crumb has gone where her friends are. And once we are out of the harbour the wind will be with us running down the coast."

Once they were out of the harbour; but that proved more easily said than done, for there was no wind at all inside the crater that evening, and Jonathan Hazell had to row his boat the whole length of the outer basin, while Dr Teal sat in the bow and fumed.

"Come *on*, Hazell," he snapped, as they drew level with the long red blade that was the *Desolation Row*. Lanterns had been lit on her high stern-castle, and her crew were busy removing tarpaulins from a boxy structure near her bows, which turned out to be a revolving gun turret.

"Look," said Teal, "they'll soon be ready for the off. Still, it's good to see that your friend Fat Jago is as wary of the Sea Goddess as every other fool in Mayda. No engines on that ship of his; just oars. She can't be very fast."

"Oh, she'll be fast," panted Jonathan Hazell. "Fat Jago employs a great many oarsmen. And she'll not be prey to the winds, as we are. We must just hope she will give us another hour or so; a sporting start. . ."

But their luck was out. Just as they passed the lighthouse at the harbour mouth and felt the first stirrings of the wind, they heard the faint, steady pounding of a drum coming up the harbour behind them.

The *Desolation Row* swept out of Mayda in the twilight under bare masts with her oars dipping and rising like the pistons of some implacable machine. Teal and Hazell watched her come, her sleek red hull like a bloodied knife, with dim lights burning in her gun-slits and that big lantern bright on her stern. Her lookouts mistook Hazell's boat for a fisherman, maybe, or maybe they were so intent on their business that they never noticed it bobbing there at all. *Boom, boom, doom*, went the drum inside her, and the white water wavered like a ghost against her ram, and the little boat pitched on her wake as she went past it and swung her prow towards the last band of golden light that lay along the western sea.

"West!" hissed Dr Teal. "They're headed west! Hazell, you idiot, you were wrong! They're making for the Ragged Isles!"

"But there's nothing there!" insisted Jonathan Hazell.

"Well Fat Jago seems pretty sure that there is! You don't set sail in a monster like that on the mere off-chance of finding something."

"What shall we do, Dr Teal?"

The Engineer looked grim, and one hand reached inside his coat. There was something in there that he kept feeling for, as if its bulk and weight reassured him. Since he was an Engineer, Jonathan Hazell suspected it must be something more practical than a lucky rabbit's foot or *The Meditations of St Kylie*. He patted it now, glared at Hazell and said, "Follow them, of course!"

Jonathan Hazell raised the sail. It might have been

russet if there had been any light to see it by, but in the deepening twilight it was just a rhomboid of deeper darkness against the sky. It flapped for a moment until Jonathan Hazell scrambled aft and pulled in the mainsheet, whereon it filled with wind, causing the boat to heel and rush forward and making Dr Teal say angrily, "I thought you knew how to sail this thing?"

Jonathan Hazell ignored him. The tug of the mainsheet in his hand was comforting, and so was the cheerful gurgling of water under the boat's foot, the slap of the small waves as she cut through them. "She's a good boat," he said. "A fast boat."

But she was not so fast as the *Desolation Row*, whose stern lantern was already dwindling in the west, racing towards those far-off islands which pricked the black horizon like fishes' teeth.

25

THE LANDING PARTY

hey had worked all afternoon, pausing now and then to eat ship's biscuits and slices of cheese, but never stopping for a meal. They had forgotten to feel hungry, or tired. Sometimes one or other of them would take a break and walk away from the tower, and once Arlo went to the beach to swim, but their heads were full of their work all the time, and they soon came back to the machine. They felt that they were close to something. To stop before they reached it was impossible.

By sundown Fever's new engine was complete. With the Aranha's torus at its heart it was as light and delicate as everything else about the *Goshawk.* As the sky above the tower grew dark and filled with stars and the angels went ghosting homeward to their roosts Arlo lit a lantern and Fever helped him fix the engine into position on the machine's back. Carefully they made it fast, boring holes through the struts and bolting the engine to them, tightening the nuts as far as they would go. Instead of the medieval armour that Edgar Saraband's engine had worn, Arlo had made a tortoiseshell basket of balsa struts and they pasted paper over it and varnished it and fixed that over the mechanisms. The torus gave off so little heat that Fever didn't think it needed any vents to cool it, but Arlo made some anyway, just to be safe. They looked like the gills of a dogfish.

And then, when the newborn sickle moon hung high over the islands, they switched it on. It buzzed restlessly, and the propeller quivered, and when Fever gave it one helping turn the big wooden blades dissolved suddenly into a circular blur of motion, and they felt *Goshawk* trembling, straining at its tethers like a live thing, a huge, newborn bird that longed for the freedom of the sky.

When they turned it off the night seemed quieter than before, the air more still. The breeze had died. Fever said, "I hope the wind comes back tomorrow. We cannot launch without a headwind."

"It will come," said Arlo, watching her, laughing privately at that busy brain of hers, the way it never rested.

"Five miles per hour would be ideal, but I suppose we can manage with less."

He said, "You never unfasten your hair."

"What?" Fever put a hand to the hard bun at the back of her head. "What does that have to do with anything?" She wondered if he was thinking of using her hair as some sort of pennant so that he could gauge the speed and direction of the wind. Surely his own was long enough?

"Even when you go to sleep," said Arlo. "Sometimes a bit comes loose, but you always tie it straight back."

"Hair is irrational," said Fever. "It is a vestige of our animal past. I had to grow mine when I left the Head just to stop people staring, but that does not mean that—"

He came around the *Goshawk*'s tail and stood close to her. He reached out and she felt his fingers busy at the nape of her neck, unravelling the careful knot she'd tied. She knew that she ought to protest, but when she tried to speak no words came out, just a little sigh, a little gasp. And then the knot was undone and around her face in wisps and strands her dry, sun-bleached hair came tickling down. He combed his fingers through it, arranging it for her, his hands brushing against her throat and her ears and the angles of her jaw.

"I do not approve..." she started to say, but she could not remember what it was that she did not approve of. She touched his face, tracing all the beautiful patterns of his freckles, thinking, *This is not rational. I am forgetting myself.* But might it not be pleasant to forget herself for a little while? Might it not be pleasant to give in to these fierce and hungry feelings? The smells of Arlo's body flowered in her mind as sprays of nameless colour. She supposed that she was falling in love. That was what Dymphna or Lillibet would call it. And although she knew it must just be a matter of chemicals and instincts, it still felt wonderful and frightening and strange. She leaned towards Arlo until their faces touched. *I am supposed to kiss him now*, she thought, thinking of all the love scenes she had watched through her periscope from her lair under the *Lyceum* stage. *I wonder how kissing works?*

White wings flared above her in the moonlight and an angel came down and landed heavily on her head.

"Weasel!" it squawked, pushing its fish-stinky beak down between their startled faces as they sprang apart. "Arlo! Weasel!"

Fever batted it away and it fluttered wildly and

settled on the Goshawk's port wing, still screaming out a mess of squawks and words. She wondered if it was angry at her for touching Arlo. Then she saw the look on his face.

"What? *What* has happened to Weasel? *How?*"

"Thir-z-aa," croaked the angel. Fever thought it was the same female she had tried to talk to about the scratches in the birdcastle. It hadn't many words or much understanding of how to put them together, but it kept trying until Arlo understood.

"She *drowned* him? Thirza?"

A cold feeling came over Fever. "What was Weasel doing anywhere near Thirza?"

"Thir-z-aa!" said the angel, doing a little agitated dance along the parapet. "Friend. Snacks."

"Does Weasel talk to Thirza often?" Fever asked.

"Often! Yesterday!"

Arlo shook his head. "Yesterday might mean last month or last year. Weasel wouldn't betray me. . ."

"Weasel wouldn't *know* he was betraying you," said Fever. "Not if she was nice to him and gave him lots of snacks."

"Thirza wouldn't. . ." he started to say.

And then more angels were around them, their voices clanging like rusty bells around the old tower. "A-ar-lo! Floatyboat! Big, big! Floatyboat come!"

Arlo and Fever turned from each other, looking out across the sea. Beyond the reefs and shoals which screened the island, a ship rode the starlit swell. Long and low and black, with lights showing here and there. Fever stared at it, trying to understand what it meant. She could not believe that it was anything good.

"Floatyboat!" cried the angels.

"It's Belkin!" said Arlo, with a catch in his voice as if he were going to cry. "That's his galley, the *Desolation Row*. It was built at Blaizey's, the year I started there. . . But it'll never get through the reefs. . ."

"Not even if Weasel told Thirza about the waymarks?" asked Fever.

Arlo looked at her. "No. She's too big. She'd rip her keel out on the rocks. . ."

"Little floatyboat!" screeched the angels, taking up a new cry. "Big floatyboat-come-little-floatyboat-come."

Arlo looked confused, but Fever, with her keen Scriven eyes, soon saw what they meant. A smaller shape was detaching itself from the black outline of Fat Jago's galley. A skiff, already starting to thread its way through the reefs. Faint sounds came to her across the water: the dull wooden clunk of a banged oar, a distant curse.

She took Arlo's hand, and felt him trembling.

"Weasel told Thirza about us," he said. "And Thirza told Belkin everything!"

"Arlo," said Fever. "It is irrational to cry over spilled milk. Can that boat get through the reefs?"

"The big ship certainly couldn't, not by night. But maybe a skiff. . ."

He made an angry gesture, scaring the angel away into the dark. He looked very frightened. Fever had the feeling that came to her sometimes when she was with Ruan and Fern; a need to protect him against the hard truths of the world. She decided to take charge.

"We'll launch the *Goshawk*. Fly to Mayda now."

"I'm not leaving you behind," he said.

"Perhaps she'd carry us both, with the new engine."

"Never. The balance would be all wrong. Anyway, there's no wind, she'll never lift in this calm."

He was right. The night was still, the air as quiet as the air in a big room, the voices of Fat Jago's men and the creak of their oars carrying clearly across the water.

"They can't come up here unless we let them," Fever said. "There's only one way in, up that ladder."

"They'll have guns."

"But they won't want to use them. The *Goshawk*'s no use to them if it's full of holes, and nor are you. We can hold them off."

"What with?"

"Where's your pistol?"

"It's not loaded. It never was."

Fever snatched the lantern and ran to the hatch and down the stairs, looking desperately around their cluttered quarters. The belt of bullets which Arlo had taken from the Aranha's gun shone faintly, abandoned under a table. *If only we hadn't dismantled it*, Fever thought. The Aranha could have kept a whole fleet from landing. But regret would not bring it back, any more than it would bring back Weasel or undo his treachery. She snatched up the bullet-belt and studied the brass cartridges. On the base of each was a raised disc which she guessed must be some sort of percussion cap. A mechanism inside the Aranha's gun would have struck that, causing the charge inside the cartridge to explode and force the bullet down the gun barrel. Ingenious, but useless, since the gun itself was several fathoms down in the old dock. . .

"What about the angels?" she asked, glancing round as Arlo came down the stairs. "Would they help us?"

He shook his head. "They'd be too scared. It's not their fight anyway. They probably wouldn't even understand. . . They don't understand much that we do. That's why Weasel thought it was all right to tell Thirza about us, I expect. I was wrong to be angry at him. Angels don't think like us. They don't understand. . ."

Fever went to him and kissed him. There seemed a strong chance that she might die soon, and she did not want to die without kissing him. She need not have worried about not knowing how; it turned out that her mouth had known all along. He tasted of the colour that you see when you lift your face to the summer sun and close your eyes.

"Fever. . ." he said, when she stopped.

It was very interesting, this falling in love. She understood now why people wrote so many plays and songs about it. But it was hard to concentrate properly knowing that those men were coming, and that one of them was the man who had tried to squash her with a house. She made herself step away from Arlo and went to the fireplace, stirring up the embers there with the poker, throwing on fresh wood. She said, "Boil up some water, quick."

"Why?"

"And gather together some logs . . . stones from the wall . . . anything heavy."

"You're going to throw *stones* at them?"

"We're going to *drop* stones *on* them. We're a

hundred feet higher than them. That's a hundred feet of acceleration. Stored gravitational energy waiting to be unleashed."

She checked the big vice attached to the old table that served them as a workbench. Fetched a hammer and a six-inch nail. When she looked from the eastern window she could no longer see the skiff, but she knew that was not a good thing; that meant it was close in now, hidden from her among the rocks and shadows of rocks just offshore. Maybe it was already off-loading its landing party along the overgrown quay.

Meanwhile, Arlo had set a big pot of water to heat over the fire, and was making a pile of the biggest logs on the platform outside, at the top of the access ladder. Fever prised one of the bullets free of the belt and clamped it tightly in the jaws of the vice, then dragged the table round until the bullet pointed at the doorway. She laid the hammer and the nail ready beside it, then fetched the heaviest things she could carry: bits of the old engine cowling, a big wrench, a loose stone from the wall.

She went outside to add them to Arlo's pile at the top of the ladder, and was about to go back in and look for something else when she heard voices echoing among the crumbled walls below, and the hollow clonk as a boat banged against the stone jetty.

"They are at the quay!" said Arlo.

The men were making no attempt at stealth. Some of them carried flaming torches, and they talked to each other in loud voices as they came up the slope from the quays. Only five or six of them, so Fever guessed that they were not expecting much resistance. She felt a fluttering sensation in her stomach. She needed the toilet, but there wasn't time now. Two of the men had detached themselves from the rest and came right to the ladder's foot. One held a torch up. The other stood in the pool of light it cast so that Arlo and Fever could see his face.

It was Fat Jago.

He shaded his eyes against the torchlight, peering up. "Thursday? Your little feathered friend told me where to find you. Will you let me up? We need to talk."

Arlo looked at Fever, and she could see that he was relieved by the fat man's reasonable tone. It would be easy to believe in that tone; to let Belkin climb up and talk to them. But Fever remembered too well her last chat with him. It was irrational to trust him. They could not let the *Goshawk* fall into the hands of a man like that.

Before Arlo could reply she picked up a big stone and dropped it over the edge of the platform. It clanged off the handrail at the edge of the landing halfway down and Fat Jago skipped clumsily backwards as it shattered on the ground just in front of him.

"Thursday! Be reasonable!" he pleaded. "Even you must see that you can't do this alone! The Oktopous Cartel will give you all you need: space, equipment, workers... They want to help you."

"They'll have to come up and get me first!" shouted Arlo, and he snatched a log and sent it hurtling down. Belkin strode to the foot of the ladder, motioning angrily for the rest of his men. They came very fast, with the torchlight splashing their running shadows on the cobbles and the weeds. Bald heads, bare arms, studded leather jerkins, wide belts with knives stuffed through them. They came barefoot, like sailors, making almost no sound.

Belkin called to them as they started swarming up the ladder, "Take them alive! I want the machine undamaged."

Fever hefted one of the weightier bits of Edgar Saraband's engine, took aim, and let it go. It struck sparks from the ladder as it dropped. A man looked up at the flash and she saw his eyes go wide in the instant before it crunched into his face. He fell soundlessly from the ladder, knocking down one of his mates, but the rest came on. She dropped another piece, and then she and Arlo started heaving logs and engine parts over the edge. The attackers were ready for them now and leant sideways off the ladder to avoid the missiles. A few glanced off shoulders and leather-armoured backs on their way to the ground, but the men came on, and were soon on the landing.

By then the pot of water on the fire was burbling happily to itself. Together, not speaking, Fever and Arlo ran to fetch it. In the short time that it took them to carry it to the ladder top one of the attackers had managed to get almost up to the entry platform. They upended the pot over him and he screamed and put his hands to his scalded face and went backwards off the ladder and down, hitting the ground with a sound like a stomped snail.

Was he dead? Fever didn't know. Did she feel bad about that? She saw no rational reason why she should. It was his own fault. If the men would just go back to their ship and sail away; if they'd only stop trying to get up the ladder. . . But the three remaining men kept climbing and after a few moments more all the ammunition was exhausted. Arlo snatched up the empty pot and it rang like a gong on the bald head of one who had made it almost to the platform, but he kept on coming.

Fever shoved Arlo inside the tower and went in after him, shouting, "Get upstairs! Smash the machine!" She thrust him towards the staircase and scrambled over to the table, where her ultimate weapon waited.

Outside, the man heaved himself up on to the platform. It was Fat Jago himself, wearing a ridiculous jacket with so many pockets that he looked like a chest of drawers. He glowered in through the doorway. Dribbles of blood covered his face like a red lace veil, spilling from a cut the falling pot had made. He was breathing hard after his climb.

Fever picked up the nail and set it against the end of the bullet. Picked up the hammer and set it against the head of the nail. Looked up to make sure that the vice was pointing right at Fat Jago's vast body as he stomped towards her.

She drew back the hammer and struck the nail against the bullet with one firm blow.

26

NIGHT VISITORS

he battle until then had been carried on in silence, broken only by scuffling noises, a few gasps and grunts and that brief shriek as the scalded man fell. The sound of the bullet exploding was abrupt and startling, like an unexpected thunderclap. It filled the tower. It sent echoes slamming from the cliffs.

Arlo froze at the foot of the stairs. Fever stood with the hammer clutched tight in her hand. The grin dropped off Fat Jago's face like a picture falling off a wall. His eyes went wide with surprise and he looked down at his own broad chest. Only the smoke moved, unfurling from the empty bullet casing.

Then Fat Jago looked up at Fever again, and his grin returned. Wherever the bullet had gone, it had missed him completely.

Fever flung the hammer at him instead, but she was rattled now and that missed too. Fat Jago lunged at her across the room, roaring, as if the sound of the shot had been a signal that everyone was allowed to start making noise now. "You interfering bloody Londoner!" he shouted. "Why couldn't you keep your nose out of this?"

Fever saw something glint in the shadows under the table. It was the Aranha's bullet-belt, and she snatched it up and swung it at the roaring face, but Fat Jago caught it and dragged it painfully from her fingers and slung it across the room. She turned to try and run but his hand was round her wrist, twisting her arm behind her; his thick forearm came across her throat from behind, cutting off her cry; she was slammed face first against the wall, his hot red breath on the back of her neck.

Behind him, two more men came through the doorway. Arlo was running towards Fever, but one of the newcomers booted his legs from under him and the other caught him as he fell, cuffing him viciously across the face when he tried to bite him.

"Right," said Fat Jago. "It's done. Where's the flying machine?"

And the fire went suddenly mad. Something sprang up and started to roar and hammer there; a leaping fire-snake, a rattling series of explosions that bled together into one long juddering noise, while tools and boxes leapt from the shelves on the walls and the walls themselves started to come apart, scattering sprays of plaster and splintered wood like wedding-rice. There were shouts and curses from Fat Jago's men. There was a shrill cry of pain and shock that sounded like Arlo's. There were whines and buzzings; a sense that the air was filled with small and speeding things; hornets perhaps, to judge by the way the men jumped and danced and clutched at themselves. Fat Jago suddenly rammed Fever still harder against the wall, pressing his immense and shuddering weight against her. "What are you *doing*?" she shouted, panicked by his brute bulk and by the noise. Fat Jago answered with a grunt, and his weight kept growing, forcing her down the wall to the floor, where he sprawled himself heavily on top of her.

It was like being buried alive.

At least the noise had stopped. There was a dwindling shriek as a man stumbled backwards through the doorway and pitched over the handrail outside; a dull clang as his head hit a rung; a distant crunch. A voice far below shouting, "What's that? Fat Jago? What's happening up there?"

The sounds came vague and underwatery through Fever's battered eardrums where she lay crushed beneath the landslide of flesh that was Fat Jago. What was he doing? Was he trying to suffocate her? She struggled for breath, sure that her ribcage would give way at any moment, her skull scrunch like an egg between his chest and the hard stone floor.

Then Arlo was shouting, "Fever! Fever!" and the weight on top of her shifted. She heaved upwards with her shoulders and elbows and Fat Jago rolled off her uncomplainingly, like an overturned sofa.

"The bullets!" Arlo was saying. "The bullets out of the Aranha – he threw them in the fire and they. . ."

Fat Jago lay on his side and stared peevishly at Fever. A dozen of the Aranha's bullets had hit him in the back. He opened his mouth and a bubble of spit formed between his lips and burst with a faint popping noise: *pok*. That was the last sound he made.

Arlo was saying, ". . .he threw them and they landed in the fire and they went off. . ."

Fever made herself stop looking at Fat Jago and looked down at herself instead, to make sure that she had not been shot without noticing it. She hadn't; Fat

Jago's body had shielded her completely. But when she looked at Arlo she saw that he was clutching a place near his right shoulder and that his shirtsleeve was dark and wet and dripping.

She made him sit down on the steps and take off his shirt. There was a hole in his upper arm, a flood of blood. She tore a strip from the shirt to bind it and told him to keep it lifted up. Arlo obeyed meekly. There was an empty look in his eyes which Fever found almost more worrying than the wound, but maybe she herself looked just as bad.

She went back out on to the platform, stopping on the way to help herself to a pistol that one of Fat Jago's companions had dropped. Outside, men were still shouting. Two of those who had fallen from the ladder had picked themselves up, though the others still lay where they'd landed. Angels whirled through the darkness, settling near the bodies, nerving themselves to start searching the dead men's pockets for snacks.

Fever didn't like to stand exposed on the platform for too long in case someone took a shot at her. So she ducked back inside and shouted, "Fat Jago is dead! That's what will happen to you too if you try coming up here again! You'll never get the *Goshawk*! Go away!"

She thought the men below might reply, but they didn't. When she peeked out again they were leaving, limping back towards their boat.

"They're going," she said. She felt absurdly pleased. She almost laughed.

"They're just taking a break," said Arlo in a flat voice. "We surprised them that time, but there could be dozens more men aboard that galley. Fat Jago may be dead, but they know there's something valuable up here, and they'll keep trying till they get it."

He was shivering. She went to him, trying not to panic when she saw how much blood had soaked through the bandages, trying not to remember Kit Solent; trying not to believe that Arlo might die. His face was pale, which made his freckles stand out even more clearly. She held him and pressed her face into the scratchy cloud of his hair and put her mouth against his ear and promised him, "It will be all right. I'll keep you safe. You can trust me."

"I don't think I'll come to this island again," he said. "Bad things always happen here."

"What about the *Goshawk*?" she whispered. "What about me? I'm not a bad thing, am I?"

"No, you're not. You're the best thing."

They sat like that a while, not speaking. Outside, the wind was rising, breathing gently in the gorse and the small trees. Through the eastern windows they began to see a faint pinkening in the sky. And from below, startling them both, came a voice.

"Fever! Master Thursday!"

Fever threw herself through the doorway, pointing her stolen gun down the ladder. How could she have been so stupid as to leave it unwatched? They were already halfway up the ladder, just two of them this time; two threatening charcoal-smudges of shadow in the gathering light; two pale faces gawping up at her from the rusty landing. She was wondering which one to shoot first when a light flicked on and she recognized the bloodless glow of an electric lantern.

"Fever, it's me!" said Dr Teal. "Hazell's here too. We've come to rescue you!"

"Dr Teal?" She lowered the pistol, trying to understand. "How did you get past Belkin's men?"

"Oh, it was not so hard. Hazell said we were sure to be smashed on the reefs or seen by the lookouts on the *Desolation Row*, but the Guild of Engineers always finds a way! We went round that long island east of here so they couldn't see us. Heard gunfire on the way, and feared the worst. But we weren't going to give up after coming so far, so we landed Hazell's boat on the southern shore and hiked over the island. No sign of anybody. They must all be on that galley. Is Thursday here? The machine. . .?"

"Who's there?" Arlo was asking worriedly.

Fever looked back into the room and said, "It's all right. They're friends; they're here to help." Wondering as she said it whether they really could, whether whatever boat had brought them here could possibly outrun Fat Jago's galley.

They were climbing the rungs now, not in silence like the barefoot Oktopous men but with a reassuring *pong pong pong* of boots on rusty ironwork. Dr Teal clambered on to the platform. He had a pistol in his hand, and he kept it ready as he came inside the tower, Fever backing in ahead of him. He stared hard at Fat Jago and the other dead man. Fever wished she'd thought to cover them up. The place looked like the *Lyceum* stage in the last act of a tragedy, except that the blood was not scarlet but dark and sticky-looking like spilled treacle, and nobody was about to jump up and take a curtain call.

"You've already had visitors, I see," said Dr Teal.

Behind him, Jonathan Hazell pulled himself clumsily up on to the platform. "Merciful gods!" he exclaimed. "What has happened? A massacre!"

"Arlo is injured," said Fever.

"Hazell, perhaps you should wait below," snapped Dr Teal.

"Not likely! Down there in the dark, with those villains likely to swarm ashore at any instant? Miss Crumb, you are not hurt? Heavens, is that Fat Jago?"

Fever was looking at Dr Teal's pistol. She had seen it somewhere before, though she wasn't sure where. In a dream? In one of Godshawk's memory-fragments? Northern workmanship: blue steel and blond wood, the long barrel decorated with a snarling wolf's head.

"This is Thursday, I presume?" he said, looking at Arlo.

"Yes. . ." she started to say, but he was already pushing past her, raising the gun as he walked towards Arlo. His face was changing. He was becoming someone else, the way the actors at the *Lyceum* did when they stepped out on stage. Becoming someone cold and graceful and absolutely without pity.

"Teal?" said Jonathan Hazell.

Fever was still holding the gun she'd picked up earlier. She turned it in her hand as she stepped after Dr Teal, gripping it by its barrel. Dr Teal glanced back, distracted by her movement, and she swung it as hard as she could. The butt of her gun hit him on the temple with a heavy, hollow-sounding thud.

In the plays she'd seen, a blow like that would

always knock a man out cold, but the plays had been wrong about that, as they had about so many other things. Teal just said, "Gah!" and doubled over, raising both hands to his head. But for a moment his pistol was pointing at the ceiling instead of Arlo, and Fever took her chance and snatched it from him.

"Fever!" Arlo shouted.

"He's Vishniak!" she said.

"Really, Miss Crumb!" exclaimed Jonathan Hazell. "This is Dr Teal: Dr *Avery* Teal, of the Guild of Engineers. . ."

"No. . ." Fever took a step backwards as the Engineer staggered and straightened up, glaring at her. She dropped her stolen gun, which she could not even be sure was loaded, and pointed his own pistol at him. It was heavy, and she had to hold it with both hands to keep it pointing at his chest and stop it drooping towards the floor. "No," she said again. "This is the man who killed Midas Flynn. This is Vishniak! I recognize the gun!"

"*He* killed Flynn?" said Arlo, trying to understand.

"You were there?" asked Teal at the same moment. "Great gods – the bathroom – I *knew* I heard someone in there!"

"Teal, is this true?" demanded Jonathan Hazell.

"His name's Vishniak!" insisted Fever.

"Lothar Vishniak is a role I sometimes play," said Dr Teal. "A mask I put on as part of my work." He took his hand away from his injured head and studied it quizzically, as if expecting blood. Then his dark eyes looked at Fever again, and she could tell that he was gauging the distance between them,

241

making ready to jump at her and try to reclaim his gun.

"And are you really an Engineer?" asked Hazell, sounding indignant. "Or is that just another role you sometimes play?"

"Of course he isn't!" said Fever.

"Oh, but I am," said Dr Teal, or Vishniak, or whatever he was called. He sighed and raised his hands, accepting that he would have to explain himself. "The duties of the Guild have evolved somewhat since you left London, Fever. I work for a new branch: the Suppression Office. It is a secret branch, answerable only to Quercus and the Chief Engineer."

"What is a Suppression Office?" asked Jonathan Hazell. "What is it that you suppress?"

"Ideas, Hazell. Dangerous ideas." He stepped sideways, and Fever moved with him, keeping herself between him and Arlo, keeping the heavy gun pointed at him.

"There are certain technologies," he said, "which must not be allowed to develop. When London is mobile it will become the most powerful city in the world. Nothing will be able to stand before it. But if we allow our rivals to develop air power, for instance, that would change. Even the new London would be vulnerable to attack from the sky. We must make certain that the secret of flight remains lost. So the Suppression Office publishes research proving that flight is impossible, and suggesting that anyone who believes it might be is a crank. And whenever we hear of some inventor experimenting with it, an agent is despatched to see to it that the inventor dies, and that his discoveries die with him."

"That's . . . *really, really* irrational!" said Fever.

"I didn't bring you here to murder this boy!" said Jonathan Hazell.

"Yes you did, Hazell," replied Dr Teal. "You just didn't *know* that was why you were bringing me here." He looked at Fever. "You know how ideas spread, Fever. They're like germs. The dangerous ones must be stamped out at their source before they can infect too many minds. I was sent to Thelona to eliminate Edgar Saraband, and eliminate him I did. I befriended him and sabotaged that engine of his. He bragged that his flying machine was all his own work, but I found some letters from young Thursday in his workshop, and I learned that he had sent a crate to Mayda shortly before his unfortunate accident. So I came here to find Arlo. It was just by chance that I found you too."

"And you used me to spy on Arlo," realized Fever. "People kept asking me who I was working for, and I said nobody. But I was working for you all along."

"I am not a monster," said Dr Teal. "Everyone told me that Thursday was just a harmless eccentric. I did not want to kill him unless I was certain that he was building a workable machine. I planned to break into that funicular of his, but when I learned that you were in Mayda I realized I could use you as my agent. I followed you out on to the cliffs that first night, and let you see the prototype glider I'd brought with me from Saraband's workshop. That whetted your interest, didn't it? The next day when I mentioned Thursday to you, I was sure you'd take the bait and go to see him, and that he'd let you in, since you're such a pretty girl. But you're also an Engineer, which made me feel confident that you would let me know if you found out anything worth knowing. . ."

Fever recalled how proud she'd felt to have discovered Arlo and his work; how eagerly she'd gone to tell Dr Teal about it. She said, "It was me who told you about Midas Flynn, and that same night you went and killed him. . ."

"I'd have got Thursday too, but when I called at his house earlier that evening he had already fled. It wasn't the first time Flynn had come nosing round one of my targets. He had to be removed from the game. I had no idea at that time that the Oktopous Cartel were involved too. Imagine the danger we'd all be in if *they* got access to flying troop carriers and bomb platforms. . ."

"But I didn't build the *Goshawk* to attack things!" said Arlo, who had been listening silently. "Fever, I just wanted to fly."

Fever turned to look at him, hoping he understood that she had planned none of this, knew nothing about any of it.

"Fever," said Dr Teal, "I have nothing personally against this young man. But even if he only used this machine to take pleasure flights over Mayda, other people would see it, and be inspired to build machines of their own, and evolution would set in, as it always does with a new technology, and before long we would be facing aerial gunships and all sorts of trouble. Don't you see? For London's sake, he must be. . ."

"Removed from the game?" said Fever.

Dr Teal smiled a thin smile. "Quite. Now, give me back my gun and let me do my job. Are you an Engineer, or aren't you?"

Fever thought about that for a second. Then she used her toe to shove the pistol which she had discarded earlier to Arlo, who picked it up and pointed it at Teal. She passed the Engineer's pistol to Jonathan Hazell and went to fetch a length of spare cord from one of Arlo's toolboxes. She dragged Dr Teal's hands behind him and tied them securely using good, rational, Engineer's knots.

"Now what?" asked Jonathan Hazell.

Fever hadn't really thought about it. She quickly considered their situation. It was not good. Dawn was coming. Offshore, Fat Jago's men would be preparing another attack. "We have to get away from here," she said. "We'll take your boat."

"They'll catch us!" the merchant objected. "There's no way we can outrun that galley!"

"They won't be after us," said Fever. "It's Arlo they want, and Arlo will be flying back to Mayda." She turned to Arlo. "You must do what you always planned to. Fly the *Goshawk* across and land it in Mayda, let everybody see what you've created. Then your idea will be free in the world and there'll be no point in anyone trying to stop it any more."

"Fever, I can't," said Arlo. He was sitting at the foot of the stairs, propping Dr Teal's gun against the handrail. "I can't move my arm. There's no strength in my hand. I can't fly the *Goshawk* like this. I'm sorry. You'll have to do it."

She started to protest, but she knew that he was

being rational. His wounded arm in its sleeve of bloody bandage looked stiff and lifeless, like something that did not belong to him.

"Don't you dare, Fever!" warned Dr Teal. "Burn the machine. The plans too. That way the Oktopous won't get hold of it, and I'll make an exception and let Thursday go."

"Really?" asked Fever.

"He's lying," said Arlo. "You can see that he's lying!"

How? wondered Fever. But she knew Arlo's instincts for such things were better than hers so she tore another strip from his ruined shirt and gagged Dr Teal to stop him saying any more. Outside, the eastern sky had turned that shade of pink you see sometimes on the insides of seashells. A brisk west wind blew scraps of cloud along.

"I've never flown before," she said.

"Nor had I, before yesterday," said Arlo. "You'll soon get the hang of it."

27

FEVER IN THE AIR

o there she hung in the harness of the *Goshawk*, wishing that there had been time to make even a short test flight with the new engine. The sky to westward was twilight grey, the sea still, a bright planet hanging just above the horizon. The wind blew in her face. Angels hung on the updraughts above the tower. Their grief over Weasel seemed forgotten now. They were just curious to see whether the machine would fly any better this time.

Fever tried to imagine herself landing the *Goshawk* in Mayda, explaining herself to the people who came gathering round to gawp and wonder. It was hard to believe that they would listen. But she could think of nothing else to do.

Arlo leaned over her, fumbling one-handed with the torus inside its new housing. After a moment Fever felt it start up. It sent vibrations rippling through all the spars and cables; through all her bones; her tensed muscles. Fever threw a switch to complete the circuit and felt the vibrations change as the propeller started turning faster and faster, the *Goshawk* straining forward. She shouted to Jonathan Hazell, "Now! Now!" and he leaned all his meagre weight against the tail-bar, pushing, running with the machine as it began to move.

The tower's edge rushed at her, sped past, and

she was in the air. She almost stalled and dropped backwards into the cliff face, but recovered in time, straining at the flap and rudder controls, easing the machine up and away over the dead quays, over the sea.

She had a dizzying view for a moment of the isles and stacks to northward. Saw a scattering of postage-stamp sails that must be Mayda's fishing fleet, and a bigger ship lying on the far rim of the sea. All she could hear was the wind sighing over paper and singing through rigging; the creak of wood and cordage. The purr of the torus was too faint to reach her. She flew with no more noise than an angel.

Then, as she turned the *Goshawk*'s nose towards the east, Mayda itself came into view, and the red galley, and three small boats lying black as splinters on the bright water halfway between the galley and Arlo's island.

They had already seen her. She could see men standing up in them, waving to each other, pointing. When she aimed the *Goshawk* at them and went swooping down a man panicked and threw himself into the sea. She wished she had brought a stone or something to drop on them, but she had nothing. All she could do was look down at the stupid, shouting, upturned faces as she wheeled above them. One man raised an arquebus and she saw the white spurt of smoke as he fired it at her, but she didn't think that he could hit her. She went higher just in case, and now the boats were behind her and she was rushing through the sunlit air, her escort of angels stretching out on either wing.

She had never felt so alive, and she found herself

thinking that if she did fall and die it would be worth it just to have felt this soaring freedom. . .

But she saw no reason why she should fall. The torus was working just as she had hoped, and the sense of impending danger that had been with her all through the launch was fading steadily as she learned to trust the *Goshawk*. She banked from side to side, veering through the flock of excitable angels. Glancing back, she saw that the boats had caught up with the galley and that their crews were scrambling up her sides, the galley herself already turning and getting under way.

It occurred to her that she should give the Oktopous men some hope of catching her. Without encouragement they might give up and go ashore in the hope of finding plans or something in the tower, and find Arlo and Jonathan Hazell too. She took the *Goshawk* down low again, remembering how mother birds sometimes feigned injury to lure predators away from their chicks. Perhaps Fat Jago's men would think that the machine was damaged. That would make them pursue it even more eagerly, and stop them wondering about who might be left behind on the island.

So she glided above the crests of the waves, spattered with water whenever one rippled into foam. On her right the *Goshawk*'s shadow scudded along, looking like some huge ray keeping pace with her just under the surface. In the north, the big ship she had noticed earlier had drawn nearer, and resolved itself into three ships sailing close together in a tight formation. That worried her faintly. Could it be more Oktopous galleys? Reinforcements, summoned by the captain of the *Desolation Row*? But surely they would not send three, and they would be coming from the south, from the Middle Sea, not from the north?

A breathy boom came from behind her. It sounded like an exhausted thunderclap and she could not think what it meant until she banked and circled and saw the galley fire a second shot; a jab of orange flame from the big gun in that swivelling wooden turret on its forecastle. The projectile went whining past, just off the tip of her right-hand wing, and kicked up a splash of spray about a hundred yards beyond her. By the time the sound came across the water to her the galley had already fired again, and she was climbing, climbing, striving to get out of range.

She had not reckoned with gunfire. Fat Jago had wanted the machine in one piece, hadn't he? But maybe whoever had succeeded him as commander of the galley wasn't so bothered about that. Maybe he would be content to smash it from the sky and see what he could learn from the wreckage.

Mayda still looked a long way off. She pushed hard on the altitude lever and the *Goshawk* climbed gamely, the torus thrumming, the distant booms of the big gun fading behind her. But there was a new noise now; a rattling, hissing sound that she was certain had not been there when she first took off. She craned her head about, trying to find the cause of it.

There was a hole in the left-hand wing. She couldn't think that it had been made by one of the shells from the big gun; it was too small, and they had not come close enough. Perhaps that man who had fired his gun at her when she circled the boats had been a better shot than she'd allowed for. At any rate, the hole was there, and getting steadily bigger as the wind worried at its edges. She felt a listing sensation, as if the right-hand wing was lower than the left. She tried altering her balance in the harness, but it made no difference. The wing was starting to break up.

She did not feel free or ecstatic any more. Carefully reciting numbers from the Fibonacci series to try and keep herself calm, she began easing the *Goshawk* back down, reasoning that if she was doomed to drop into the sea it would be better to do it from six feet than six hundred. She glanced over her shoulder and saw the galley coming after her, perhaps two miles behind. She wished now she'd not tried to be so clever; wished she hadn't taunted them or tried to be a mother bird. Hoping to get well ahead, she adjusted the torus control to give her more speed.

It was a bad mistake. As the *Goshawk* powered forward the stresses on its injured wing increased. A supporting strut snapped with a sound like a pistol shot; a loose cable lashed Fever's face, the *Goshawk* flipped over, and suddenly she was not the pilot of a flying machine any longer, just a frightened girl dropping into the sea in a tangle of ripped paper and splintering wood. The horizon cartwheeled over her. She heard the angels screeching. Then the sea slapped her hard and she was underwater; blue and white and a blizzard of bubbles, some of which were caused by all the air in her lungs rushing out and making for the surface.

She struggled with the buckles of the harness. She couldn't tell if she was ten fathoms deep or if the wreck was floating on the waves and she just happened to be underneath it. It didn't matter much anyway, since she could drown just as well in either place. The buckles were too stiff. She strained at them and couldn't shift them and then at the last moment, as her vision darkened and coloured stars started to swim inside her head, she wrenched herself free of the straps without undoing them, fought against the drowning machine for a terrified moment and burst up gasping into the sunlight.

The *Goshawk* was afloat. Crumpled, shattered, barely recognizable as the graceful thing of thirty seconds earlier, it rode the long swell like a clot of flotsam. Which, Fever supposed, as she dragged herself on to the rudder, was all it was now. One wing, held upright by a taut tangle of rigging, poked into the air like a boat's sail. Like a paper tombstone. Like a signpost, telling the lookouts at the masthead of the *Desolation Row* where they could find their fallen prey.

She lay on the rudder and tried to catch her breath. The waves that washed over her washed away pink, and she realized that the stinging pain she could feel on her face was a deep gash, caused by that flailing cable-end. If it weren't for the goggles, she might have lost an eye. She pulled them off – they'd filled with water anyway – and started trying to think what she should do next. It was hard to concentrate, for loss of blood was making her feel dizzy and stupid. She wondered if she would bleed to death before the galley reached her. *But whatever happens, they mustn't find the torus. . .*

The thought of that powerful little device in the hands of another man like Fat Jago cut through the fog that was starting to wrap her brain. She made herself grope her way along the wallowing fuselage to the place where the engine housing was attached. The torus was silent now, broken in the wreck or drowned by the sea. But she couldn't be certain that it was not repairable, so she pulled her knife out of her pocket and set to work, loosening one screw and then the next until the torus came free in her hands. She looked at it, at the battered pale metal which had survived through so many centuries, which her grandfather had held before her. All that power, and all that mystery. *I can't just throw it away*, she thought. *It needs to be studied. The Order of Engineers should see it. . .*

But then she looked up and the *Desolation Row* was much closer than she'd thought, and anyway the Engineers weren't an Order any more, they were a Guild, and even if she could give them the torus they wouldn't use it to fly, only for something irrational like making an even bigger, faster mobile city. So she opened her fingers and it slid down the slope of the wing and silently into the sea, where she watched it for a moment going down, fading away from her into the blue depths like her offering to the Mother Below.

The beating of the galley's drums came steadily to her across the water, and with it now there was another sound; a steady pounding, a throaty throb. She thought at first that it was the blood whooshing and booming in her ears, but then she looked at the *Desolation Row* and saw that they had heard it too. Men were running about excitedly on the galley's decks, and the gun turret was swivelling, and it wasn't pointed at her any more but at something else, something in the north.

Sleepily, she sat herself up, bracing herself against the struts of her foundering machine. The swell was steepening, and for a moment, down in the combe between two waves, she could see nothing but sea and sky. Then the next wave heaved the wreckage upwards and her view widened.

There was a second ship coming towards her. It was the same one which she had glimpsed earlier, and which she had mistaken for three ships sailing side by side. Now that it was closer she could see that it was really one ship with three hulls linked together by thick struts and gantries. A trimaran, she supposed you'd call it. All three hulls were studded with gun emplacements, and as Fever watched one of the guns went off, and a white spurt of water was flung up just ahead of the *Desolation Row*.

The sea swung her down again into another trough; nothing to see but blue water. When she came up again she was just in time to watch the galley let off its big gun, the shot falling harmlessly just short of the strange ship. She could see people hurrying along brass-railed walkways on the upper decks of the newcomer, a flag flapping on a tall mast. She squinted at it, and knew it. It showed a wheeled white tower on a black field. The flag of Quercus. The flag of London.

Fever Crumb, she thought, flopping down on her side, *you're hallucinating. Your mind is making up a rescuer for you. There's no point looking at it; it isn't real.*

But the waves kept hoisting her up, like friendly grown-ups lifting a child to see a passing parade. She couldn't help but watch. She couldn't help but see the way the *Desolation Row* started to turn uncertainly as the new ship bore down on it; the way the new ship's central hull swept forward into a ram longer and sharper and even more vicious than the galley's. A shell glanced from its ironclad prow. Another made part of its upperworks unravel into smoke and splinters, but it kept moving at the same speed, the thump of its engines drumming across the sea, steam and smoke and sparks pumping out of its tall chimneys. It swept past the wreckage of the *Goshawk*, and its wake lifted Fever even higher so that she could watch as it sliced the *Desolation Row* in half.

The galley's stern rolled over and sank instantly. The bow section floated for a few seconds, the oars still going up and down as if some of the rowers there hadn't noticed that they no longer had a ship to pull. Then something exploded down beneath the gun turret, blasting orange flame high into the air, sending shards of splintered wood turning over and over up among the circling angels. A man went with them. Fever watched him waving his arms and legs as he soared up and up, and seemed to hang for a moment in the sunlight, as if gravity had forgotten him before he fell with all the other wreckage, and vanished into the rash of white water where the galley had gone down, and did not surface.

A black clot of smoke rose and spread above the wreck-site, trailing long cloudy tentacles like a phantom squid. The victorious steamship backed its engines and began to turn towards Fever, and had she been watching still she would have seen that boats were being lowered from davits on its sides. But by then she had seen enough. Her eyes closed. It felt peaceful just to lie there with the salt water prickling as it dried on her skin and the sun making hot patterns behind her eyelids, the colour of Arlo's kiss. She relaxed her grip on the struts she'd been clinging to. Her own weight slid her gently down the wing, and the waiting sea folded over her like a coverlet.

She didn't notice the angels descending. She didn't feel their beaks and fingers hooking her wet clothes, or hear the flap of their wings as they struggled together to keep her from slipping under the water. But somewhere in her dreams she heard the shouts of the sailors in the approaching boats, who thought that the big birds were trying to eat her. "Get out of it! Gahn! Blog off, you great fevvery cloots!" *London voices*, she thought. *London has come to find me.*

28

MOTHERSHIP

 ever, dearest?"

Her mother was bending over her.

Her *mother*?

She tried closing her eyes and opening them again.

"Fever," her mother said, "it's me."

And so it was. Wavey Godshawk, with her ash-white hair wound in an elaborate chignon around her beautiful head, and wearing a costume that had been designed by some expensive dressmaker to look slightly like a sailor's uniform without concealing any of her natural curves.

"But where. . .?"

Fever sat up, and felt salt prickling where the seawater had dried on her skin. The cabin was luxurious: all wood and bronze, with curtained windows, glass-fronted bookcases, soft chairs, a scent-lantern playing something cool and minty. There were paintings on the panelled walls and one of them was a portrait of Fever's father, looking awkward in a stiff-collared tunic. Only the beat of big engines trembling through the walls and floor let her know that she was still at sea. She seemed to be always waking up on strange boats these days.

"What ship is this?" she asked.

Wavey leaned over her, smoothing a soft hand over her face. "You are aboard the steam-ram *Supercollider*, my darling, and you are perfectly, perfectly safe."

*

When Wavey Godshawk received word from Dr Teal to say that he had found her missing daughter, she had gone straight to Quercus to ask for a ship that she could take to Mayda, and Quercus had lent her the *Supercollider*. He had built the great steam-ram to protect the convoys of shipping which helped feed his new city's hunger for raw materials, but the northern seas were clear of pirates now, and he saw no harm in letting the barbarous southerners see how powerful London's new masters was. He had lent her to Wavey with his blessing.

The voyage south had been brisk, pleasant, uneventful. It was a sort of honeymoon for Wavey and her latest husband, who had both been busy since their wedding working on the immense task of mobilizing London. They had stopped at Cape Bretagne to see the famous Petrified Car-Park, and touched at Nowhere and Evora too. They had retired to their cabins the previous night with the lights of Mayda twinkling in the south, looking forward to going ashore next day and finding Fever. But before sunrise Wavey had been woken by the *Supercollider*'s captain, who reported a war-galley flying the colours of the Oktopous Cartel at anchor off the Ragged Isles.

She had gone up on to the quarterdeck in that pearl-pink dawn to see it for herself. A red ship upon a pastel sea. What was the Oktopous doing there? she wondered. And then, as she watched, she saw that white wing rise from one of the islands, and she knew. So the Thursday machine was really flying, and the naughty Oktopous had stretched out a tentacle to try and steal its secrets!

"Full ahead," she told the captain, and sent a sailor below to rouse her husband. They stood together on the ship's prow in the blown-back spray and watched the new machine sweep eastward, dip and fall, and never guessed that it was Fever flying it.

"Take us to where it came down," Wavey ordered the captain. "We must not let that galley reach it first."

It wasn't until the galley was sunk and the sailors brought Fever aboard – sodden, lifeless-looking, that red weal across her face still welling blood – that she realized who the pilot of the machine had been.

"What about the kite, lady?" they asked her, as she knelt down on the deck to take her daughter in her arms. "What about that old-fangled flying contraption?"

"Sink it," said Wavey quickly.

She did not even bother to stay and watch as the boatmen smashed and weighted it and let the sea take it.

Fever knew none of that, and there was no time to ask, no time to wonder. This ship, her mother, it all felt like a mystery she could never hope to fathom, like the torus, something unreasonable that she would simply have to accept.

She looked down at herself. Someone had taken off her wet clothes while she slept and replaced them with a sailor's too-big trousers and smock. She touched her face and there was a soft pad of lint across her gashed cheek.

"Don't worry," said her mother. "You're healing remarkably fast. I don't think you'll have a scar."

Fever didn't care whether she had a scar or not. She was thinking about Arlo, left alone on that island again. "How long have I been sleeping?"

"Not long," said her mother. "You haven't missed much. We've been searching the place where that galley went down, picking up survivors – it was *dreadfully* boring, but apparently it's a Rule of the Sea – the captain was most insistent. At present we're off Mayda-at-the-World's-End, negotiating with the authorities there to let us moor in their harbour. They have some silly prejudice against motor vessels, but I expect they'll come round. Now, where is Arlo Thursday, I wonder?"

"Arlo is still on the island," said Fever. "So is Master Hazell. And Dr Teal. . ." She looked sideways at her mother. Her beautiful, brilliant, dangerous mother. "How do you know about Arlo? And the machine? Dr Teal said he reported only to Quercus and the Chief Engineer. . ."

Wavey laughed. "Oh, Fever! You *are* out of touch! Did Dr Teal not tell you? He must have wanted to let me surprise you. He's *such* a sweet man! You see, I *am* the Chief Engineer! Dr Stayling kept raising stuffy objections to all Quercus's plans, so Quercus fired him and gave me his job. Oh, Fever, you simply *must* come back to London and see how well things are going. . ."

"He was going to kill Arlo!" said Fever, pushing herself upright.

"Well, he had good reason," said Wavey. "That

flying machine was most impressive. We can't have things like that flapping around, they would ruin everything. We'll send a boat to the island and deal with Senhor Thursday."

"You mean kill him?" said Fever.

"Well, if you will insist on being crude about it, yes. . ." Wavey looked curiously at her. "Does he mean something to you, this Thursday boy?" She reached out and stroked Fever's hair. "Poor Fever! He's only a common-or-garden *Homo sapiens*, you know. There are *loads* more where he came from."

A knock at the cabin door interrupted her. It opened, and a young sailor leaned in and said, "Captain's compliments, ma'am. A small boat is approaching from the islands."

"Is Dr Teal aboard?" asked Wavey sharply.

"No, ma'am. Two gentlemen, ma'am; strangers both."

"Arlo and Master Hazell," said Fever. Wavey glanced quickly at her, and Fever could see that the news had worried her. If the Suppression Office was as secret as Dr Teal had said, the chances were that no one else aboard this massive ship knew what she had planned for Arlo Thursday. If he had stayed on the island she might have been able to have him killed and claim it was an accident, but she could hardly have him assassinated aboard the *Supercollider* with her whole crew looking on. . .

Wavey, being Wavey, recovered almost instantly. "Come," she said pleasantly, offering Fever her hand to help her off the bunk. "Let's go and meet your friends." To the sailor she added, "We shall have to send a boat

261

to the island to collect Dr Teal. And will you please tell Dr Crumb that his daughter is awake?"

Fever, who had been thinking frantically of ways to keep Arlo safe, thought she had misheard at first. "Dr Crumb is here too?" she asked.

Wavey looked at her with that expression of mischievous delight which meant that she knew something startling which Fever didn't. "Of course he's here! It would have looked most peculiar if I'd left him at home. He is my husband!"

They met Dr Crumb on the way to the quarterdeck. He had got Wavey's message and he was running to find them, but as soon as he saw them he stopped running and tried to look as if he had not been hurrying at all, because although he had a wife and a daughter he was still an Engineer, and displaying emotion was difficult for him.

Difficult for Fever too. It had been such a long time since she had seen him, and she still wasn't sure how she felt about her discovery of two years earlier that he really was her father, not just her guardian. She had no idea what she should make of his marriage to Wavey, but she didn't think she liked it; she thought she wanted him all to herself. She wanted him the way he had always been; bald and indoors-y and white-coated.

But he had changed as much as she had. He looked better-fed and better dressed and he had let his grey hair grow until it was about a half inch long and stood upright all over his scalp like an experiment with magnets and iron filings.

She started to run to him, and slowed, and stopped an arm's length away and gave him a neat little Engineerish bow. "Hello, Dr Crumb."

"Fever!" he said, fidgeting uneasily with a small telescope which he had brought with him from the quarterdeck.. "This is – I mean – oh, that we've found you – that is – it is – most satisfactory."

He couldn't stop looking at her. Her hair, her clothes, her long, tanned hands, the dressing that she wore like a mask. "Your face. . . You are hurt. . ."

"It's not bad," lied Fever. "Wavey says. . ."

Wavey took her hand, took Dr Crumb's. It was the first time that their strange little family had ever been all together in the same place, and it silenced them. They stood there together on the swaying deck, while sailors hurried past them and the sun slid into their eyes. The *Supercollider* was turning, spray from her paddle wheels drifting like a cool mist across her upperworks. Fever saw that the cliffs of Mayda and the harbour mouth were quite close on her left-hand side, and that a small boat was sailing up on her right.

"Dr Crumb," she asked, "might I borrow your telescope?"

He gave it to her, very glad to find that she still needed him for something. She extended the telescope and trained it on the boat. After a moment's trouble focusing she saw Jonathan Hazell at the helm, and Arlo sitting in the front, leaning against the mast.

Her father had turned to look at the boat, too. Marines were running to the *Supercollider*'s rail to aim muskets at it and shout at the merchant to lower his sail, but the boat was already slowing, the sail already rattling down. Jonathan Hazell had stood up uncertainly in the stern and was shouting something, his words lost in the slap of the waves against the *Supercollider*'s side.

"Who are those people?" Dr Crumb was asking.

"The young man is Arlo Thursday," said Fever.

"The inventor of that remarkable flying machine!" Her father looked pleased, and she knew that at least he did not know about Wavey's plans. "He must be a very talented Engineer! I was most vexed when our clumsy sailors let his machine sink. I shall look forward to making his acquaintance!"

"I imagine that Wavey will want to hand him over to the Suppression Office," said Fever, looking at her mother.

Wavey flushed a little.

"The Suppression Office?" asked Dr Crumb. "What is that?"

"Nothing," said Wavey. "A misunderstanding, nothing more. . ."

The boat was close now, and sailors were throwing down lines, advising Jonathan Hazell to "Hook on, mate!" Dr Crumb went hurrying along the *Supercollider*'s deck towards the place where the newcomers would climb aboard, and Wavey would have gone with him, but Fever caught her by a sleeve and held her back. She knew that there was no point in trying to persuade her mother that the Suppression Office was irrational, but maybe she could meet its madness halfway; suggest some compromise that could keep Arlo safe.

As quickly and as calmly as she could, she said, "You can't hope to stamp out flying machines in this piecemeal way. Murdering inventors won't work in the long term. Someone else will always have the same idea. Even if you. . . Even if you deal with Arlo, there must be dozens of people all over the world working towards the conquest of the air. What about me? I've flown. I helped build the *Goshawk*. Are you going to kill me?"

"Of course not, Fever," said Wavey irritably. "You're one of us. Now be sensible."

"I *am* being sensible!" said Fever. "If *you* were sensible you'd see that it can't work. If you really want to stop people thinking, you don't use guns or bombs. You use religion."

She waved one hand towards Mayda and hurried on, not sure where her words were coming from or where this idea was going, but blurting it out anyway. "Look at this place! They don't even use engines! Why not? Because they think their goddess has forbidden it. Out there to westward somewhere, beyond the sea, there's a whole continent waiting to be re-explored, but no one goes there, because the gods have cursed it. Down south, in Zagwa, they destroy every scrap of old-technology they find because they say it offends *their* god. All over the world, all sorts of good things are banned and forbidden in the name of one religion or another. You don't have to hurt Arlo. Please don't. You can stop his ideas being used. Just bribe a few priests. It's the job of priests to control knowledge and stand in the way of progress: it's what they're *for*. Let them spread the word that the gods never meant us to fly."

Wavey watched her with those Scriven eyes of hers, those grey and golden eyes which seemed both more and less than human. "You *are* a clever girl, Fever," she said.

Fever went rushing on. "I'll go and talk to the Maydan's high priestess myself as soon as we dock. I think I know how to make her listen. But you have to promise me that Arlo will not be harmed." She knew what Arlo would have said if he had been able to hear her; that he would not want to live if he could not fly. But she did not care. All she cared about was that he be spared.

Wavey looked away from her towards the rail. Jonathan Hazell must have succeeded in tethering his boat alongside, for his nervous face had just appeared over the *Supercollider*'s gunwale. The rest of him followed, hauled aboard by helpful sailors, and after a moment Arlo came after him. Wavey watched the young man; watched the sea-wind tousling his dark hair, the uncertain, winning smile that spread on his face when he saw Fever waiting there.

"Oh, he *is* rather lovely," she admitted, and looked round smiling at her daughter. "Very well. As long as he gives up his work, I shall tell Dr Teal that he is not to come to any harm."

29

WORD FROM THE GREAT DEEP

y the time the *Supercollider* had docked in Mayda's outer basin the sun was already past its zenith and the cool blue shadow of the western wall lay across the Quadrado Del Mar. The great driftwood temple of the Sea Goddess looked like a wreck on the floor of the ocean, with blue-robed priests darting in and out of its ever-open doors like inquisitive fish.

Quite a crowd followed Fever as she walked towards it: her mother and father, a squad of marines from the *Supercollider* and a whole shoal of Maydans, shopkeepers and gentry, dockers and children and harbourside riff-raff, who had been drawn to the quay to watch the strange new ship come in and were eager now to see what happened when its passengers met Orca Mo.

The priestess had been warned of their coming. Indeed, she had watched the fall of the *Goshawk* and the arrival of the *Supercollider* that morning from the temple's precincts, through a vast old telescope cased in mother-of-pearl. She had objected at first when the steam-ram asked permission to dock, reminding the council that the Goddess abhorred motorized ships. But when its captain sent word that he would like to make a large donation to the temple funds, she prayed for a while and came to understand that the Goddess would not mind making an exception for the *Supercollider*, just this once.

She was waiting for its passengers at the top of the temple steps, dressed in all her regalia, with the tentacles of her squid-hat waving on the breeze.

Fever, striding towards her across the cobbled square, felt a quick, nervous fluttering in her stomach. "Stage-fright", the actors on the *Lyceum* called it. She stopped at the foot of the temple steps, looking up at Orca Mo.

"Why have you come here?" asked the priestess sternly.

"I have come—" said Fever, but her voice was just a hoarse little whisper so she had to start again. "I have come to ask for forgiveness."

She wasn't an actress, and she'd always hated lies. But she thought of Arlo, and the look that Arlo had given her as they parted at the foot of the *Supercollider*'s gangway, of disappointment and betrayal and despair, and she said, "I've come to ask the Sea Goddess to forgive me," and it sounded sincere.

Orca Mo smiled at her. Not a smile of triumph; quite a kindly smile. "Then come in, child," she said, holding out one hand to Fever, and the other to stop all Fever's friends and followers who would otherwise have come with her up the steps.

Shafts of dim blue daylight lanced through skylights into the temple's dim interior, slanting down between barnacled wooden columns. All sounds seemed muffled. The distant voices of chanting priests were as vague and echoey as whale song. A water-organ was playing softly somewhere. If you could let yourself forget how dotty it all was, thought Fever, it would be quite beautiful.

Orca Mo sat Fever down on a driftwood pew close to the altar and settled beside her. She studied the wound on Fever's face, the purpling bruises. "You are already forgiven, child," she said. "The Goddess has already forgiven you. I saw it all. You flew with the birds, and fell into the sea, and our Mother Below chose not to let you drown."

Fever wondered how she knew all that. She couldn't possibly have been able to see through her telescope who the *Goshawk*'s pilot had been. But probably part of the job of being a priestess was making people believe you knew everything, so she did not ask how the woman came by her knowledge.

"When you were under the waves," said Orca Mo softly, "did the Goddess come to you? Did you see Her? She has been known to appear to those who fall into Her realm. Even to unbelievers."

Fever looked down for a moment at her hands, folded in her lap, then up again at the priestess. *Don't do this*, Arlo had shouted at her, when he learned what Fever was planning. *You mustn't!*

"Yes," she said. "I saw her."

She could feel herself blushing, her ears warming up like twin electric elements. She felt sure that Orca Mo would know she was just making this up. But when she looked into the woman's eyes she saw only a wistful yearning. Orca Mo longed to believe, and that made her easy to lie to, even for a novice liar like Fever.

"What did She look like?" urged the priestess. "How could you be sure it was Her?"

Fever glanced up at the altar, where the statue of the goddess smiled down insipidly from its aquarium. It was the same age-old, sacred statue that she had watched being carried on its litter across the lock-gates at the Festival of the Summer Tides. Now it was back beneath the water, surrounded by bright shoals of darting fish, and on the white sand at its feet were the *Mãe Abaixo*'s three sacred symbols: the bubbling clamshell, the treasure chest and the skull.

"She looked just like her statue," said Fever. "Those blue and white clothes. The circle of gold above her head, exactly like that. But her eyes were green and her hair was dark and she had freckles."

"Freckles?"

"Freckles."

"And did She speak to you? Did She ask you to carry any message to us out of the Great Deep?"

"Yes," said Fever.

You mustn't! Arlo had screamed at her. She had gone to see him in the *Supercollider*'s medical bay, where Wavey's surgeon was tending to his wounded arm, but when she told him what she planned to do he had driven her away. *If people start believing flight is wrong we'll be barred from the sky for centuries!* he had shouted. *Flight is possible! We've done it! The* Goshawk *flew! You can't murder the truth!*

But Fever thought she would rather murder the truth than let the Suppression Office murder Arlo.

"What did She say to you, child?" pleaded Orca Mo.

270

Fever bowed her head. "She said that it was she who had made my flying machine fall, and that she was letting me live so that I could come to you with her message."

"And what is Her message?"

"That people are not meant to fly. That is one of the reasons why she smote the Ancients with, um, smite-y things. Because of all their flying machines, dirtying the sky. . . Only the Goddess may make flying things."

She broke off short, sure that she'd gone too far. Surely no one could believe this bilge? But Orca Mo's eyes shone, filling like tide-pools, spilling salt water down her cheeks. "Oh yes!" she said, taking Fever's hands in hers. "Oh yes! It makes such *sense*!"

"Does it?"

"Of course! The sky is Her realm too, you see. Science has taught us that the air is mostly made of water, so what is the sky but another sort of sea?"

"Well, that's not *quite*. . ."

"And does not even the moon herself obey the pull of the Sea's tides?"

"No, it's the other way round," Fever started to explain.

Orca Mo did not notice. "Pray with me, child," she said, pulling Fever off the pew, shoving her down on to the sea-worn planking of the temple floor, kneeling there beside her. "We must give thanks to our Mother Below for this new revelation. And then we shall go forth into the city, and make sure that all of Mayda knows Her will."

But all Fever could think of was the last look that Arlo had given her, that empty look of shock and loathing. He'd been betrayed by Weasel, and betrayed by Thirza Blaizey, and now he had been betrayed by Fever Crumb.

30

WESTERING

wo days later the *Lyceum* rolled back into Mayda, still garlanded with flowers from the fiesta at Meriam. The flowers were fading now, but Ruan and Fern had fresh bright memories of their adventure which they were eager to tell Fever about. The dolphins in the harbour! The great walls of Meriam, high as high! The fountains they had played in by the light of the festival fires! The kindness with which the caliph had received them! The way Ruan had worked all the lights and stage-effects himself, without ever once burning the poor old barge to flinders, which Fergus Bucket had said he was sure to do!

But they had no chance to tell Fever any of it, because she had news of her own. That strange warship anchored in the outer basin had come from London just to find her. These people were her parents; this lady, tall and kind and beautiful, was her mother, this shy, quiet gentleman her father. And what would that mean? What would happen now?

When she told them, Fern started to sniffle, and Ruan couldn't even look at her; he had to go away and walk along the harbourside by himself. There was no one he could talk to about what he felt. How can you explain that you have a broken heart when you are only ten?

But the show must go on; if he had learned anything

in his two years with the Persimmons, it was that. So he went back to the *Lyceum*, back down into the crawl space under the stage that had become his now. He was determined to let Fever see how well he could work her lights.

That evening, back on the waste ground behind the harbour, the tale of *Niall Strong-Arm* unfolded once more in the summer twilight, and this time Fever watched it from the audience, seated in the front row between her mother and father. She was worried at first that they might not approve of this make-believe world she had spent the past two years in, but Wavey laughed at all the jokes and applauded at the end of every scene, while Dr Crumb, who had never seen a play before, seemed quite fascinated.

Fever was fascinated too. She had never really understood before the strange alchemy that AP and his company could work. Now, although she knew the script by heart, she found herself moved by the improbable story; by the love of Selene for her astro-knight; by AP's voice, which served up slabs of poetry as rich and dark as fruit cake; by Laura Persimmon's autumn beauty; Lillibet's ballet; Max and Dymphna's clowning; by the excitement of the fights and battles, and most of all by the skilful way Ruan worked the lighting and effects, and by little Fern. AP had padded out the handmaiden's role with extra lines, and Fever realized that Fern must have been watching and learning during all her time aboard the *Lyceum*, for she could steal a scene as slyly as Cosmo Lightely and ride a joke as well as Dymphna.

And she knew that that would make it both harder and easier for her when the play ended and she had to go to AP and tell him what she had already told the children: that she would not be travelling onward with the *Lyceum*. Wavey and Dr Crumb had already decided what would happen to her, and Fever had not had the strength to argue. She would be leaving with them on the morning tide, going back north aboard the *Supercollider*. And Fern and Ruan would not be going with her. It would not be fair, she thought, to take them from this summer country back to the snows and sloughs and smokes of London. They would miss her for a little while, she thought. But she had never really been a parent to them, or even a proper guardian; she had just been the person who delivered them to their new home, the *Lyceum*, and there aboard the *Lyceum* she must leave them, among all these good people whom they loved, and who loved them better than Fever had ever managed to.

It might have been different if Arlo had been there with her. He might have given her the strength to stand up to Wavey and Dr Crumb. She might have stayed on with him in Mayda. Or taken him with her aboard the *Lyceum* and let him be drawn into AP's messy, cheerful family. But Arlo had gone off alone as soon as the *Supercollider* docked, refusing to even look at her. Gone back to Casas Elevado, Fever guessed.

And what would he do there? What could he do, with the *Goshawk* gone and the common folk of Mayda so stirred up against the idea of flight that they were burning even their children's kites on the bonfires in the Quadrado Del Mar?

Dr Teal, rescued from Thursday Island by the *Supercollider*'s launch, had taken Fever aside when he saw those fires and said, "I have to admit, Miss Crumb, you've put the whole Suppression Office to shame! You've got the Sea Goddess to do our job for us. If this spreads – and I mean to make sure that it does – you'll have set back the development of flying machines by a generation!"

From the smile he wore while he said it, she gathered that she was meant to feel good about that.

The play reached its end. The audience stood up, applauding as the actors formed a line along the stage-front, no longer characters out of the lost past but just themselves again, holding hands, bowing, waving. "Extraordinary!" Dr Crumb was saying. "I had no idea. . .!" AP brought Fern centre stage and requested a special round of applause "for young Fern Solent, who will one day be the brightest star of Bargetown". And then the division between actors and audience dissolved and there was talk and laughter and drink and music, with Fever in the midst of it somewhere, being hugged by Dymphna and Lillibet and Cosmo. Ruan was showing Dr Crumb the backdrops he had helped to paint and explaining to him about perspective. Dymphna was having a long and serious conversation with Jonathan Hazell. Wavey was flirting with AP, telling him, "You must come to London soon! If not, London must come to you!"

Fever, all unnoticed, walked away. Through the throng and racket of Bargetown she went, and then along the quays to the Southern Stair. Although it was so late, the light still lingered in the western sky, and above the crags of the eastern wall a vast and sulphur-yellow moon had risen.

All the way to Casas Elevado she was working out in her head what she would say to Arlo. *I had to do it; Dr Teal and my mother would have found a way to kill you otherwise. What I told Orca Mo will be a nine-days wonder. It probably won't spread much beyond Mayda. You'll be able to go to another city and start working again. One day people will fly. . .*

Or should she suggest that Arlo come back to London with her, and offer his services to the Engineers? But Arlo's fragile, beautiful machines had nothing in common with the huge, crude, all-devouring thing the Engineers were building. Like Fern and Ruan and all the good things in her life he belonged in sunlight, not in London.

And when she reached his house she found that she was too late anyway. His gate was not just open, it had been torn from its hinges. Angry feet had tramped a broad path through his garden. His house stood smashed and vandalized at the bottom of its rails, its windows shattered, its walls daubed with religious symbols; slogans; threats. The followers of the *Mãe Abaixo* had not forgotten Arlo Thursday and his gliders. When they had finished burning all their kites they had come for him.

Fever wandered through the ruined, moonlit rooms. In the bedroom, the picture of her grandfather and Arlo's had been torn down, slashed and trampled until the two men's faces were unrecognizable. Arlo's clothes had been ripped and flung about. Books had

277

been torn up, the pages lying in thick drifts on the floors. The people who had done it probably couldn't read, and they'd imagined that these poems and stories were instructions for building godless flying machines.

Fever began to cry. She had never really done it before, although she had sometimes felt like it. She'd always been able to control herself till now. But suddenly she was sobbing. Sitting down in the wreckage of the kitchen where she had sipped Arlo's coffee and listened to Arlo's plans, she let the salt tears flow out of her.

When there were no more she went outside. Wavey was waiting for her in the day-bright moonlight on the veranda. She looked at Fever's tear-stained face and said, "Surely, Fever, you knew this would happen? You of all people ought to know a bit about the madness of crowds."

"What have they done with him?" asked Fever, feeling angry at herself because she knew Wavey must have heard her sobbing and mewling in the kitchen.

"Oh, Arlo wasn't here," said Wavey. "I seem to remember promising you that he wouldn't be harmed. I think Dr Teal would have liked to interpret that as meaning that *we* would not harm him, and letting the Maydans do the deed for us. But that would have been cheating, don't you think? So I made sure Arlo went aboard his cutter yesterday night, and stayed there. Some of our people sailed it for him from Thursday Island. It's moored in the outer basin."

"What will he do?"

"Leave Mayda, I imagine. After that, who cares? The Suppression Office will keep an eye on him, of course, but I doubt he'll ever get another of his flying machines off the ground, not with so much feeling against it."

She sighed, sensing Fever's unhappiness, searching for some way to comfort her. "Honestly, Fever, it's not your fault. Forget it. What are flying machines anyway? Just toys for children. Wait until you see the new London; see the *power* of it, I mean. . . We'll walk together through the Engine District, you and I. Those immense turbines, like the mills of God. . . You'll soon forget your silly *aëroplanes*. . ."

She smiled, and reached out to rearrange Fever's hair. "He is a handsome boy, Fever. But he is not for you."

Fever pushed her hand away and ran, back through the garden, along Casas Elevado, down a narrow stair to Rua Círculo. A restaurant was starting to descend, and Fever leaped aboard. Waiters came to show her to a table but she waved them away, hurrying through the building, the diners all turning in their seats to stare at her. Some reached out to touch her as she passed, for luck. *That's the girl – the girl who flew – the girl the Goddess spoke to. . .*

She ignored them, ran out on to the veranda at the far end; potted palms and bougainvillea, Chinese lanterns swaying in the breeze, the static buildings of the cliff side sliding by on either side. Below her, moonlight sprawled silvery across the waters of the harbour. In the outer basin a cutter had raised its sail.

She vaulted up on to the rail that ran around the veranda and balanced there, waiting for the restaurant to arrive at its lower buffers. The manager appeared behind her, pleading with her to get down, telling her that she was endangering herself and disturbing the diners. But Fever didn't care about the diners, and this didn't feel like danger, not compared to some of the things she'd done lately. When the buffers were still six feet away she sprang across the narrowing gap, landed hard and ran, leaving the watchers on the veranda behind her to shake their heads and tell each other that her encounter with the *Mãe Abaixo* had deranged her wits.

"Arlo!" she shouted, haring through the shadowed canyons between the warehouses.

The *Jenny Haniver*'s pale sail slid across a slit of moonlit water between two walls. Fever ran on, out on to the harbourside. It wasn't rational, but she needed to talk to Arlo before he left, to stop him leaving if she could. If she could only get his forgiveness, then at least she would have salvaged something. . .

But the *Jenny Haniver* was making for the harbour mouth, and as she gathered speed and moved out into the wind-ruffled water beyond, a ghost-white storm of angels detached themselves from the bridges and cliffs and rooftops of the city and went soaring after her, surrounding her, wheeling around her masthead, flying low over her straight silver wake like gulls behind a trawler.

Fever ran and ran, right out to the uttermost end of Mayda's long mole. She could see Arlo at the cutter's helm, his injured arm bound up in the white sling the *Supercollider*'s surgeon had given him. "*Arlo!*" she shouted.

He did not look round, and Fever had no way of knowing if he was ignoring her or if he simply hadn't heard. She thought at first that he must be heading back to the Ragged Isles, but as the cutter cleared the harbour mouth it turned due west.

Where was he going? Maybe he didn't care. Maybe he just wanted the solitude of the open ocean. Maybe he wanted to die out there. *It may be that the Gulfs will wash him down...* thought Fever, half-recalling some fragment of verse from one of AP's poetry recitations. *It may be he will touch the Blessed Isles...* And it may be he was going where the angels had gone of old; letting their atlas guide him to whatever forgotten coastlines lay beyond the sea's blue edge. And the angels were going with him. She could see skeins of them lifting from their eyries on the Ragged Isles, blowing like white banners across the sea.

"Arlo!" she screamed, standing at the end of the harbour wall in the moonlight, the sealight, in the spray of the steep salt waves. "Take me with you! Aa-a-a-r-lo!"

But the cutter just kept on getting smaller, shrinking into the huge emptiness of night and sea and sky, taking Arlo and the mysteries of flight away from her, no more than a flash of white sail now, smaller than a handkerchief, smaller than a pillow-feather, and after a while, when even her sharp Scriven eyes could not tell the *Jenny Haniver* from the whitecaps on the waves, Fever knew that she would never see him again.

She turned away and started walking slowly back along the harbourside towards the lights of the city and the black, waiting bulk of the *Supercollider*. There was nowhere for her to go now except home.

WITH THANKS . . .

. . . to my editors, Marion Lloyd and Alice Swan; to Kjartan Poskitt, my Chief Scientific Advisor; to the Moorland Merrymakers and particularly Dave Booty, who told me about the scary home-made lighting-rigs of yesteryear. To Eamon O'Donoghue for the illuminated capital letters. And to David Wyatt, whose drawings of the people and places in the World of Mortal Engines have done so much to help bring it to life.

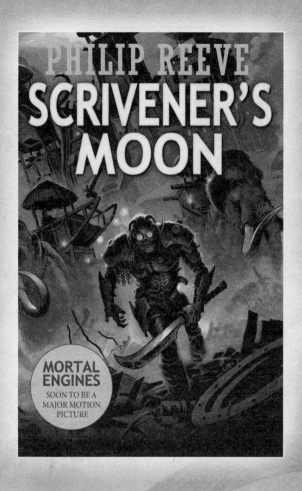

THE
MORTAL ENGINES
QUARTET

THE
FEVER CRUMB
PREQUEL SERIES